The Baasi
(Slow T

By Michael Bershay

Cover art by Steven Novak.

Many thanks to Pat Lichen for her editing and technical input. Also thanks to Murr Brewster, Dan Fiebiger, Roy and Brenda Trammell, and Joyce Lackie for their constructive criticisms.

CHAPTER ONE: CLOVER

The purple flowers smelled so wonderful that the girl could not resist grabbing handfuls of them and rubbing them on her skin before devouring them. Nearby, her older brother crawled through the meadow, fist-sized rock in hand, searching for food. Normally, the siblings would have to settle for field mice or small fish from the nearby stream for their meat. But today, the brother was lucky—he surprised an opossum whose pregnancy made her run even more slowly than usual. Sentiment was a luxury in those times; the brother slammed his rock into the opossum's head, securing dinner for the evening. He grabbed the dead animal and stood to locate his sister. He yelped sharply to get her attention. The girl hastily gathered up the flowers, roots, and berries she had collected and ran toward him.

The brother squinted hard and scanned the meadow until he saw his little sister bounding toward him. From several yards away, she was just a blur to him. Rushing up to him, her smiling, round face finally came into focus. The girl looked at his catch and grinned, then presented her shopping for the day. He peered at the pile of goodies in her hands and smiled back at her. The two had successfully survived another day—a safe distance away from their tribe.

Ever since their mother had died from disease, there was no one to care for the siblings. Their father spent all his time with the other hunters of the tribe, avoiding his son who could not hunt worth a damn and who was taunted mercilessly by the other youths because of his poor eyesight. By association, the little sister was also taunted, but that was when her brother would demonstrate his ability to draw blood at close range. By the time the brother was 16 years old and his sister was 12, they were spending less time with the tribe and more time exploring the minutiae of the nearby fields and streams. While the tribe dined on deer, buffalo, and the occasional unfortunate member of another tribe, the siblings had to settle for smaller fare. Yet they found much fascination in their world outside the tribal compound. They had become their own little tribe.

Though shunned, they were tolerated to live near enough to the compound to be protected from animal predators.

This truce was shattered the day when the girl experienced her first menstruation, making her a candidate for mating. Yet she seemed more interested in checking out flowers and small animals with her brother than engaging in Neolithic sexual politics. Overtures to her by various males in the tribe were met with growling, scratching, and biting by both her and her protective brother. Despite his poor eyesight, however, the brother was not the worst-shunned eligible male in the tribe: that dubious distinction fell to one eighteen-year-old whose excellent hunting and fighting skills could not compensate for his excessive hair growth and withering body odor. This brute figured that the outcast girl was his best candidate for sex, since the other females weren't keen on defending her—in fact, they too were hoping that the brute would take the girl and leave them alone.

Since the brother needed his sister to guide him for long distances, he wasn't going to lose her without a fight. He knew from experience that the brute was better at fighting than he was. But his low-level safaris in the nearby meadow inspired other methods of combat.

The brute stalked up behind the outcast girl, grabbed her, and stroked her hair affectionately. The girl figured that she would need all the flowers in the meadow to mask this suitor's stench, so she fought to get away from him, yelling for her big brother. Fortunately, the brother was nearby with a tubular weed in his hand. He broke the weed open and squeezed a white liquid into his hand. Then he crept behind the brute and slapped him in the face with the liquid. The brute was at first surprised, but then the obnoxious juice stung his eyes mercilessly, causing him to let go of his intended mate and furiously rub his eyes as he screamed in pain. The girl beat her fists on the brute's back until her brother pulled her away. She gave the brute one last bark of contempt as her brother took her by the hand and had her lead him toward the small grove of trees that they slept in, away from the tribe. The tribe members who witnessed this were too far away to get involved, and evening was fast approaching. The brute rubbed and blinked his eyes until enough tears flowed to wash out the juice. Ignoring the dying daylight, he looked for a blunt object—he *would* be satisfied that day!

The grove of trees was advantageous for the two-sibling tribe. It was well-situated in the middle of a field, so predators could be easily spotted. The trees were thin and required opposable thumbs for climbing. The girl had spent many hours carrying stones and more of those stinky weeds up the trees and wedging them into the branches for ammunition. It was their little haven.

It was getting dark by the time the outcast siblings reached the grove. Trying to get something to eat before retiring for the night, they spent time foraging in the grass around them. Intent on finding food, they inadvertently split up and ended up on near-opposite sides of the grove. The brother held up a small stone, disappointed that it wasn't a snail. Too late, he noticed a large blur that swung the femur bone of a bear at his head. His right arm reflexively went up to catch the blow, but the impact still sent him reeling. He fell into the grass in pain.

The sister heard his cries and ran to check on her brother. To her shock, she found the stinky brute trying to beat him with a large bone, while her brother desperately rolled around to dodge more blows. She ran behind the attacker, jumped on his back, and dug her fingernails into his cheeks, shrieking. The brute screamed in pain and tossed her off his back and pinned her to the ground. His hormones overcoming his rage, he made his move. The girl tried to fight him off, but he was almost twice her size. The brute excitedly started to accomplish what he'd set out to do earlier that day. He failed to realize that he had dropped his weapon close enough for the nearsighted brother to locate it.

One of the blows had grazed the brother's lower back near the kidney. He grabbed the bone, painfully arose and took direct aim at that spot on the brute's back.

The girl was crying in terror until her attacker suddenly froze, wide-eyed and speechless. Another blow to his opposite kidney, and he fell on his back to one side of her, in helpless agony. Carried away with adrenaline, the brother straddled him and brought the bone down between the brute's legs. The brute screamed and cried until the brother swung the bone to the side of his head.

The sister stood shakily, taking in what her brother had just done. He held the bone aloft and yelled angrily at the brute, daring him to get up. But the danger from the brute was over with forever. The sister looked in dread toward the tribe's compound as she saw an even bigger danger: the tribe was running to the trees to investigate. Trembling, she grabbed her brother's free hand, grunted urgently, and pointed toward the angry mob. Knowing that the tree grove would not protect them, the two fled into the vast field.

The sister knew they could only travel so far before the daylight was gone. After a mile and a half, she guided her brother to a small clump of trees in the middle of nowhere. Exhausted and in fear, the two huddled together in the middle of the trees and tried to fall asleep.

The rest of the tribe, although furious at the loss of one of their better hunters, returned to the compound and let the two outcasts escape. It was too dark to chase after them without imperiling more lives.

It was a clear night with a full moon. The nocturnal insects were out in force, their songs combined into one long, continuous drone. It was the kind drone that can lull one to sleep. But the sister's senses were on high alert. A rustle in the grass nearby jolted her sleepy eyes wide open. She frantically shook her brother awake. As he stirred, the sister spun around and saw the source of the sound the silhouettes of two female lions charged from fifty yards away.

She screamed and scrambled up one of the trees, calling for her brother to join her.

The next thing the sister saw was the last of her brother. Both lionesses had easily taken him off the tree and proceeded to shred him. He had no chance to scream. The girl could now think only of escaping while the lionesses' attention was diverted. She had no choice. The trees were too easy a climb for the lionesses, so the girl ran away at full speed.

By the time she had stopped running through the plains, the morning sun was barely peeking over the mountain range in the distance. She stopped out of a combination of fatigue and a left ankle throbbing from a brief stumble. Gasping for breath, she hid behind a large rock and peered back where she'd been. Soon the gasps dissolved into sobs. She crouched fetus-like next to the rock and cried inconsolably. She was alone. Her brother had been killed before her eyes. Her tribe would only take her back as a meal. With her hurt ankle, it was almost certain that she would soon be joining her beloved brother in the same lionesses' stomachs.

A roar nearby confirmed her fear. As she peered from behind the rock, and her eyes widened. The two lionesses were attacking ... a creature she had never even imagined to see. The lionesses' intended prey stood about twice as high as the girl. It seemed to be a large, purple ... salamander? It stood on four legs. It had four arms. Its head was at least twice as large as hers, but elongated with a mouth at the lower end, two large eyes surrounded by impossibly thick eyelashes in the middle, with a thick mat of brown hair that crowned the top of the head and cascaded down its back. A smooth brown—pelt?—cradled its crotch and was fastened at its shoulders. It was pointing something at the lionesses—something that made a strange shrieking sound and spat lightning! A lightning bolt hit one of the lionesses, enveloping her in a ball of blue plasma. The other lioness held back, roaring at the being, wanting to strike. Another lightning bolt from the weapon enveloped her. Both lionesses fell dead into the grass.

The girl couldn't even blink. In amazement, she saw the salamander prod each lioness with one large front foot to make sure they were dead. From farther afield, a weird buzzing noise called the being. It was another being, this one a little lighter in color (crimson) and shorter. It joined its colleague, and the two traded buzzing sounds with each other. The girl wanted to run away, but when she turned, she was confronted by a third being a mere ten yards from her. It looked at her with a face that displayed no expression that the girl was familiar with. She shrieked and fell to the ground, terrified. At least she knew what lions *were*.

The third being made no threatening move. It merely looked at the girl curiously. The other two beings carefully walked up and also regarded her with interest. More buzzing noises were exchanged from the beings' mouths. The one who'd confronted her first reached out one of its hands—the girl saw it had only three long, muscular fingers—and buzzed to another being holding a sack. The sack-bearer produced a large pear and placed it in the outstretched hand. In turn, the outstretched hand held the pear toward her. The famished girl desperately wanted the pear, but was too terrified to accept it.

The being with the sack buzzed at the pear-giver. The pear-giver thought for a second, then brought each limb to its immediate adjacent limb, in simple imitation of a hominid. In unison, the pear-giver's two left arms re-offered the fruit to the girl. Seeing that she was still too scared to accept it, the being crouched down and gently rolled it to her. Hesitantly, she accepted it, but did not take her eyes off the three strangers as she devoured it.

The buzzing sounds began again.

"It was rather unexpected," said Toochla, the pear-giver whose role was ground expedition leader, "but it looks like we've made our first contact with an extraterrestrial person."

"I was hoping to avoid this," said the sack carrier, Drasher. "These beings don't have a verbal language yet. This may become more complicated than we can handle."

"No verbal language," Toochla replied. "But they are not stupid. This young female has an especially well-developed curiosity."

The girl finished the pear, seeds, stem, and core. She still trembled with fear, yet she didn't run away. She studied the three strangers more intently.

Xashan, the lioness-killer, added, "A thought has occurred to me: perhaps she could be a live specimen to study on our journey. Since her tribe has rejected her, she would fare far better with us than she would out here."

"But only because there would be no predators," Drasher interjected. "Care for a live specimen is exponentially more complicated than care for a dead one in terms of compatible foods, water, and air. And even if all her material needs are met, her *psychological* needs may be impossible for even our best intentions to satisfy."

Toochla glanced at the girl, who seemed rooted to the ground by fear and curiosity. Toochla turned to her colleagues and said, "Let us sit." As they sat, the girl relaxed, though her caution remained.

"We still have two days before the Reconnaissance Ship can retrieve us," Toochla said. "My suggestion is this: you two keep up your observation with rest of the tribe. I will observe this hominid myself and try to gain her trust. If she accepts me by tomorrow, then I think we should take her with us."

Drasher was perplexed. "But I just informed you—"

"I'm well aware of the risks you mentioned," Toochla interrupted patiently. "Now here is my reasoning: the key to long-term survival of a species is adaptability. If this hominid can adapt to being in a new environment, both physically and psychologically, then her species descendants have more potential to achieve full sentience. Thus, we may have potential friendly relations with them."

Drasher observed, "She most likely will act differently in captivity."

Toochla smiled. "Our terrarium on the Mothership is over fifty square miles in size. I would hardly call it captivity if she lived there. Her reaction to us displays a very healthy mind. As you can see, she is observing us as well."

Drasher thought for a moment. She turned to Xashan and asked, "Comment?"

Xashan shrugged and said, "I must confess that she has caught my fancy as well. If she does accept us, her presence on the ship may boost morale. But why should you split away from us, Toochla?"

"Less intimidating for her," Toochla explained. "After all, we have just met. So, Drasher, if she accepts us, are you willing to accept her?"

"Absolutely! But I don't want us to be blinded by the novelty of her company."

Toochla carefully rose to her feet. Her colleagues did the same. The girl sprang up and was reminded that her ankle still ached. She was primed to sprint away at the first hostile move.

"Then it is settled," Toochla announced. "We will rendezvous back at the camp this evening. I will keep you informed of how she responds to my company. In the meantime, Drasher, I want you to prepare a sedative for her and slip it into another piece of fruit. If we are to take her, I want to spare her the trauma of going through the Gate. Xashan, take the remains of one of those large predators and place it with the rest our samples."

"Yes, Leader," Drasher and Xashan chorused as they walked away.

Toochla looked at her new charge with a benevolence that was foreign to the young hominid. Toochla smiled warmly and said softly, "My people are exiles like you. I hope you will accept us." She placed all her hands on her chest and deliberately uttered, "Tooch-la." Then she pointed at the girl and gave her an obvious name: "Clover."

The newly-named Clover stood quietly, still staring at the large purple salamander. It was now clear that it presented no danger to her, and in fact, had fed her. Toochla reached into a small sack and held out something very familiar to the girl: clover. She cupped her hands hesitantly, accepted the gift, pressed the little field flowers to her nose and inhaled deeply. She then ate the flowers and sighed with relief. Toochla turned slightly to walk away. Stopping after several steps, she looked back at the girl. Clover took a step toward Toochla, but shyly hesitated. Toochla smiled. She studiously kept both sets of her arms beside each other, and motioned with one set of arms for Clover to come along. Realizing that she would at least not be alone, Clover followed Toochla through the field.

CHAPTER TWO: CLOVER'S NEW TRIBE

Most of the rest of that day was devoted to exploration. Toochla knew that Clover was dehydrated from her long sprint earlier that morning, so the first stop was a nearby stream that ran near the Baasians' encampment. Clover gratefully ran ahead to the stream and eagerly scooped water into her mouth. Now rehydrated, her hunting instinct emerged, and she scanned the stream for fish. A small trout soon swam close enough for Clover to seize it, and seize it she did, falling into the stream. She scrambled back to the embankment, throwing the trout forcibly to the ground. She grabbed a palm-sized rock, pinned the floundering trout to the ground, and bashed its head several times. She then bit into the fish sideways and stripped its flesh off its bones. In her frenzy, she was halfway through her meal before she noticed that Toochla was looking at her, grinning. "The others will enjoy seeing this," Toochla said to herself as the small camera attached to her head recorded the spectacle.

Clover stared at the lead salamander, momentarily forgetting her meal. What was that thing that the salamander wore on her head? She saw Toochla take another strange object from her pack, which had a long gray twig sticking out from it. Toochla started touching various leaves with the gray twig and staring at the object. A small chirp emanated from the object along with the flash of a light. "No nutritional value," she muttered. Toochla noticed that Clover had stepped closer, eyes widely transfixed on the object. The comparison between their tools dawned on Toochla: Clover's found rock meeting Toochla's high-tech nutritional value analyzer. Keeping an eye on Clover, she touched the analyzer to a fern leaf. Again, a chirp, and a light. The fern was of no nutritional value to Toochla's body, but it was nonpoisonous. Clover gasped. Toochla was concerned that Clover might try to grab the instrument, but the girl kept a respectful distance. Toochla knew that Clover couldn't understand verbal language, but figured that the young hominid should get used to hearing her voice. So she said aloud, "You'll see a lot of our technology, young girl. We need it like you need your rocks."

The large purple salamander started to move farther downstream, collecting more data on the local flora. Clover followed her more closely than before. By the end of the day, Toochla found their way back to the Baasians' campsite. Seeing Clover with the leader, Xashan said, "It appears we have one more passenger."

"I believe we are her new tribe," Toochla replied. She turned toward Clover, who had stopped farther back. She was still shy about going near the group of purple salamanders. Toochla beckoned with her right set of arms. Clover took a couple steps toward the camp, then hesitated. Xashan, taking that as her cue, brought out an apple and carefully offered it to Clover, emulating Toochla's example from earlier. Clover glanced at Toochla for reassurance; Toochla nodded. Clover walked up and timidly accepted the apple.

Drasher was busy setting up a large, domed object in the middle of the campsite. "It will be another cold night," she said. "From observations, her tribe huddles together for warmth and comfort when they sleep. I don't think she's confident enough to huddle with any of us yet."

"Ah, I think you're right," Toochla said. "Perhaps the heater you've set up may be enough?"

"She needs contact with something warm," Drasher said. She walked behind one of the artificial shelters and came back holding a large, beige pelt. "I took the liberty of skinning the other dead predator."

"Very good!" Toochla replied. "You seem to care for her more than I thought."

"We are all responsible for the well-being of our guest," Drasher said dryly as she handed the pelt to Toochla. She twisted a knob on the heater, which glowed softly. Clover stared widely at the heater, but made no move toward it. Still, its heat seemed quite inviting.

Toochla handed the pelt to Clover. Although it belonged to the lioness that killed her brother, Clover accepted the pelt. It was heavy, but the fur was soft. She fumbled with the pelt until it was wrapped around her. It was very comfortable, and it actually produced a little smile on her lips. Xashan grinned and said to her, "You have now avenged the death of your sibling!"

Toochla was pleased. "I must say, you are both displaying excellent instincts in dealing with her."

"On her home planet, yes," Drasher noted. "She may respond differently in an alien environment."

Xashan looked at Drasher. "Always the worrier," she said.

Toochla said to Xashan, "If our leaders on Baas had listened to the worriers more closely, we would still be able to inhabit Baas."

"Yes, Leader," Xashan mumbled, acknowledging the well-taken point.

The rest of that evening was devoted to conjecture of how to deal with Clover on the Mothership. They sat in their blankets near the heater and talked until the dead of night, when they decided to get some sleep. As Drasher and Xashan retired to their tents, Toochla glanced at Clover. The young hominid was curled up in her pelt, fast asleep. Toochla made herself comfortable near Clover, still thinking of Drasher's concerns. It would be, she thought, a horrible decision to take Clover if she couldn't adjust to their world.

Just before daybreak, the camp was awakened by terrible wheezing and coughing sounds. Clover bolted awake, ready to run, but stopped when she saw the source: Drasher, who was being attended by her colleagues. Toochla applied a mask connected to a tube to Drasher's face. The filter coating in her lungs was almost depleted. "There is simply too much nitrogen in this atmosphere for us," Toochla remarked. After several breaths into the mask, Drasher's coughing spasm lessened. Toochla asked, "Are you feeling better?"

"Yes," Drasher said through the mask. "I don't think I should travel any more distances on this mission."

"Understood," Toochla said, patting her on the shoulder. "You can stay here and get things ready for the Gate opening. Xashan and I will do some final observations of the tribe. Xashan, prepare breakfast. I believe it is close enough to our wake-up."

"Yes, Leader," Xashan said as she dug into a large box. She paused. "Do think Clover might eat some of our food?"

"It is worth a try," Toochla said. "Her species is omnivorous, after all."

Through her air mask, Drasher said, "My analyzer has the metabolic data on the dead specimen we found several days ago."

Drasher adjusted her analyzer to "Target organism: hominid specimen," then handed it to Xashan. Xashan chose a long, parsnip-like tuber from the food box, touched the tip of the analyzer to it, then announced, "Edible; adequate nutritional value. Judging from the acidic content, it may be a little sour for her taste. Clover sniffed the tuber, then bit a piece off and chewed it. Her expression didn't show any extreme reaction as she swallowed it. "Perhaps not her favorite dish," Xashan observed, "but at least she can tolerate it."

When breakfast was over, Toochla scanned the horizon with her monitor. "No major predators or other hominids nearby," she reported. She said to Drasher, "We won't be gone long. Is your weapon sufficiently charged?"

"It is. Repelling animals isn't too difficult. My main concern is other hominids, especially Clover's tribe. If they see anything unusual, no matter how threatening, their curiosity will bring them back in greater numbers. That is what I have observed, Leader."

"Xashan and I won't be more than a two mile radius from here. If you see any potential threat, call us immediately."

Toochla and Xashan turned to leave. Clover, sensing that Toochla was the leader, followed them. Drasher looked on, then started breaking camp. I wish my lung coating didn't break down so fast, she mused to herself. What should have the adventure of a lifetime had been spoiled somewhat by the headache she'd felt for the last several days because of the Earth's air.

Toochla, Xashan, and Clover arrived at the Baasians' usual observation point in a meadow over a mile from Clover's tribe. Turning her long-range monitor toward the hominid tribe's camp, Toochla saw something worrisome: the tribe's older males—18 of them—were heading toward the Baasians' campsite. "Xashan!" Toochla hissed. "There is a hunting party coming this way—they could be here in less than 5 minutes! We need to go back now!"

Xashan froze. It sank in: the Baasians were faster runners and had better technology. But the hominids were tenacious hunters who far outnumbered them. The meadow had acres of very tall grass, which was good to hide in, but impossible to sneak away in without detection. An added worry was Clover's safety. And the Baasians' lung filters wore off more quickly with increased physical exertion. Their entire mission was now in jeopardy.

Clover sensed that the hunting party was nearby, and was getting nervous. She was already taking a step back toward the Baasians' campsite.

Toochla holstered her monitor and said quietly, "We'll have to lure them away from our camp and alert Drasher. I hate to say it, but we may have to use our lasers on them as a last resort."

Suddenly, Clover started running back toward the campsite—practically a homing device for the hunting party, whose voices now became audible. "Damn!" Toochla hissed. "I'll grab Clover. You cover our rear. Keep low!" She took off after Clover.

There was rustling of tall grass within earshot of Xashan, and it was getting closer, and grunting noises were growing more excited. Xashan came up with a plan. "Sorry if you don't approve, Leader," she muttered. She quickly set her laser on "incendiary" and crouched low to the ground. The rustling and the excited grunts were a mere few yards away and closing in. Xashan aimed the laser parallel to the ground and waited for the right moment.

As she ran, Clover felt herself suddenly scooped up by two strong arms and her speed accelerating. Toochla carried her like a baby and tore through the field. Coming from a planet with very high winds, the Baasians were well-evolved for low-level scrambling. It was imperative that the Baasians not be seen by the natives.

Xashan could make out the hunters' approach through the thick grass. When the closing distance was about 30 yards, she sprayed fire from her weapon in a roughly 75° arc.

The hunters' war whoops turned to terrified screams. A quarter of a mile away, Toochla stopped and looked back. A large ball of flame loomed up between the scrambling hominids and the now-running Xashan. Clover looked on helplessly from Toochla's strong arms, in awe of Xashan's mastery of fire.

"That," Toochla admonished Xashan when she was within earshot, "was a very dangerous maneuver."

"Forgive me, Leader," Xashan replied. "My aim was to scare them away with something they are at least familiar with—fire."

Toochla looked at the burning meadow. Despite its initial burst, the fire appeared to be dying down faster than it was spreading. The ground was still slightly dewy, the grass still had some green in it, and the wind was only a gentle breeze. She felt Clover clinging tightly to her. As far as she could tell, none of the hunters were close enough to get seriously burned—a massacre would have been hard to live down. Xashan's decision seemed quite sound.

Drasher was standing at the front of the camp when the others returned. "What happened over there?" she asked through her air mask.

"The tribe's hunting party was heading this way," Toochla explained, setting a much-relieved Clover on the ground. "Xashan used the flame-thrower to scare them off."

Drasher turned to Xashan. "Are you insane?" she demanded. "We can't contain a field fire!"

"It's not dry enough to spread far," Toochla assured her. Clover stared at Drasher: was this how the salamanders show anger? she wondered. Should she be afraid of the one wearing the thing on her face? No aggressive moves, at least. Clover decided that she was in no danger and kept her trust in the salamanders.

"Still," Toochla observed, "we cannot contain the tribe either. We had better be on alert for the rest of the day." She consulted a communicator from her pack. "The Reconnaissance Ship isn't in range yet. Xashan, put out a Level Three urgency signal from the transmitter. Let's see if we can have the Gate opened somewhat earlier. Drasher, how much more preparation is needed before we are ready to leave?"

"With the three of us working together, maybe a couple hours."

Toochla unholstered her long-range monitor. "I'll check on the hominids' camp," she said as she walked toward the vantage point. "Hopefully, they won't try to come this way until we're gone." Ever the loyal one, Clover followed her. In a few moments, they returned. "Their camp is deserted," Toochla reported. "They must have run the opposite way to escape the fire. Let's have everything ready so we can leave as soon as the Gate opens."

The three took turns periodically looking out for the tribe as they packed. It was the equivalent of 3:00 pm when everything was packed and ready to go. There was no sign of the tribe for the rest of that day. There was nothing to do except wait until the Reconnaissance Ship responded. The Baasians sat around and chatted to pass the time. Again and again, they returned to how to deal with Clover. The girl, seeing that nothing of interest was happening, walked around the campsite, checking out the cargo: there were 10 large hexagonal enclosed carts, each the size of a bison, and supported by six wheels—the invention of which on Earth was still millennia away. The carts had strange markings on them— some held plants, some held soil and rocks, some held dead animals and insects. One held the mountains of data files that Baasians had collected with their equipment. They were all tightly sealed, so all Clover saw were 10 large things on round rolling things. The only things of the Baasians that weren't packed were Xashan's weapon, Toochla's communicator, and that evening's dinner—with a specially-prepared apple reserved for Clover.

Finally, at dusk, the call came. "Reconnaissance ship to Landing Party. Signal received. Status report?"

Clover, almost nodding off, was jolted awake. She wondered which salamander had spoken.

Toochla sighed with relief and brought the communicator to her mouth. "Toochla reporting. All in Landing Party safe; all healthy, though lung filters are almost depleted. We are ready to enter the Gate."

"Very well," Captain Mrovinta, the voice on the other end, replied. "You sent a Level Three signal. Were you in jeopardy?"

"The hominid tribe we were observing approached our camp as we were preparing to leave. We successfully scared them off, but weren't sure if they would return."

"The Gate is in its final preparations for opening. Are there any special preparations we need to make for you or any material you will bring on board?"

Well, Toochla thought, this is it. "We have adopted a young female hominid into our camp. She was forcefully rejected from her tribe."

A pause on the other end of the line ensued. "A hominid ... in other words, a live specimen?"

"Affirmative. If we leave her here, she would most certainly perish. She is a very social one. We think she would be a valuable study. Our research shows that she could survive quite well in the terrarium."

Another pause. "Let me check with the High Council. Will return momentarily." This time, the pause was an interminable 10 minutes. Finally, Mrovinta answered. "Permission granted with stipulations. One, that the hominid be rendered unconscious when taken through the Gate—"

"Already intended," Toochla said.

"Good. Second stipulation: the hominid be kept under total sedation until her body is decontaminated and her bodily fluids thoroughly analyzed. Third stipulation: that if she is unfit to live on the Mothership, her life will be terminated."

Xashan jumped, wide-eyed at the third stipulation. Toochla held up a stifling hand and said to the communicator, "All stipulations understood. Will fulfill first stipulation, then all will be ready for the Gate upon my signal."

"Very good," Mrovinta said. "We hope this extra effort is not in vain."

Drasher brought out their final dinner on Earth. The special apple was held out to Clover. Clover accepted the apple and devoured it—too quickly to notice a peculiar taste to it. The Baasians regarded her sadly as they ate their own fruit.

"Leader," Xashan asked Toochla, "how could you agree to that third stipulation? I think it is barbaric!"

"It is purely protocol. Her death by our hand would be far more merciful than any death she would meet here." More softly, she said, "Don't worry. I'll make sure there won't be any rash decisions regarding her fate. I think that she is very adaptable and will adopt the Mothership as her new home."

While the buzzing sounds went back and forth among the salamanders, Clover started to feel very sleepy. She wanted that lioness pelt that she slept in the previous night, but it was packed away with everything else. Not that it mattered now; she curled up in a fetal position and fell peacefully asleep. Drasher was the first to notice. "Well," she sighed, "it's time."

Toochla got out her communicator. "Landing team to Reconnaissance Ship."

"We hear you, Toochla."

"Live hominid specimen is now rendered unconscious. We are ready to return."

"Commencing Gate opening. We look forward to your safe return."

A mere twenty yards away from the campsite, loose gravel and dirt started to gently clear away from the coordinated spot. With a low humming sound, a frenzy of light particles quickly grew into a super-charged halo of brilliant cyan light that rose over twenty feet. The Baasians peered into the center of the halo until they saw what they were looking forward to: the shadowy features of the Reconnaissance Ship's decontamination/decompression chamber.

"Let's go!" Toochla exclaimed as she picked up Clover and carried her into the Gate. Drasher and Xashan wheeled in the first two carts. In a few minutes, all the carts were loaded into the Gate. The halo quickly shrank into nothingness. The space where the Baasians' campsite was now reverted to its previous anonymity.

CHAPTER THREE: CLOVER'S NEW HOME

Clover had been carried into a smaller room in the Re-entry Chamber while the Landing Party patiently waited in the main chamber to be cleansed and their bodies to be slowly reacquainted with their own native air pressure. Toochla listened as Gorhanna, the genetics specialist, reported her analysis of the sleeping girl:

Specimen: Live mammal; four limbs, bipedal

Age: Approximately 12 years

height: 4'2"

weight: 83 pounds

Skin pigment: Dark beige

Health findings:

> *Microscopic skin parasites in head hair*
>
> *Minor tooth decay*
>
> *Overexerted muscle tension in left ankle*
>
> *Overall health status: excellent*

Standard Mothership environment compatibility to foreign organism's needs:

> *Air: No major issue*
>
> *Water: No major issue*
>
> *Food: Most foods edible, though our peppers may cause stomach upset and diarrhea. Best to monitor what she eats*
>
> *Gravity: Slightly lighter than native planet, no major issue*

"That is ironic," Toochla observed. "Clover can adapt more easily to our world than we can to hers."

Drasher relished the fresh air that the chamber provided. "Well, we have been in an artificial environment for so long, our bodies aren't quite as robust as they used to be. Had I visited this planet within the first year of our mission, my reaction to the air probably would have been less severe."

"I was starting to feel rather queasy myself by the time the Gate opened," Toochla admitted. "That burst of running I did yesterday depleted my lung filter quite noticeably."

Xashan was stretched out on her chair, reflecting on her time on planet Earth. "Too bad. It's such a beautiful place. I hope we return to it soon."

Toochla said, "It would have to be restricted to shorter visits. The nitrogen in that atmosphere is too much for us. But I would like to see it again soon myself."

"I'm willing to give it another chance," Drasher said. "I will not allow my adverse experience to deter me from visiting it again."

A voice from outside the chambers announced, "Decontamination and re-integration time completed. Welcome back to the ship."

Gorhanna called from the smaller chamber, "Go and get some sleep. The girl will be sedated until we get her to the terrarium. She is quite a specimen."

"Treat her well, Gorhanna," Toochla remarked as she left the chamber.

"I will treat her as if she were my own child," Gorhanna said with a smile.

*****

While waiting for the moon to rotate into the position now held by the sun, Mrovinta reviewed the Landing Party's analyzers. She marveled at the sheer diversity of plant and animal life on the blue planet. True to Toochla's prediction, there were many specimens that could diversify the Baasians' new planet's ecosystem. Very exciting finds indeed, she thought. But the video observation of the indigenous tribe both fascinated and disturbed her. These creatures were proto-sentient, but they were also savages, and cannibals at that. The live specimen that the Landing Party had adopted seemed harmless and displayed above-average curiosity and intelligence. But the girl was also entering puberty, a time of life, Mrovinta knew, that could wipe out many endearing social qualities in children. One bite from her could mean illness or death to a Baasian. Yet, the captain thought, there was a presence in that girl's eyes that suggested deep empathy—she was a very social creature who needed companionship. She put aside the analyzers and started making out her report to the High Council. She suggested, "The benefits of having this live hominid specimen with us outweighs the risks. If she can be tamed, she could be good for the morale of the crew."

The trip from the moon to the Mothership was about eight hours. The Landing Party slept while the Reconnaissance Ship fired its ramjets and headed for the Mothership. Clover slept peacefully, strapped to a bed with a tube down her throat. She was not afforded the luxury— or the trauma—of saying goodbye to her home planet.

When she woke on the Mothership, she felt groggy due to over 48 hours of heavy sedation. As her eyes focused, she saw the now-familiar figure of Toochla sitting peacefully beside her. Underneath her was the lioness pelt she had slept in before. Focusing more, she noticed the brilliant green sky—

Brilliant GREEN SKY? Clover's eyes widened. She glanced again at Toochla for reassurance, but then looked around her. There were trees and plants everywhere, but they didn't look at all familiar. The nearest tree had full-grown ferns for leaves; the ground was a burnt rust color; the flowers looked like elongated pink tulips. She unfurled her lithe body from the ground and spun around, taking in her surroundings. She stopped and looked at Toochla again. Toochla tried to seem reassuring, but Clover's face expressed in no uncertain terms: WHY DID YOU BRING ME HERE?!

She emitted a worried whine as she staggered about in confusion. The whine grew to a panicky shriek as she started to flail about helplessly in her new environment. She jumped up and down in a frenzy, then collapsed to the ground, a shivering rag doll of abandonment. Toochla rolled an apple to her—soon, the botanists on the Mothership would be able to grow full-fledged trees for her— but she failed to recognize it. Toochla sighed and said gently,

"Please don't be sad, young girl. In time, I hope you will appreciate this place." She picked up the pelt and placed it near the terrified hominid. Clover's trembling hand grasped the pelt and drew it over her prostrate body—it was her only possession.

Toochla wasn't the only Baasian in that part of the terrarium. Xashan was several yards away, watching with great anticipation, then concern as she saw Clover's violent reaction to her new environment. She approached Toochla and said, "Will she be okay?"

"It's too soon to know," Toochla replied. "Her mind is still dominated by her instincts. When confronted with the unfamiliar, her first instinct is to flee to something more familiar. I hope she will calm down soon enough to allow her curiosity about this place to emerge."

"So does most everyone else on the ship."

"*Most* everyone? I've been assigned to watch over her for the next several days, so it's hard for me to hear any rumors. Who objects to Clover's presence?"

"Most objections I've heard come from the Terrarium keepers," Xashan replied. "Specifically, they're concerned about her feces and urine contaminating more the sensitive plants and groundwater here. Plaabutin looked at our footage of the hominids' waste habits and was disgusted by them. She said to relay her concerns to you."

Toochla glanced at Clover, who still seemed catatonic. "Yes," she muttered. "They don't exactly localize their waste, do they? What does the High Council say about those objections?"

"The High Council is weighing the issues. For now, they have a wait-and-see attitude. Plaabutin respects their decision, but she will be monitoring Clover's presence very closely." Xashan looked at the ground. "I hate to say it," she said softly, "but I'm starting to more deeply understand Drasher's concerns about keeping Clover. Were you and I blinded by our fascination with her?"

Toochla thought for a moment and then responded, "One way or another, if we want to interact with an alien species, we need to develop a rapport with them. This is pioneering work we are doing, so we have to start with someone." She put one hand on Xashan's shoulder and declared, "Clover will have to do something *extremely deadly* to make me give up on her! I will do my best to train her where she can relieve herself, but you can tell Plaabutin that this moon that we converted into the Mothership is not our native home either, and that she needs to worry about other things."

Xashan smiled slightly. Glancing over Toochla's shoulder, she noticed that Clover was now standing behind Toochla. Clover had the pelt draped over her shoulders, held in place with her left hand. Her big, soulful eyes were looking directly at Toochla. Turning slightly toward her, Toochla extended one hand. Clover, not breaking her gaze, reluctantly, then firmly, grasped the hand with her right hand. It was time for Toochla to show her around. Toochla grinned and said to Xashan, "Apparently, our conversation felt familiar to her! Would you care to take a walk with us?"

Xashan shook her head, and replied, "I'd love to, but I have other duties to attend to. Incidentally, most people I have spoken with are truly excited about Clover. She won't lack for love in our world!"

Toochla smiled. "Tell them she needs to get more familiar with our ways before we allow her more visitors. We'll meet later." She turned and escorted Clover down the path.

The terrarium was the largest green space on the Mothership. It was as large as the island of Jamaica and was divided into three sections. The largest section housed the food garden and fields that fed the entire population, which was not to exceed 600,000. The smallest section was the marshes, which were the natural water filtration system for the ship. The middle-sized section, where Clover currently lived, was the forest, which was the air filtration system. The High Council decreed that it would be most suitable for her, though Toochla conjectured that she might eventually become acclimated enough to live in the housing sector.

They hadn't gone far when Clover stopped walking. Her burst of adrenaline had subsided, and she was now tired and very hungry.

Toochla had remembered to bring the apple she offered earlier and gave it to Clover, who practically inhaled it. She scanned the surrounding foliage. Toochla plucked one of the elongated tulips and offered it to her. Clover took a test nibble of one petal, raised her eyebrows, then devoured the rest of the flower. To Toochla's delight, Clover started eating more of them. Good thing these are common flowers, Toochla thought.

Many crooked streams flowed throughout the terrarium. Toochla led Clover to one of them. She broke away and lapped water. This was rather unsanitary, though not catastrophic for the ecosystem. When Clover climbed back to the path, Toochla guided her over to a simple piece of technology that even a hominid could use: it was a small column that stood several yards from the stream. Toochla pressed a ceramic lever at its top. To Clover's astonishment, water sprouted gently from a hole, from which Toochla drank. Then it was Clover's turn; she pushed the lever down, and the water did the same for her! She gasped, took her hand off the lever, then pressed down again. For the first time on the Mothership, Clover smiled. She drank from the fountain and found the water tasted even better! Clover squealed with delight. The two then made their way farther down the path. Toochla's own delight diminished as she considered Clover's nutritional needs: hominids needed animal protein. And meat was a luxury item on the Mothership.

As they walked, Toochla brought out her communicator and pushed buttons on it. She paused then said into it, "Terrarium Keeper's office." Another pause. She then said, "Plaabutin? This is Toochla, leader of the Landing Party. I understand you have concerns about the hominid in the terrarium ... Yes, there are so many things to consider ... so far, she has been very well-behaved. She is a good child ... No, she hasn't defecated yet, but I'm keeping watch over her for that first moment ... I AM aware of your concerns on that matter, Plaabutin ... I will make sure she stays away from the canals when it happens ... Fine. Now I have a question of you ... isn't controlling the jander mole population in the gardens one of your crew's biggest peeves? ... It takes a lot of time and effort, doesn't it ... yes, they are good composters and ground aerators, but they breed so damned fast ... I have a proposal for you: the hominid is a good hunter, and she needs animal protein for her diet. Perhaps she can be of use to your crew?" Toochla smiled. "I thought you might be attracted to that offer ... I think in several days, she might be acclimated and trained enough to help you out on that ... Yes, her mind isn't as advanced as ours, but she is a fast learner and she is very social ... We will keep in touch about this ... As to you. Goodbye."

As Toochla put away her communicator, she noticed that Clover had wandered off. Not good, Toochla reprimanded herself. Clover's curiosity may have overruled her sense of safety. Remembering the tiny homing tag (the size of a grain of sand) that was embedded unnoticeably behind Clover's right ear, Toochla took out her monitor and was about to turn it on, when the smell wafted past her nostrils: Clover's first bowel movement in her new home. Looking to her left, Toochla saw Clover emerge from behind a large shrub, smiling at her mentor. The Head Salamander calmly walked over to where Clover had done her business and summoned the hominid back to the scene. Giving Clover a very direct look, Toochla pointed at the mess, then scooped up a handful of dirt and covered it. Toochla pointed at the mound and gave Clover another direct look. Clover looked at the salamander, then looked at the mound. To drive home the point, Toochla placed two fingers over her own nostrils and turned away from the mound. Hoping that Clover had gotten the message, Toochla guided Clover back to the path and continued exploring.

For the benefit of the terrarium's plants, the artificial lighting in the massive room was dimmed every 27 Earth hours to simulate the Baasians' home planet's daily rotation. By the time the night cycle began, Clover was exhausted. Toochla guided her back to where Clover had originally awoken, which wasn't too far from one of the Terrarium's entrances. Clover laid on the ground and covered herself with the pelt. It was also Toochla's time for a bowel movement of her own. She made her way to the restroom near their camp, and sat down, exhausted. From behind the closed door, she heard a whimpering sound—Clover was still terrified of being left alone. "I'm in here," she called soothingly from where she sat. She heard rubbing and slapping noises all over the small privy, with even more frantic whimpering. Toochla quickly concluded her business and opened the door, startling the young hominid who looked at her with the most pleading expression. Smiling, Toochla led her into the privy and showed her the simple toilet. Toochla sat back down on it and made a grunting sound, demonstrating its use. Clover looked into the hole that the salamander had sat on, but then recoiled in disgust. It was the first time Clover heard a salamander laugh.

"Maybe we can build one for you," Toochla said, very amused as they left the privy. "Come, it's time to sleep." Toochla had a small mattress not far from Clover's pelt. The climate in the terrarium was an agreeable 20° Celsius. The lighting was now provided by the stars visible from outside the Mothership. From under her pelt, Clover gazed up at the display in awe. She always loved looking at the stars, but there was something different about this sky: the stars did not twinkle, and a large blue ball with white streaks was slowly growing smaller as it drifted across the horizon. Nudging Toochla and grunting excitedly, Clover pointed at the blue ball, got up and ran a short distance to get a better look at it, gawking in amazement. Far from being excited herself, Toochla looked with uncontrollable sadness at the receding planet and Clover's innocent excitement. She closed her eyes, looked away from the young girl and burst into tears in realization of scope of her decision to adopt her. "I am so sorry, Clover!" she whispered as Clover continued to gaze at the shrinking blue ball in the sky.

CHAPTER FOUR: THE TAMING OF CLOVER

It was late in the artificial morning when Toochla awoke. Normally, she was an early riser. Hominid-watching, however, required a more flexible schedule, and Toochla treated it as a working holiday. What woke her were the footsteps of Drasher, who had brought some provisions. "You two must have had a long day yesterday," Drasher said brightly.

"Long and productive," Toochla replied as she yawned and stretched. "I showed her many plants she could eat, how to work a fountain, and where we relieve ourselves." She looked at Clover, who was just starting to wake up. Toochla pointed at the other Baasian and asked Clover, "Drasher?" which was short for "Do you remember Drasher?" Clover looked bleary-eyed at Drasher and nodded.

Drasher handed Toochla a small bag, saying, "Here is breakfast for you." Then she pulled out a dull-pinkish, floppy piece of something. "And here's what, I hope, is a treat for Clover."

Clover perked up when she smelled the piece. It smelled like—bison meat! Ignoring the rubbery texture, Clover took the food and greedily devoured it. Toochla was curious. "What was that?"

"Lakkafraa curd infused with genes from the bison we collected," Drasher replied with a smile. "The genetics department volunteered to clone the cells of the plants and animals we brought back, in case our cuisine isn't to Clover's liking."

"Excellent! I wasn't sure that was possible," Toochla said as she peeled a green fruit. She remembered her conversation with Plaabutin. "Actually, I was hoping today to see how she likes the taste of jander moles. It would certainly please Plaabutin and her crew if Clover could help curb their population."

"Pleasing Plaabutin is a hard enough task," Drasher said dryly. Then her nostrils picked up an unpleasant odor. She looked past Toochla and saw Clover emerge smiling from behind a tree. "Oh, dear," Drasher winced. "I can smell what Plaabutin has been complaining about!"

Toochla immediately stalked over to where Clover had done her deed. Clover, startled, ran ahead of her to the site, hastily scooped up some soil and tossed it on her pile. She looked anxiously at Toochla. Toochla looked at the pile, then looked at Clover and bowed her head, smiling. The smile returned to Clover's face. Drasher saw this and remarked with a grin, "Ah, almost forgot, didn't we?"

Toochla turned to Drasher and said, "I wish to take her to the fields today, and I need a roller. Did you drive one here?"

"It's just outside the entrance. Since I have no duties today, I can drive you there and back."

Moments later, Drasher drove up in medium-sized six-wheeled topless car. Clover hid behind Toochla and gazed in wonderment at the contraption. Toochla climbed into the back seat and motioned for Clover to follow. Clover stood rooted, intimidated by this rolling thing. Toochla climbed out, picked up Clover and carried her into the back seat. Clover shivered and whined. What were the Salamanders doing with her now?

From the driver's seat, Drasher sighed. "I was afraid of this."

"She will have to get used to our technology," Toochla said as she used her two powerful right arms to restrain the squirming hominid. "Start slowly."

Hoping for the best, Drasher barely pressed the accelerator with her front right foot. The vehicle crawled quietly to life and languidly down the path toward the fields. Clover was even more terrified, and squirmed even more, her whine evolving into a shriek. Toochla gripped her with all four arms and gave her a direct look accompanied by a low growl. Clover froze. The message was very clear: sit down and shut up. Clover relaxed, and started looking at the passing scenery. After a while, Toochla didn't need to restrain her. Clover's indefatigable curiosity reemerged and she marveled at the ever-changing surroundings. She looked at Toochla at one point for reassurance. Toochla looked at her, smiled, and patted her on the shoulder. Clover smiled, then returned to her sightseeing.

An hour later they arrived at the fields. From a distance, this reminded Clover of the savannah. The roller slowed to a halt and they disembarked. Clover looked at the grass. It was tall and light brown. She was feeling more at home already. If it wasn't for the green sky, the illusion would be complete. The peaceful vibe was jarred by Drasher, who emitted a disgusted, "Ecchh!" as she inspected the seat that Clover had used. Toochla saw it: a small brown streak on the soft padding. Toochla turned to Drasher and said sheepishly, "It looks like the next lesson will be on *wiping!* Sorry."

Drasher took out a cleaning leaf, spat on it, and wiped off the streak. "On the trip back," she snorted, "we will COVER her seat!"

Clover was too enamored by the new scenery to notice the salamanders' conversation. She felt more comfortable in the field than she had in the cloistered atmosphere of the forest. Seeing no predators, she decided to go exploring. Drasher saw Clover wandering off, and asked Toochla, "Shouldn't we keep her closer to us?"

Toochla thought for a few seconds, then answered, "She spent all of yesterday by my side. She could probably use some freedom. Besides, I don't think there is anything out here that can harm her." The two Baasians followed the hominid at a respectful distance.

It was quite a long hike. Clover spent most of her walk with her gaze pointed slightly downward—as always, she was looking for food. She sampled some grains and flowers along the way, but with little apparent enthusiasm. The *faux* bison meat she ate for breakfast kept her filled for the first half of that day, and with Toochla and Drasher following a short distance behind, she felt no danger. But there was nothing very stimulating in this field either. She was safe and fed, but also bored and tired. She sat down on a large rock, stared off into the distance, and started to brood. Would she ever see any of her own kind again, she wondered. And where were her favorite clover flowers?

Then Clover heard something rustle in the tall grass nearby. It seemed to be something small enough for her to catch and eat. She scrambled into a crouching position on top of the rock and stared intently at the rustling grass. Then she saw the head: a brownish-purple, flat-faced head with four small eyes and two antennae, its broad nose sniffing at the ground. Its hairy, squat body had six legs. Clover saw that it was the size of a wolf cub. She slowly reached down to grab a rock large enough to kill something. The six-legged mammal didn't seem to notice the hominid poised to attack; it sniffed blissfully on. Clover slowly drew back the rock. A brief hesitation, then the pitch: the rock flew straight into the front left leg of the mammal, crippling it. The animal emitted an ear-piercing cry, then scrambled back into the brush. Clover reclaimed the lethal rock and chased after her prey.

Drasher recognized the squeal. "That was a eug!"

Toochla pursued Clover, saying, "Not good! Let's get her!" Eugs were slow breeders and prized for their fur; many were kept as pets.

Two members of Plaabutin's staff were inspecting the fields nearby. They had the same reaction as Toochla and Drasher to the eug's squeal. They ran to investigate, contacting Plaabutin along the way. It was a close race, but Plaabutin's people got to Clover first. "Wind of the East!" cried the larger of the caretakers, using a popular expletive. "That must be the Blue Planet person!"

"She caught one of the eugs," cried the younger caretaker.

"It *would* be one of Plaabutin's," muttered Drasher as she and Toochla rushed up to the scene. To the caretakers, she cried, "Don't go near her, please!"

Clover stood surrounded by the four salamanders, two of whom she did not recognize. Her terrified gaze darted all around as she clutched the now-dead eug. She turned to the unknown salamanders and took a defiant stance, baring her teeth and hissing at them in imitation of deadly snakes her people had encountered. The larger caretaker made a grab for the dead eug. Toochla ordered, "We said don't go near her!"

Clover took a swat at the caretaker, who replied frantically, "But that eug belongs to our leader! She's going want that hominid flayed!" She tried to grab the eug from Clover's grasp. Clover gnashed again, stepping toward her to take another swat. The caretaker retreated a bit—just enough to make Clover more bold. The hominid took several more stamping steps toward the caretaker, acting even more intimidating. In reality, the caretaker could outfight the hominid, but neither was aware of this.

Plaabutin raced up to the scene on her three-wheel pedaler and disembarked, running. "How DARE you bring that foreign creature into my field!" she shouted. "I'm notifying the High Council about this!"

This was a moment Toochla had hoped wouldn't come. She walked behind Clover, grabbed her free arm, and spun her around to face her. Toochla grabbed Clover's hand with the eug. Clover looked surprised at her guardian, them screamed at a higher pitch and struggled as mightily as she could, as Toochla used her free hands to wrench the eug out of the hominid's clutch. Incensed, Clover screamed even louder, kicked her feet, and tried to bite one of the powerful hands restraining her.

Enough was enough. Toochla braced her four feet firmly on the ground, then used her lower hands to grab Clover's ankles. With all four of the hominid's appendages secured, Toochla lurched her into a spread-eagle position, shocking Clover out of her anger. Toochla took a deep breath, then let loose a heart-stopping, ear-shattering, "RRRROOOOOAAARRRR!"

Clover screamed in terror. She knew that the Head Salamander was going to rip her to shreds.

Toochla knew better. After the roar, she glared witheringly at Clover in dead silence. The other four Baasians watched the standoff, mesmerized. Finally, Toochla relaxed her mighty grip, dropping the hominid on her feet. Clover stared at Toochla, tears in her eyes, not knowing how to react. The girl then let out a despairing cry and ran away into the field.

Plaabutin picked up the dead eug, examined its lifeless body, turned to the larger caregiver and ordered, "Find that animal, then bring it back to me, dead or alive!"

Toochla jumped between the caretaker and the departed Clover. "Leave her alone! I will take full responsibility for this mishap."

Plaabutin whipped out her communicator and snarled, "Be careful of what you volunteer for, Toochla." She punched a button, and said, "High Council, North Sector."

The smaller caretaker, about the equivalent age as Clover, walked up to Toochla while Plaabutin made her complaint. "I guess that hominid doesn't know any better," she observed shyly.

Toochla, scratching her own head contemplatively, sighed. "No. But *I* should have known better."

Drasher kept tabs on Clover's location with Toochla's monitor. The hominid had run many yards away, then stopped for some time. Probably having a big cry, Drasher assumed.

Plaabutin put away her communicator and looked directly at Toochla. "Cossakki herself will be here soon. I suggest that you make as strong a case for yourself and the hominid as you can. My estimate is that the hominid will face much stricter confinement, if she's lucky! As for you," she shook her head, "you may lose your custody of her and get an official reprimand." Softening somewhat, Plaabutin asked, "Why didn't you inform me that you were bringing the hominid here today? I wanted to show her the creatures we want her to catch."

"We meant no disrespect," Toochla assured her. "My purpose was to show her as much of the terrarium as possible." More pointedly, she added, "Also, the only restriction I was given about where to take her in the terrarium was away from major food producing areas. This is a nonfood area."

Most of the talking was between Toochla and Plaabutin before Senior High Councillor Cossakki arrived. It was a spirited conversation. Plaabutin was well-known for her volatile temper; inflaming that temper was never a good idea. During the Great Debate, Drasher, seeing Clover slowly making her way back to them, surreptitiously stepped into the field for a few moments with the remains of the eug, then returned just as surreptitiously, resting the eug corpse to the side of the path as she rejoined her colleagues.

Cossakki arrived in her vehicle with her valet. All present bowed. High Councillors were the most venerated people on the Mothership. It was respect that was well-earned. All Baasians on the Mothership knew of the great responsibilities the High Council had to deal with, as well as their great sacrifice: by tradition, all of its members had to give up all privacy for the duration of their terms. This involved having cameras imbedded in their skulls. Their every move, their every conversation, even their meals and potty breaks were recorded for everyone to witness. This meant no secrets, no hidden agendas, no cabals, no special privileges—nothing escaped public scrutiny. The High Council's word was law, and one had to be a crackerjack debater to justify any transgression of that law. Cossakki, a little short and slight in stature, had a very powerful mind and was not easily fooled or flattered. Both Toochla and Plaabutin were especially aware of this now.

Cossakki returned the collective bow. She then said, "I have been eagerly anticipating meeting this Blue Planet person. Too bad it had to be under these circumstances. Where is she?"

Toochla replied, "She ran away after I disciplined her, Senior. She does have a monitor chip in her head."

Cossakki squinted at Toochla. "Are you sure it is wise to leave her unattended, Researcher? She has already killed one eug and may be a danger to every living thing in this area."

"The hominid tried to bite us," Plaabutin interjected. "She—"

"I'm still addressing Toochla, Caretaker," Cossakki cut her off. To Toochla, she continued, "What is your reason behind your faith in that hominid's behavior?"

"She recognizes me as her leader, High Councillor," Toochla replied calmly. "She doesn't wander too far from me, and she is a fast learner. She just needs more time to adjust to our ways."

Cossakki pointed at the dead eug, asking, "What about that?" Plaabutin's expression silently echoed the High Councillor's concern.

"I had no idea that eugs were in this part of the field," Toochla stated. "In fact, yesterday Plaabutin and I were hoping to eventually put her to work here controlling the jander mole population. I will take full responsibility for Plaabutin's loss, and will try to compensate. But I wish you to consider the hardships that the Blue Planet person has had to deal with these last few days, and her youth."

Drasher felt it was time to interrupt. "The hominid is approaching us now, High Councillor."

Cossakki saw her first live glimpse of Clover coming through the field. There was a frightened look in the hominid's eyes as she shyly shuffled up to the group of salamanders. To everyone's surprise, she held a crude bouquet of common field flowers in both her hands. She stopped several feet away, then gently tossed the flowers to the feet of the salamanders, stepped back a couple paces, and dropped to her knees. Her hands were folded in front of her, eyes looking beseechingly at Toochla.

A big grin stretched across Toochla's face. She carefully knelt down, scooped up some of the flowers, then bowed her head at Clover. The message: all is forgiven. Clover quickly bowed her head in return.

Drasher smiled and picked up another flower. The two caretakers gawked in astonishment. Plaabutin gawked, then shook her head with a hand against it, embarrassed.

Absolutely charmed, Cossakki laughed with delight. She asked Plaabutin, "THAT is the terrible monster you described to me?" She reached down, picked up one of the remaining flowers, grinned, and bowed to the hominid. Clover returned the bow. The caretakers and the valet did likewise. Clover bowed again.

The only Baasian without a flower was Plaabutin. "With all due respect, Senior," she said testily, "this is still no assurance that she won't kill more eugs."

Drasher picked up the dead eug and said, "No. But perhaps this is." She walked over to Clover and offered the eug to her. Clover hesitantly accepted the eug, but then sniffed it. Recoiling in disgust, she thrust it back into Drasher's hands. Drasher leant closer and gave her a sharp, curt nod. The message Clover received: don't mess with these creatures. Still, the girl was hungry. She looked up at Drasher miserably, held her stomach and whimpered like a baby. Drasher smiled and pulled from her bag another slab of the bison-flavored bean curd. Cheering up immensely, Clover accepted the slab and tore into it, grinning at Drasher with appreciation.

The others were astonished. Drasher handed the animal back to Plaabutin, who asked in amazement, "Why does she suddenly not want the eug?"

Drasher smiled and replied, "I peed on it." Plaabutin immediately tossed the dead eug to the ground in disgust. Drasher put a reassuring hand on Plaabutin's shoulder. "She learns by example," she explained tactfully. "Consider it a sacrifice for all eug-kind."

"Very inspired, very inspired!" Cossakki applauded. Toochla smiled admiringly at Drasher. The younger caretaker barely suppressed a giggle. Cossakki asked Plaabutin, "Tell me, Caretaker, have you ever raised children?"

"No, High Councillor," the Head Caretaker replied, "I have not."

"I have raised three," Cossakki declared. "And I can say, with experience to confirm my words," she leaned closer, pointing at Clover, confiding, "I've seen them act worse than her!" To the rest of the group, she proclaimed, "My decision is thus: the hominid is still our welcome guest, and we should keep her well. Toochla, you and your crew have handled her astoundingly well. But for this one lapse in her supervision, you do owe compensation to Plaabutin for her loss. Plaabutin, you may set the terms of that compensation, but I recommend that you base it more on material loss than your own emotions. If there are no more relevant comments ..." she paused as was the custom, "then my business here is complete. Oh, you all may want to watch the sky tonight. We will be passing by the sixth planet in this system at about Hour One tonight. The astronomers say it should be quite a sight. Good day." She turned with her valet and departed.

Drasher looked up at the massive window ceiling above the terrarium, which was located about half a mile under the surface of the converted moon they were riding on. "We'll need to get back to my vehicle," she said. The lights will be dimming soon."

Toochla said calmly to Plaabutin, "My offer about Clover catching moles still stands."

Plaabutin, embarrassed and exasperated, could barely look at the Researcher. "One day helping my crew for compensation," she grumbled. "We will deal with the mole issue some other time."

"Fair enough." Toochla carefully approached Clover and gently helped her to her feet. She put a protective arm over the young hominid's shoulder and smiled. Clover managed a nervous smile and let the Head Salamander guide her back to Drasher's roller.

*****

Back at the campsite in the forest that night, Clover lay on her pelt. Despite the emotional scene earlier that day, meeting more of the salamanders put her more at ease in her new environment. Most of them (except that large, grumpy one) acted very kindly to her. She had not seen any large predators, and the food was good (except for that stinky six-legged thing). Soon, memories of her brother invaded her thoughts. She imagined how much fun they would have had exploring this strange new place together. The crushing realization that she had to explore it without him forever made her choke back sobs. But she did manage to fall asleep.

A low, steady, unfamiliar roar awoke the young hominid late that night. She bolted upright, wide-eyed. In the terrarium, she could make out the silhouettes of thousands—tens of thousands of salamanders gazing up at the sky, many pointing long fingers upward. Looking up, she saw a large, yellow moon looming in the night sky. As it zoomed closer, she saw huge rings around it. There were other, much smaller moons surrounding the ringed moon. Clover sat on her pelt, transfixed at the awesome sight. Moments later, the roar reached a crescendo as the big yellow ringed ball filled half the horizon. Clover's eyes widened so much that they seemed to push her back onto her pelt. As she was about to scream, the giant yellow moon began to recede toward the opposite horizon. Over that horizon, she saw a larger-than-usual star.

The roar eventually shriveled to a din. In need of reassurance, Clover made her way to the Head Salamander. What she found gave her pause: Toochla lay on her blanket, naked. The Fire-Making Salamander (Xashan), also naked, lay next to her. They both were on their backs marveling at the awesome sight, conversing softly.

Clover softly whimpered to get Toochla's attention. Toochla looked up with a grin. "Quite a display, isn't it?" she asked the confused hominid.

"Which?" Xashan deadpanned. "The ringed planet or us?"

"Shut up!" Toochla mock-ordered good-naturedly. She sat up and took the girl under both her right arms and held her to her side. For the first time, Clover hugged her surrogate mother. Eventually, she would fall back to sleep under those arms.

As the morning broke, the Mothership sailed past what another species of hominid would later name the Oort Cloud. Its ramjets shifted to near-light-speed. Imperceptibly, the atmosphere and air pressure were altered and the metabolism of life on the Mothership entered the waking hibernation condition of Slow Time. Unaware of this marvel of Baasian science, Clover slept peacefully on. It would be another five Slow Time Years before she would see her home planet again. In linear time, it would be another 400,000 years.

CHAPTER FIVE: MEETING CHARLIE SCHWITTERS

Charlie Schwitters waited patiently in line at the Transition Project soup kitchen for his dinner. A native of Seattle, he was now living in Portland, Oregon. Charlie's 43 year route from Seattle to Portland had taken him through Gonzaga University in Spokane for his bachelor's degree in biology, to Cornell University in New York for his bachelor's in paleoanthropology, to a teaching gig at Aterwood Middle School in Wichita, Kansas, to a short prison term in Waco, Texas, and finally to Portland, one of the most progressive cities in the United States.

It was the elements and events in Wichita that kept replaying in his mind every time he stood in a breadline. There was his training in paleoanthropology, which convinced Charlie of the validity of Darwin's evolutionary theories. There was the Aterwood PTA, which was staffed (or, in his mind, stacked) by predominantly hardcore Intelligent Design advocates. There was that cockamamie rule imposed by the Kansas State Board of Education about teaching Intelligent Design in his science courses to the students. There was the first court case, where Charlie led most of the local scientific community to successfully have the rule overturned. Briefly after that came his feeling of security that he could go back to his true calling as a science teacher and get away from the power politics of the Intelligent Design crowd. Then came the event that would lead to the second trial: when he gave a failing grade one his students, Monica Ludlake.

Monica was the oldest child in a large family of strict evangelical Christians. She presented a science paper that espoused Intelligent Design theories in direct defiance of Mr. Schwitters' teachings on evolution. To Charlie's well-trained mind, the paper contained the same hackneyed arguments that creationists had screeched about since the first edition of *The Origin of Species* saw print. Ever the professional, Charlie called Monica into a small meeting room at Aterwood to privately discuss her failing grade, as well as her constantly disruptive behavior in his class. Discussion, nothing more.

Soon after he started talking to Monica, she flinched and yelled, "Don't!" This startled Charlie, whose hands had been chastely clasped together on his chest. He tried to calm her down, but she ripped her blouse open and shouted even more loudly, "No, DON'T!" Then she ran out of the room, down the hallway, screaming, "RAPE! RAPE"!" Charlie emerged from the meeting room wide-eyed, and stammered to witnesses, who moved away from him. Then came the arrest. Then came the second trial. Accompanying these was the sensational media coverage: "Charlie Schwitters, the winner of the controversial *Schwitters vs. the Aterwood Board of Education* lawsuit," announced one anchorperson, "now faces a new trial, this time in criminal court for allegedly trying to molest one of his students."

As he accepted his plate of we-try-our-best-with-what-we-got supper at the soup kitchen, Charlie was feeling a little more thankful that his current homelessness offered him some anonymity. During the trial, his mugshot had been all over the news—"Tonight's top story: the latest on the evolution teacher's trial for sexually assaulting a student ....coming up later in our broadcast, more on the war in Afghanistan and the famine in Somalia."

Under ordinary circumstances, Charlie Schwitters would have been cleared of all the charges that the Ludlake family brought against him. Monica Ludlake's testimony on the witness stand was kaleidoscopic in how often she changed the details of her story. But what she lacked in evidence and consistency, she made up for in political connections: her father was an elder in her church, which had strong ties to Rev. Allen Graves and his "Fellowship America" movement. In turn, Graves had extremely powerful connections to every branch of the United States government, as well as most major media conglomerates. The reverend was known for his arch-conservative politics and his bullying debate tactics. His own sensational claims against people he "would pray for" (i.e. despised) would've seemed comical, but he was a powerful salesman. And he passed his selling points on to those of his members who could further his agenda, such as the district attorney who prosecuted Charlie Schwitters, and the judge who presided over the case. Then there were Monica's supporters, who were plentiful, loud, and scary.

Instead of throwing Monica's case out, the judge called a closed conference of the D.A. and Charlie's lawyer, Greg List. The judge, a woman in her late 50s, strongly recommended that Mr. Schwitters accept a plea bargain. List was outraged—the jury had not yet heard all of his client's character witnesses—but the judge held stonily firm. Charlie himself was outraged, and refused to cop a plea for a crime he didn't commit. The jury, which had been difficult for Greg List to balance out, found Charlie Schwitters guilty of sexually assaulting a minor in his care, and he was sentenced to seven years at the Waco Maximum Security State Prison. After more than a brutal year of prison politics that he tried desperately to block from his mind, Charlie's case was reopened, and he was eventually exonerated and free to go.

But go where? Thanks to Rev. Graves' masterful media manipulation, many people still believed that Charlie got some slick-ass lawyers to work the system for him, and that included many potential employers. Every teaching job he applied for, local news media would mention the trial, concerned parents would raise their voices, and Charlie Schwitters wouldn't get the job. Eventually, he lost his savings, his belongings, and his spirit. Bitterly, he figured that Rev. Graves and his minions knew damn well that the Monica Ludlake case would eventually be declared a mistrial. The true goal was the destruction, not the incarceration, of Charlie Schwitters and anyone who dared oppose Fellowship America. Though his fellow scientists gave him as much moral support as they could afford, they knew that the same fate could happen to them as long as Fellowship America enjoyed so much political influence. And so to the soup kitchens Charlie Schwitters went.

It was a relatively light turnout at Transition Project that afternoon, so Charlie had little trouble finding a seat at one of the tables. He was a semi-regular here, but he had few people to talk to.

Most of the other clientele there had little to say to him. To them, he was just some yuppie scum who had lost everything in some dumb-ass investment deal. At least it was a step up from thinking he was a child molester.

The small, wall-mounted TV was showing network news. The anchorwoman mentioned a story that caught Charlie's attention: NASA reported a mysterious dark streak across the latest photos from the Hubble Space Telescope, and astronomers were baffled what caused it. One brief soundbite from a NASA spokesman —"The object would have to be traveling about half the speed of light"—then it was back to the anchorwoman. Having a few extra seconds before the next commercial, she squeezed in a story about the upcoming "Fellowship America" rally being held in Colorado Springs, hosted by evangelist Rev. Allen Graves. Charlie nearly threw his loaded plate at the TV, but he restrained himself; getting himself kicked out of a soup kitchen would only continue Graves' victory over him.

Soon after he started eating, he heard a thick French accent from behind him say, "Hallo." He turned his head, and stooping close behind him was a man in his mid-40s dressed in ill-fitting, ill-matched clothes. The Frenchman seemed eager to strike up a conversation. "Are you constant here?"

Definitely English as a second language, thought Charlie. "You mean, do I come here often?" he asked.

"Yes, yes," the Frenchman replied. He seemed jittery. "I am new here. I do not know my way. You may help me?"

Between bites, Charlie answered, "Not much I can do besides give you directions. If you need money, this definitely not the place to ask for it."

"No, no, no," the Frenchman replied, with waving hands. Then he had to find the next words to say. "I just arrive here with others. We need to know where to get things." He extended his right hand. "My name is Didier."

Charlie accepted the handshake. "Don Anderson," he said, using his pseudonym to protect his hard-fought-for anonymity. "Nice to meet you." He saw Didier staring at him. "So," he asked, trying to restart the conversation, "what's so special about me that you would ask me for help?"

Didier, smiling nervously, said, "Oh, well, you look, er, different from those men here. You look well-schooled for to be here."

"Well, thank you," Charlie replied guardedly. "I must say that you don't seem to fit in here either."

"No?"

"No. I mean, you're dressed like the others, but you talk like you've just stepped out of the Sorbonne."

"Oh!" Didier grinned shyly. "*Merci*. That is flattery." More seriously, he continued, "My attire, I get from donate, er, donation box. We need more."

A squat, curly-haired man in his mid-50s sitting across from Charlie and Didier dropped his fork under the table. "Agh," he muttered as reached down to retrieve it. Charlie paid it no mind. "There is more than just you, I take it?" he asked the Frenchman.

"Yes. Eight others than myself."

"Eight?" Charlie asked, astonished. "Are they, like, your family? Are they all French?"

Didier seemed to be choosing his words very carefully. "I am the only Frenchman. Others are from other places. They are like my family."

Charlie turned his attention from his dinner. "There must be some weird story behind all this, dude. Can you elaborate?"

"Ee-laborate?"

"Give me more information?"

"Ah, yes," Didier replied discreetly, "but we leave from here first."

Something is wrong here, Charlie thought. Why did this Frenchman single me out for help? He leaned toward Didier and said earnestly, "Look, guy. If you're in some kind of legal trouble and are trying to hide, there is nothing I can do for you. I'd rather stay lost myself after the shit I've been through. Sorry, but I don't want to be burdened with other peoples' secrets!"

Didier was taken aback. "I did not wish to offend, *Monsieur* Schwi—*Anderson!*"

Charlie's eyes widened at the first syllable of his last name. Didier—and, no doubt, his people—knew more about Charlie Schwitters than he let on. Then his eyes narrowed. "Yes," he said, "my name is Anderson. And that's all I feel like telling you now. *Au revoir!*" With that, he grabbed his backpack, and made for the door.

Didier appeared frantic. "No, no, *monsieur*," he pleaded. "I am not of those who hurt you! My people can help you if you help us!"

"*Je tres bien, merci beaucoup!*" Charlie called back as he walked briskly down Glisan Street toward the Northwest Hills.

Didier stood helplessly, dabbing his forehead with a handkerchief as he watched the homeless paleoanthropologist disappear around a corner. A moment later, the squat man who had dropped his fork stood beside the nervous Frenchman. "It's okay," he told Didier. "I was able to stick the tracking particle into the strap of his pack."

"I know," Didier said, still looking in the direction of Charlie's departure. "I'm afraid I may have given him the wrong impression of us, Iannis."

Iannis grinned knowingly. "Can you think of the *right* impression of us?" Putting an arm around Didier's shoulder, he said, "Come, let us finish our meal."

"If the meal itself doesn't finish us!" Didier replied with slight revulsion as they reentered the soup kitchen.

None of the other occupants there noticed that the easily-flowing conversation between the two foreigners was in two very different languages: modern French and ancient Greek.

*****

It was almost dusk when Charlie made his way to the middle of Forest Park, the largest inner-city park in Portland, as well in as the Western Hemisphere. The main trail was Leif Erickson Drive, a winding, unfinished road closed off to motor vehicles. There were many hiking trails, but there were even more places where a homeless man could temporarily lose himself from the rest of society. Charlie was getting to know most of the park, having spent more than a year there. The park maintenance staff knew that the real identity of "Don Anderson" was Charlie Schwitters, the unfairly disgraced science teacher—in fact, it was one of the poorest-kept secrets in the Portland area—but they had a "don't ask, don't tell" agreement with him. More fastidious than most homeless people, he had earned the staff's trust by helping pick up litter along the trails, and was a champion destroyer of the English ivy that plagued the park. In return, the staff looked the other way while he camped illegally. But their largesse existed only during their working hours, which ended every day at 5:00 PM. After that, until 9:00 AM the next morning, Charlie was on his own.

Charlie stood six-foot-one inch at 173 pounds. Despite his hardships, all the hiking and light meals he ate had him in as good physical shape as he had ever been. But no amount of exercise or dieting could help him outrun two punks pedaling furiously on mountain bikes after him. Walking along Leif Erickson Drive, just a quarter mile short of his usual camping site, he heard them. He turned around and saw two ski masks and two sawed-off golf clubs atop two bikes heading straight for him. "Shit!" he hissed as he bolted off the wide trail and into the trees. The bikers followed him, taking slightly different directions to surround him.

Rushing frantically through the woods, Charlie saw both bikers gaining on him. He was terrified that these weren't amateur cyclists; they were making some truly expert maneuvers as they negotiated their way among the trees and bushes. What Charlie didn't see in time was a sudden drop in the forest floor that sent him tumbling. Sensing the attackers were only a few yards away, he instinctively curled up in a fetal position and covered his head tightly with his arms.

That first blow came immediately to his exposed right thigh—an attempt to make the victim uncover his head. Another blow landed on his right shoulder. A steeled-tipped shoe kicked him in the ribs twice, joined by another steel-tipped shoe. Several times. Two more blows to his arms. Despite the intense pain, Charlie kept himself tightly shut. The blows ceased. One of the masked maulers said to his partner, "Damn, he's a tough nut to crack."

"Well," replied the partner in crime. "you just have to know the right spot to hit." He raised his truncated three-iron and slammed the back of Charlie's left hand. With an agonizing cry, Charlie's fetal position unravelled, leaving his head exposed. This is it, Charlie mourned to himself as he awaited his forceful exit from life.

But both attackers and their victim heard a rustling of bushes at the top of the steep slope. The two attackers saw a strange figure dressed in a tattered overcoat, a battered fedora, and rubber boots. The face looked familiar to the attackers: it was a rubber Halloween mask of Bull Mountain, the pro wrestler. The attackers turned on the Mystery Man to chase him off.

Charlie opened his eyes and saw the whole thing: his assailants rushed up the slope, brandishing their three-irons. The Mystery Man reached into the overcoat and pulled out what looked like a thick cattle prod. Then came a blue light and a shrill screech from the prod. Suddenly, one of the attackers was enveloped, with a gurgling scream, in a blue, plasma-like blob as thousands tiny electric jolts coursed through his body. The prod gave the same treatment to the other assailant. While the two punks writhed in agony in their electric plasma prisons, the Mystery Man turned back and made a come-here motion with his arm, accompanied by a weird, muted-trumpet-like call. A moment later, two women arrived.

Charlie wanted to get up and run, but was in too much pain to move. The two women made their way down the slope and picked Charlie up, draping one arm over each of their shoulders. One of the women looked in her early 40s, Caucasian with long curly red hair; the other looked Arabic and in her early 20s with lustrous, jet-black hair. Charlie wanted to speak, but the Arabic woman put a stern finger to her lips and shushed him. The two women and Charlie climbed the slope, away from the scene, with the Mystery Man leading the way. As they left, the two small plasma storms faded away, leaving the bicyclists trembling violently and helplessly until they both lost consciousness. The Mystery Man looked back on the two well-nuked bike punks, shook his head, and joined the two women and Charlie.

They did not go back to Leif Erickson Drive. Instead, they followed a barely discernible trail deeper into the woods. It was now twilight, and the Mystery Man led the way with his flashlight. Charlie, too stunned and in pain to comment, noticed something very unusual about the Man's walk: his legs straddled widely, but took unusually large strides.

CHAPTER SIX: EVERYTHING EXPLAINED

Eventually they came upon a long-disused cistern that Charlie recognized. The top of it stuck out about seven feet from the ground and was covered with graffiti and ivy, sporting a weathered metal plaque above the access door that read "1919." The cistern probably hadn't been used in about 40 years—at least to hold water. Light emanated from the cracks of the door, however. Arriving at the door, the Mystery Man emitted another muted-trumpet sound, answered by a similar voice. They all went in and climbed down the concrete stairs to the bottom.

Inside the round, musty cistern, were several smaller, dome-shaped shelters made of what looked like silver mylar. Light was provided by three tall, tubular lamps placed in an equilateral triangle pattern on the floor. Four six-wheeled metallic carts were parked neatly at the far radius from the door. There were only two people in the room that Charlie could see: one was a dark-complexioned man about Charlie's age, weight, and height, clothed head-to-foot in shabby clothes similar to what that Didier weirdo had been wearing, showing only his bearded face; the other was seated at a table holding some very sophisticated equipment, wearing only a blue sheet draped over his (her?) entire body, deliberately facing away from Charlie. Soon, everyone in the room was conversing animatedly in different languages, except Charlie, who couldn't understand any of them. The ladies escorted him to a chair, and the red-haired woman rushed to one of the carts to get some medicine. The Arabic woman assisted Charlie in removing his heavy backpack. Charlie finally noticed that the women were also shabbily dressed, and he immediately realized that these people must be the "they" that Didier had referred to! Nervously, he uttered his first words to his hosts: "I'm sure there is a logical explanation for all this."

Everyone turned toward their guest. The Arabic woman let out a laugh and said something to the others in Arabic. The others seemed equally amused. The redhead started tending to Charlie's wounds.

The draped figure at the desk handed something to the dark man, who walked carefully with a cane over to Charlie and handed the object to him. It looked like a stylish ear plug. Charlie looked at the object, then at the man. The dark man pulled up his stocking cap and revealed a similar object in his ear. Taking the hint, Charlie inserted the object into his ear and looked around. The Mystery Man approached, leaned down, and said to him through the rubber mask, "You may now join our conversation, Mister Schwitters."

The effect to his virgin ears was hearing a voice-over translator on the radio or TV. In the unaided ear, he heard the same trumpet-y voice as before; in the aided ear, the same voice instantaneously translated to English. Charlie's amazement made him forget how much pain he was in. "This is insane!" he gasped.

The others looked at him strangely. "I think it's perfectly logical," said the redhead.

The draped figure said, "We recommend that you refrain from slang and colloquialisms when you speak with us. These translators have their limitations."

Charlie uttered an elongated "Okay ..." Composing himself while the redhead daubed a minty-smelling ointment on his bruised bicep, he asked , "So, how many of you are not from Earth? I mean, after what you did to those guys who attacked me ..." ending his sentence with a silent shrug.

The Mystery Man answered, "My name is Toochla. At the control center there is Drasher. We are from a planet we call Baas, which is located in another arm of this galaxy. We are very pleased to finally meet you, Mister Schwitters."

"*Finally* meet me?" Charlie asked, somewhere between curiosity and suspicion. "So, what's the attraction? Am I that famous on your planet?"

The Arabic woman laughed again. "You are so funny!" she exclaimed, patting his shoulder. "My name is Taza. I am from this planet, from Arabia."

His nurse said, "I am Clodagh. I was born in England. This" she pointed to the dark man, "is Yehudi. He is from Palestine."

"Hello, one and all," Charlie said shyly. "Is a Frenchman named Didier part of your group?"

"He is, you may say, the newest member," Toochla replied. Then she raised a hand and said, "Before any more questions: since you have ascertained that Drasher and I are of another planet, would you be comfortable if we remove our disguises? Our appearance can be alarming to humans at first."

Charlie spread his arms and answered, "As long as you're not wearing masks, I don't care what you look like!"

"Thank you," Toochla said as she removed her trench coat. "These clothes are very uncomfortable."

Drasher stood up from her chair. "Prepare your eyes, Mister Schwitters," she said as she methodically pulled off her all-covering blanket. Charlie shuddered, but kept his composure. Purple, two set of arms and legs, elongated head with large eyes and thick eyelashes, impressive mane of hair from the top of the head down the back— Charlie took these in. Toochla eventually got all her disguise off. Both Baasians were dressed in sleeveless body suits that wrapped under the crotch and buckled in front of the waist. After the initial shock, Charlie figured he'd seen scarier-looking monsters in horror movies and video games. "I can get used to looking at you," he said amiably.

"Excellent," Toochla said. "Now, in answer to your question of why we chose you, the answer is rather involved. To be brief: when we visit your planet, we try to find someone who will act as our guide. There is only so much information our long-range devices can tell us. Your fellow humans here have been our guides in the past."

"Holy shit," Charlie muttered. He immediately turned to Drasher and gasped, "Sorry, I forgot!"

Drasher smiled knowingly and replied, "We will allow for expletives."

Charlie then turned to Clodagh and said, "You said you were from England, but I still needed the translator to understand you."

Clodagh smiled and replied, "The year of my birth was 1045 AD, by your calendar. Most people in my town spoke Saxon."

The control panel emitted a beeping sound. "Toochla? Drasher?" A male, assertive-sounding voice came through a small horn-like speaker. "Iannis speaking."

Toochla spoke into the horn, "Toochla speaking. Are you nearby?"

"We are," Iannis replied.

"Mister Schwitters is now safely with us. You both did well. You and Didier should return immediately."

"We will," Iannis replied, and signed off.

Toochla turned back to Charlie and explained, "You saw Iannis with Didier at the poor place. He planted a tiny tracking device in your pack."

Charlie made the connection. "He dropped his fork while Didier distracted me." He nodded. "Well, it worked, didn't it?"

"Anyway," Taza said, "I was born in Dibba in your year 621 AD. Iannis was born in Greece in 339 BC, Didier was born in France in 1750 AD, and Yehudi—"

"Taza, please!" Yehudi snapped at her. Taza clammed up. Yehudi turned to Charlie with entreating eyes. "I must be extremely careful about revealing myself. In my experience, people have a worse reaction to me than they do upon seeing the Baasians."

Confused, Charlie shrugged and said, "No problems here." He turned to Toochla and asked, "So what's the criterion that you use for choosing guides? Did we win a lottery or something?"

All went silent. Taza finally spoke softly for all the humans in the room, "It's not what we have won, but what we all have lost."

Clodagh explained, "We were all unjustly rejected by our own peoples. I was to be burned as a witch by the Christian bishop in my region."

Taza said, "I refused to convert to Islam when the Muslims sacked my city."

Toochla said, "Iannis offended local authorities with his Cynical philosophy. Didier barely escaped death under Robespierre's regime." She paused and said, "And you were ostracized under a false accusation. In brief, Mister Schwitters, we adopt those whom their societies reject unjustly. They are more willing to come with us and educate us about your people and other things on Earth."

"Are you Baasians also banished from your planet?" asked Charlie. "You talk as if you're in the same situation as we are."

Toochla looked at the floor for a moment. She then explained, "In a way, the remaining population of our planet banished itself. When our Mothership was built, it was an era of great cooperation between nations—there are natives of seven nations on the Mothership. Our aim was to find another planet to terraform and colonize. But when we returned from initial terraforming maneuvers, we found that the international cooperation we enjoyed in our time ...had deteriorated."

Charlie furrowed his brow. "I think I know where your story is going."

Toochla nodded. "The leaders of Baas' two largest nations, including the one that hosted the building of our Mothership," she sadly continued, "were in a terrible war over dwindling resources. The Mothership was to be conscripted by its host nation to attack the other nation and end the war more quickly. The Mothership's leaders, the High Council, voted not to get involved in the war. As a result, we became their new enemy." She sighed and said, "So we left our native solar system and redoubled our efforts to terraform the new planet. We estimate that it will be ready for us to live there unaided by artificial means by the time we return from this visit.

"When we arrived at the new planet, we had two pleasant surprises. First, the terraforming was going on as scheduled, so we had renewed hope for our survival. The second was that your planet came within range of our sensors and we were delighted that it showed signs of abundant life. While waiting for more changes on the new planet, we paid a visit here. Unfortunately for us, your atmosphere has too much nitrogen for us to breathe comfortably. We use a special fungus to coat our lungs, which filters out the nitrogen, but we don't have the resources to mass-produce it."

"This may sound treasonous on my part," Charlie said, "but couldn't you have terraformed the Earth to suit yourselves?"

"It was suggested," Toochla replied, "but our studies indicate that such an act would cause massive extinctions of most of your planet's lifeforms and cause more ecological problems than it will solve." She grew deathly silent, then added, "We have already seen one extinguished planet in our lifetimes. It was our own."

"Oh, no! I am so sorry!" Charlie said, mortified.

Toochla nodded sadly. "It is futile to mourn about it anymore. I will continue: we have been returning to your planet periodically to collect plant and animal specimens to diversify life more fully on our new planet, since our original plan was to return to Baas for that purpose. Having a human who could show us possible uses for those specimens has been of great help to us. We keep hoping that human society will mature enough so that all our human guests may return safely to your planet. But this Fellowship America organization that condemned you is very similar to the Frachetor Alliance on our home planet—they are the ones who forced the Mothership to flee. For us Baasians to witness how much power Fellowship America exerts in your government is like a recurring nightmare."

"We decipher your television news broadcasts," Yehudi added, "but we humans still do not know if we should return to Earth this time, or spend the rest of our days on the Mothership. Humans cannot survive on New Baas."

"The way I feel right now," Charlie replied, "I think you people have a better option on the Mothership!"

There was a knock on the access door. "It's us," called Iannis. Taza dashed up the stairs, unlocked the door, and opened it. Didier and Iannis followed her back down the stairs.

Charlie rose from his chair, Clodagh's medicine easing his pain, and extended a hand. "Didier," he said, "I'm sorry for how I behaved toward you back at the soup kitchen."

Didier warmly accepted the handshake. "You behaved most appropriately, my friend," he replied with a smile. Indicating the Greek, he said, "This is Iannis, the fork dropper."

Charlie shook Iannis' hand, saying, "Hello! I remember you now."

"Yes," Iannis responded with a sly grin and an eye toward Didier. "I have gone from Cynical Philosopher to Fork Dropper!"

Taza said, "Iannis is our representative to the Baasian High Council. He can explain many things to you."

"Later, later." Iannis waved her off. "I've walked many miles today, and I need a rest."

Another few beeps from the work station. "Xashan here," buzzed a Baasian voice. "We are just minutes away from the base."

Drasher responded, "Good. Mister Schwitters is in our care here. How is Clover managing?"

"She is fine," Xashan replied. "She killed and ate a small rodent, so she is happy."

Charlie was curious. "Clover?" he asked Toochla.

"She is our first passenger from your planet, Mister Schwitters," Toochla explained. "This is another factor in why we chose to contact you. You study humans from your ancient past, correct?"

"Very much, yes," Charlie answered.

"Clover is a female hominid from over 500,000 years in your past."

Charlie's eyes bloomed in amazement. "No shit!" he exclaimed. "I—I mean, really? What part of our planet did you get her from?" Drasher conjured up a map of the Earth and pointed to eastern Spain. "Oooh, that would mean she is *homo antecessor*. Oh, man, this is big —BIG!"

"We adopted her after she was banished from her tribe when she was about 12 years old," Toochla continued. "She is 27 now."

"I can't wait to meet her," Charlie said, calming down. Then he thought for a moment about the age and time discrepancy. "Mathematics were never my strongest suit," he said, trying to find words for his next question. "One of our greatest scientists, Albert Einstein talked about how people age at different speeds of travel. His theory of relativity, you know, $E=mc^2$?"

"Very good, Mister Schwitters," Toochla said with a smile. "Yes, to travel such long distances without aging ourselves too much, we enter a dimension we call Slow Time Space. It is where we on the Mothership function at our normal pace, while linear time accelerates enormously. The time distance between our two planets is roughly one Earth year in Slow Time, and 96 years in linear time. The longer we remain in Slow Time, the exponentially longer we are away in linear time. The process itself you may not fully comprehend, but you do grasp the idea."

"Yeah," he answered heavily, glancing at the humans in the room, "but it must be one hell of a price for all of you to pay."

"It is," Iannis said, his voice less boisterous than before. Then a brief silence enveloped the cistern until another knock on the door interrupted it. "We're back," called Xashan.

Didier let them in. Xashan, dressed in a similar disguise and mask as Toochla's, trotted down the stairs with Clover, who dressed in the same style of bodysuit as the Baasians, only it was light purple. Charlie's eyes widened in wonder. He had studied ancient hominids since he was in middle school and had seen many artists' depictions of them. But seeing one alive took his breath away. "Wow!" he slowly uttered as he gazed upon Clover for the first time.

Clover saw the bearded stranger looking at her and froze in her tracks. She didn't know what to make of him at first. She studied him carefully.

"She is very shy of newcomers," Iannis told Charlie. "Don't be deceived by her animal looks. She is a very nice girl."

Charlie couldn't take his eyes off of her. She stood at four feet eight inches tall, but was definitely an adult woman. Her lithe body —borderline-gymnast—had very little visible hair on her limbs. Her round face did have a long jaw and prominent eyebrows, but she had large, alert eyes and a supple mouth. Her long black hair looked very well-combed (courtesy of Taza). A huge smile overtook Charlie's face as he whispered, "Animal looks, nothin.' She's beautiful!"

The look of awe in Charlie's face seemed to mesmerize Clover. She took a couple steps closer to the newcomer. Charlie carefully walked up to her until they were within handshaking distance. Charlie leaned down and beamed at her warmly. Not knowing how to greet an ancient hominid, he shrugged his shoulders, and simply said, "Hi!"

Clover kept gazing at him. She took a deep breath and, in a hoarse, whispery voice answered, "Hiiiii."

Everyone else in the room blinked and gawked. Toochla summed up their reaction: "She has never warmed to anyone so quickly, Mister Schwitters. You have made quite a good first impression on her."

Charlie blushed. "I don't normally have that effect on modern women."

Xashan broke in. "So you must be Charlie Schwitters."

Charlie turned his gaze away from Clover. Nervously grinning, he replied, "And you must be President Ronald Reagan."

Xashan was confused by Charlie's response. Then she remembered that she was still wearing the rubber mask that Didier had scrounged up for her yesterday. "Oh! I may remove my disguise then. My name is Xashan."

"Pleasure to meet you," Charlie said as he shook one of her hands. It suddenly occurred to him—he had just touched the skin of an extraterrestrial being. It was warm and leathery. He flinched apologetically. Turning to Toochla, he shook his head and asked half-jokingly, "Did my attackers hit me in the head? This is all seems like a crazy dream."

"Fortunately, no, Mister Schwitters," Toochla responded. "This is all very real."

"Attacked?" Didier gasped to Charlie. "Good heavens, man! Are you badly hurt?"

"It could have been far worse," Charlie reassured him, rubbing his sore arms.

"Toochla ionized them within inches of their lives," Taza stated, grinning. "They won't be bothering us anymore!"

Charlie turned to Toochla. "'Ionized?' What was that thing you shot those guys with?"

Toochla produced the thick cattle prod and held it safely. "The name of this," she said, "translates in your language as a Hyper-Ionizing Plasma Gun. It shoots plasma that excites the static-electric ions in your atmosphere immediately around its target, causing electrocution. When I used its 'stun' setting on your assailants." She paused and sighed, "But I realized too late that their weapons were metal."

"Oh," Charlie drawled, "and the metal conducted the electricity even more!"

Toochla bowed and smiled. "Your grasp of science is quite good," she complimented him. Then her smile faded. "I fear I may have done irreparable damage to them. We have not come here to kill your people."

A sneer crept into Charlie's voice. "It's too soon after their attack for me to feel sorry for those assholes," he said. "But when they are found, the police are going wonder how they were damaged, and they will be searching this area for clues."

CHAPTER SEVEN: SALVATION VIA VADUZ

The room was silent for a moment. It had sunk in that the two now-incapacitated punks who attacked their guest had complicated the Landing Party's mission even further. Charlie asked the Baasians, "How much longer do you plan to hide in this cistern?"

"Four more of your days," Drasher answered. "We cannot leave this planet until our Reconnaissance Ship on your moon is positioned correctly to retrieve us. According to your broadcasts, if we are discovered, the response of your governments could be catastrophic for both our peoples."

Charlie limped over to his backpack on the floor, dug into one of the pockets and pulled out a roll of yellow "CAUTION" ribbon and a paper sign in a clear plastic sleeve. Charlie read the sign to the cistern occupants: "'Caution: pesticide spray used for garlic mustard'—those are nasty weeds—'in this area. Do not enter.' I can hang this up at where the trail to the cistern begins, and people should leave you alone."

Iannis was astounded. "Why do you carry this with you?"

"Privacy," Charlie replied simply. "People leave me alone while I sleep out here."

"You fiend!" Didier laughed. "How absolutely clever!"

The only one in the room who wasn't impressed was Drasher. "A sign?" she asked incredulously. "We are to be protected by a *sign*?! That is preposterous! We need to act quickly!"

"Be still, Drasher," Iannis said. "You should amazed at how we humans can deceive each other."

Drasher raised her voice in frustration. "We can't take that chance, Iannis! Those attackers have put us in further jeopardy! We need to plan our escape now!" She slammed a fist on her desktop.

Toochla put two firm hands on Drasher's right shoulder. "Our guest says we should be safe for tonight. You must have gathered enough information from their internet service by now to help us formulate a plan for tomorrow."

Drasher slumped against the desk, fatigued. "There is so much worthless information to sort through," she complained, a slight tremor in her voice. "It keeps inundating our system! I have spent half my day today deleting frivolous garbage, advertisements, puerile erotica—"

"Have you spent any time at rest?" Toochla asked.

Drasher stopped her rant and let her head sag. Toochla leaned closer and gently scolded, "I told you to *rest* periodically! Drasher, you are relieved of your duty until you have had sufficient sleep. Go to your tent. Xashan, take over the work station until further notice."

The room was silent as Drasher arose tiredly from her workstation. She faced the others, bowed her head and mumbled, "I'm very sorry." She then slunk into one of the mylar domes and closed the flap.

After an appropriate pause, Charlie said, "You seemed to know so much about me before you met me. You got that information from the internet?"

"Yes," Toochla replied, "as well as past video and audio broadcasts."

"How hard did you have dig? I mean, did you have get through much encryption code to find out where I was?"

"Some encryption code, yes. Our system can decode fairly easily. The trouble is that your peoples' technology can now easily detect the presence of our Mothership and its Reconnaissance Ship, which is currently landed just out of sight on the dark side of your moon. This was an unprecedented problem that we were not prepared to deal with when we reentered your solar system."

"I heard on the news that our telescope satellites did detect your Mothership, but they don't know what they saw yet. Where is it hidden, anyway?"

"On the far side of your sun, in a tandem orbit to your planet."

"Okay," Charlie said. "And now the big question: why choose me to help you? I study ancient humans, but I only have so much knowledge of our technology."

Iannis decided to explain. "The Baasians have great machines. But those machines need informed minds to find things on our world. They still ask all of us humans for our advice, regardless how long ago we lived here."

"Mister Schwitters," Toochla stated apologetically, "we would love to let you have some rest so soon after meeting us. But we cannot return to the Reconnaissance Ship for another four days, and our food supplies are almost gone. Anything you could do for us will be enormously appreciated."

Charlie rubbed his chin thoughtfully. He addressed Xashan, "Can you navigate our internet, or will we need Drasher?"

"Let Drasher sleep. It is well within my abilities."

Clover observed that this newcomer commanded respect from everyone, even her surrogate mother, Toochla. She made no move, but she felt she wanted to get closer to him.

Toochla asked, "What is your idea, Mister Schwitters?"

Conspiratorially, he answered, "To put it bluntly, we are going to steal money from Reverend Graves."

Everyone in the room gawked at Charlie. Toochla asked, "Steal? I thought you had more integrity than that, Mister Schwitters."

"Desperate times call for desperate measures, as the old saying goes," Charlie said with a shrug. "Besides, the money I have in mind for us to steal has been earned in less-than-honest ways."

Curiosity piqued, Toochla said, "Explain these 'less-than-honest' ways."

"It's a crime called money laundering. I'm sure you know, from reading about me, who Rev. Graves and Fellowship America are. Well, I can tell you from personal experience that Rev. Graves will stop at nothing to get what he wants, both politically and financially. One of his many organizations was a charity called Operation

Righteous Path. It was officially a mission to provide passable roads in Niger, which is a very poor country in Africa. Not long ago it was exposed as a front for illegal mining operations in Niger. The only roads the mission ever paved were for mining companies, which used Graves' planes and boats to smuggle precious materials out of Niger and onto the black market. In return, they paid him a percentage of their profits, which he deposited into a secret bank account to conceal where the money really came from. Do you follow me?"

"Stealing from the poor?" Didier asked incredulously. "That doesn't sound very Christian of him at all!"

Clodagh added, "But he was caught, correct?"

"Yeah," Charlie replied with an agitated nod. "But because he has such powerful friends in our government AND the news media, the scandal was briefly mentioned, and then," he fluttered a hand, "it magically went away!" He paused and looked meaningfully around the room. "Call me a vengeful son-of-a-bitch if you wish, but I am *not* the only person whom Rev. Graves has harmed because of his lust for power and money!"

Again the room was silent. Finally, Taza spoke, "It sounds tempting. Do you know where this money is?"

"Not yet. But with your computer's help, I think I can locate it AND access it."

"I want nothing from this!" Yehudi snapped. "Stealing is against God's will, even if it is from another thief!"

Iannis said, "Also, such an effort may make our whereabouts detectable. I don't know if it is worth the risk."

"I hate to say this," Charlie stated, "but Drasher is right about your situation. Tonight may be the only time we have to make a plan before the police investigate this area. What my plan will do, hopefully, is buy you all enough time on Earth until your ship can retrieve you." Turning to Yehudi, he said, "I'm sorry, Yehudi, but one cannot function in this country without money. If we are caught, I will take full responsibility to the authorities."

Yehudi demanded, "Would you also take your full responsibility to God?"

Although an atheist, Charlie replied, "I would. My aim is to help the people who saved my life and gave me refuge, not to cause great harm to Rev. Graves. Compare my motives with Rev. Graves' motives: whom would you hope that God will favor?"

Yehudi closed his eyes and sighed. "That is a terrible question," he muttered, "and I have no answer for it. Do as you must." Clodagh smiled and patted Yehudi's gloved hand.

Charlie turned to Toochla. "I guess you have the final say."

Toochla mulled it over. "No one else has thought of a better plan," she finally said. "Xashan, follow Mister Schwitters' instructions as best as you can."

Charlie took a deep breath, clapped his hands and said, "Right! Xashan, sir, if you can—"

"All Baasian people are female, Mister Schwitters," Xashan corrected him.

Charlie hesitated. "Really?" he asked in surprise. "I'll ask later. Anyway, first I want to find out the serial number of Rev. Graves' private jet."

Xashan worked the computer and found the answer. "VG789004"

"Okay, now we need a complete list from all airports in the world *outside* of the United States where his jet has visited in the last five years." Xashan's effort produced a very long list. "Right. Now comes the fun part: we need to find the airport that the jet has visited most frequently, especially for just a couple of days between arrival and departure."

Xashan entered Charlie's described parameters. "Zurich, Switzerland," she eventually announced. "Eighteen times within five years."

"Too easy!" Charlie exclaimed. "Keep that information and let's do some real hacking." Xashan turned to Charlie, befuddled. "Encryption decoding," he clarified. "We need to look into the deposit records of all the banks in Zurich. What we're looking for is the bank account number whose deposits times coincide with most or all the airport visits." More hand waving and virtual typing. Then more of the same.

Xashan turned to Charlie and sighed. "No recognizable pattern or matches."

Charlie's shoulders slumped. "Shit," he muttered. Still looking at the translated English screen, he studied the map of Switzerland, wondering if he had reached the limit of what he could suggest. Then he saw a little anomaly along Switzerland's border with Austria, about an hour's drive east of Zurich. "Liechtenstein!" he gasped in recognition.

"Liechtenstein?" Didier asked. "It still exists?"

"Like so many of the world's smallest countries these days," Charlie explained, "Liechtenstein supplements its economy by being a tax shelter. Sad but true." Back to Xashan, he spelled "Liechtenstein" for her. One bank in its capital, Vaduz, registered 18 out of 18 matches with the Zurich airport's records of Rev. Graves' jet.

Xashan exclaimed, "One account number matches all 18 times."

"Save that number!" Charlie ordered excitedly. "Now, get all the bank's information on that number: name—which is most likely an alias—address, current balance, everything relevant." Xashan produced everything Charlie needed. Naturally, Charlie looked at the account balance first: "$11,386,782.46. Looks like he's just sitting on that money. Let's make sure it's his. Xashan, match the address of the account to the address his jet is licensed under." It matched.

"Ow!" Charlie whooped in triumph. As he spun around, he almost ran into Clover, who had edged closer to him while he did his work. "Oh! Sorry," he said, surprised. "I didn't see you there."

Clover jumped back from the newcomer's outburst, but kept looking at him, fascinated. Charlie addressed the rest of the room, "Ladies and gentlemen, we have struck gold!"

Everyone in the room, even Yehudi, was impressed. "Amazing!" Taza exulted. "How did you know to do this?"

"When one is destitute," he happily exclaimed, "one tends to fantasize about things like this a lot. But I never had the skills or technology necessary to pull it off."

Bringing the reverie to a halt, Toochla asked Charlie, "But how do we access this money?"

Still jubilant, Charlie pulled out his wallet and retrieved his old bank card. "I'm glad I held onto this. My account has been closed for over a year, but this card can still function in cash-dispensing machines. Xashan," he said as he handed it to her, "just add this card's number to the list of numbers that Rev. Graves' bank account will accept. Tomorrow, I'll withdraw $800, which is the daily maximum, from an automatic teller machine, or ATM. That should provide you all with enough food and some decent clothes for the remainder of your stay here. If we need more, you can erase the ATM's record of my withdrawal and fool another machine into giving us more money."

Toochla shook her head uncertainly. "It is possible that authorities may detect this chicanery."

"This chicanery happens every day," Charlie assured her. "Authorities may detect what we're doing, but by the time they get around to looking into it, you will all be safely back on the Mothership."

Clodagh looked worriedly at Charlie. "But what about you? Wouldn't you like to come with us?"

Charlie froze. "Come with you?" he asked, amazed.

He looked at Toochla, who said, "If your plan works, you will have proven yourself worthy of joining us."

Charlie remained awed. "Man, I'll have to think about that. I mean, this is a once-in-an-eon opportunity, but—wow!"

"You don't need to answer now," Toochla assured him. "Tomorrow is a crucial day for us. It is best if now we get some sleep." It was then that the others noticed the snoring in the room. It was Iannis, who was sacked out in a chair. Toochla pointed at the sleeping Greek and said, "Just follow his example."

Some tittering in the room resulted from that comment. Clodagh told Charlie, "We have an extra tent and pad for you, Mister Schwitters."

"Thank you," he replied. "Hopefully, my bruises won't keep me awake." He again noticed that Clover looking at him. The look, by this time, had evolved from curiosity to admiration. Charlie smiled warmly, pointed at her, and said, "I want to learn more about *you* as part of the deal."

Clover smiled coyly, but stepped away. She was still rather shy with the newcomer, but the feeling was mutual. In fact, she desired to sleep with him that night, but decided to wait until she knew him better. She also heard a sad moan from Drasher's tent.

Drasher had heard the whole plan from her sleeping pad in her tent. She felt fatigued and depressed. She had worked diligently all day trying to alleviate her group's dire situation, with only stress to show for her efforts. The fact that the new guy figured out a viable plan in a matter of minutes made her feel even more depressed and useless. Her moan was the Baasian way of crying softly into her pillow.

A soft, cooing voice interrupted her funk. She looked up and could barely make out Clover's familiar features in the dim light. Clover had crept in and gently laid a hand on her shoulder. Clover's expression read: are you okay? A wan smile came to Drasher's mouth. With one hand, she gently stroked Clover's long, lush black hair, which she loved the feel of. Drasher then laid her head back down on her pillow and let Clover curl up next to her. Soon, both were asleep.

CHAPTER EIGHT: TAZA'S CONTROVERSIAL DANCE

Early in the next morning, Charlie was awaken by a hand gently shaking his shoulder. He rolled face up with a moan to see the shaker. It was Yehudi. "Oh, g'morning," Charlie muttered. He sat up and saw that he was still inside the tent in the large cistern with the motley crew he had spent the night with. Yehudi handed him the yellow "Caution" ribbon and sign. "Oh, right. Got a sign to hang," Charlie said as he accepted the things and got up. His bruises were still smarting, but thanks to Clodagh's medicine, they hurt far less than they would have.

In the slowly brightening glow of the lamps, Charlie saw Clover emerge from Drasher's tent, eyes zeroed in on him. She smiled sweetly as she stood upright in front of the tent, hands folded in front. Drasher then poked her head through the tent flap. She smiled faintly and whispered, "Good morning, Mister Schwitters. I see you are going to hang your sign."

"Yeah," Charlie replied, looking at his watch (it read 5:43 AM). "The sooner, the better. There shouldn't be anybody this far into the park this early."

"Allow me to check," Drasher said as she retreated back into the tent. Seconds later, she emerged with her monitor. A few buttons pushed and a couple soft "beeps" later, she reported, "Only two living humans one mile away, but they are not moving. I believe they are your assailants."

Charlie thought for a moment. Then he asked, "Maybe you and Clover can come with me. We can use that device of yours to warn us if someone comes near. Besides," he added tactfully, "you seemed very stressed last night. Perhaps a little walk in the daylight might refresh you."

Drasher looked at Charlie with surprise. "I appreciate your concern for me, Mister Schwitters, but perhaps Toochla or Xashan would be better suited—"

"Permission granted, Drasher," Toochla's voice butted in from her and Xashan's tent. "I think that is an excellent suggestion."

Drasher looked toward Toochla's tent. "Yes, Leader," she answered reluctantly. To Charlie, she shrugged and said, "Clover and I need to relieve ourselves anyway." Everything settled, the Baasian, the hominid, and the paleoanthropologist left the sanctuary of the cistern.

It was a quiet walk until halfway to the trail's intersection with Leif Erickson Drive. All three did their business in separate areas at the same time, with Drasher carefully sterilizing her pile before burying it. As they continued, Charlie felt they were far enough away from the cistern to ask Drasher, "If you don't mind me saying, you seem to be the 'odd one out' of you Baasians here. I mean, the other two sharing a tent and you sharing one with Clover ..."

"Toochla and Xashan are life-mates," Drasher explained. "You were told that all Baasians are female."

"Yeah, I've been curious about that."

"How we reproduce is that all of us have a gland in our bodies near our ovaries that produces sperm as well as our equivalent of testosterone. For those like myself, this gland doesn't develop enough to produce those elements, so we are not as desirable as life-mates, even though we are still capable of pregnancy. This, you might say, makes me even more female than the others."

Charlie looked at Drasher with concern. "Does this cause you problems?"

"The affliction itself does not," Drasher explained with resignation. "In the time that I was born, my people were more understanding of its cause, but there were those who still insisted that I was less than a true Baasian. I exert myself very much to perform my duties to keep proving my worth—sometimes too much. What happened with me last night had not happened to me in a long time, but it does remind me of why I have never been chosen as a life-mate. Toochla and Xashan have always treated me with dignity and respect. They are as close to a family as I will ever have."

"It's too bad for the rest of your people. You seem like you'd be a very good life-mate. I think your exclusion is more your peoples' loss than your own."

That remark surprised Drasher. Usually, new human contacts took several days to warm up to Baasians. Charlie Schwitters had not only immediately befriended her, but was even giving her moral support. His comforting words triggered feelings within her that she felt had long ago withered away, feelings that seemed to be mirrored in Clover's reaction to him. She decided to reassert her professionalism. "Perhaps I should not discuss this much longer," she politely suggested. "I must remain alert at this time. But I do appreciate your observation, Mister Schwitters."

"I understand," said Charlie. "So tell me how my peoples' internet system overwhelmed your computers. I would think that our primitive technology would be no threat to yours."

Drasher briefly checked her monitor, saw that they were still alone, then replied, "When our receivers detect a signal from far away, they are able to trace the signal farther into time and space so that it is read faster than it takes the signal to travel. When we set up our work station in the cistern, it immediately started pulling in all internet traffic faster than it could process the information it was getting. To keep up with the flow, I frequently had to delete many unnecessary things." She snorted, then concluded, "Your communication technology has advanced more than what we were prepared for. During our last mission, it was easy for us to continue monitoring without detection. For this mission, it is next to impossible for us to stay hidden."

Charlie nodded. "Hence," he suggested, "your need for someone like me."

Drasher finally smiled. "Everyone has chosen very well in you, Mister Schwitters."

They arrived at the trailhead and Charlie hung the yellow ribbon and sign across the entrance. Charlie noticed Clover plucking the ribbon with her finger. He grinned and motioned for her to follow him and Drasher back to the cistern. As they walked, Charlie felt Clover's hand coyly touching his forearm. Obligingly, he grasped her hand and continued walking. He turned to Drasher and remarked, "I think I have an admirer!"

"Indeed," Drasher said. "First impressions are very important to her. Unfortunately, most of our human guests have been initially shocked by her appearance, so it is harder for her to bond with them. You, however, greeted her with happiness ..." She paused, then said, "You have adjusted to us very quickly, Mister Schwitters. You are one of the few positive aspects of this mission we have experienced."

"Hey, meeting you folks has been of the few positive aspects of my *life!*" Charlie remarked cheerily.

Back at the cistern, all were awake and eating their ration of breakfast. Plans were made, protocols were set, provisions were packed. Charlie told them, "The first thing we need to do is get rid of those guys who attacked me."

"How?" Clodagh asked warily.

"No violence," he assured her. "It would be best if I just 'happened to stumble upon them,' then have our authorities take them away. Once they're gone, it should go back to business-as-usual in this park, and we'll be safer than we are now."

Drasher checked her monitor. "You had better go soon. Two people are entering the park's south entrance."

Charlie checked his watch. "They are probably maintenance people. They know me, so my plan should work. Let's go!"

"Let's" referred to Charlie, Didier, Taza, and Iannis. Everyone else needed to stay at the cistern for the time being. Clover wanted to stay least of all. She gripped Charlie's forearm and tried to walk with him. Toochla intervened, gripping Clover's shoulder and indicating that it was too dangerous outside for ancient hominids and Baasians. Clover stubbornly grunted and stamped her foot, not wanting the newcomer to leave her so soon. Taza shook her head and complained, "I hate it when she behaves like this."

Iannis then put his right hand on Clover's shoulder, pointed to himself, then made a circular walking gesture with two fingers, then pointed to the floor. He smiled reassuringly at her. Clover couldn't bring herself to smile, but her body language suggested that she understood.

"You make it look so easy!" Charlie observed under his breath. Without further ado, the venturing quartet departed. Clover looked longingly at Charlie until he and the others were out of her sight.

Charlie walked several yards ahead of the others. As planned, when he passed the approximate place where the punks chased him off the road, he ventured down the slope to where they were zapped by Toochla. They were not too hard to spot—their bicycles lay near where the attack and the zap took place. Until then, Charlie had been rehearsing in his mind how he would react to his attackers to cover his own tracks. How he reacted when he saw them needed no rehearsal: their skin was extremely red, blotched black and blue, and alternately swollen and wrinkled; their heads were still covered with ski masks, but he could see what was left of their eyes—dribbles of dried jelly down their puffy cheeks. "Shit!" Charlie shouted as he started to retreat. "Oh, christ, oh god ... *fuck!*"

"We can't move!" moaned the conscious one. "We can't see! I can't feel anything! Help ..."

"Okay! Okay!" Charlie cried, scrambling up the hill. "I'm on it! ... Son of a bitch!" His ill-feeling toward his attackers temporarily erased, he tore down Leif Erickson Drive and came across Molly and Jim, two members of the Forest Park maintenance staff who knew him. Gathering his composure, he urgently told them, "There's two bikers lying in a gully in bad shape. Call 9-1-1!"

After using her cell phone to give instructions to the 9-1-1 operator, Molly asked Charlie for a description of the victims. Charlie carefully selected the truths to tell. "They're wearing ski masks and there's a couple of sawed-off golf clubs near them. I didn't want to get much closer."

"You think they're muggers?" Molly asked.

"I'm sure they are," he said, again telling the truth. "I've heard about us homeless people being attacked by guys like that."

Molly relayed his words over the cell phone. She turned to Charlie and said, "Can you go back and mark the entry point to where you found them? He says that's all you have to do for now."

"Sure," Charlie said, and ran back up the Drive to the site. The two words, "For now," had an uncomfortable resonance to him, but he let it go for the time being.

Fifteen minutes later, an ambulance, a Fire Rescue Unit, and several police cars were allowed up Leif Erickson Drive to retrieve the two fried muggers. Lieutenant Paul McLaughlin of the Portland Police Bureau muttered, "Jesus Christ! What the hell happened to them? They look like overcooked hotdogs!"

Detective Dale Ryerson, who had just set up the area for the forensics people to do their work, answered, "It looks like electrocution, Paul. Apparently, their intended victim was ready for them with some nasty weapon."

"No shit. Must be some souped-up taser gun, or something."

"The head EMT says they'll have to spend a couple days under heavy sedation before they're in any shape to talk," Ryerson said. "This should be interesting."

"What about the homeless guy who found them? Where's he?"

"Don't know. The two park people say he's a regular here. Don't know how much more he can tell us, though."

McLaughlin mulled it over for a few seconds. "Yeah, he probably heard about that homeless vet who was murdered in Macleay Park last month by two shits on mountain bikes. Can't blame him for not wanting to get much more involved, 'cause our victims here may be the suspects in that case. Still, it would be nice if we can get his testimony firsthand. For now, let's see how far we get with what we have. If we come up short, we'll look for him."

It seemed that Charlie Schwitters had indeed bought the Landing Party more time. When his group found the nearest ATM, he was ready to buy them material things.

Knowing that most ATMs were equipped with built-in security cameras, he casually inserted his bank card, secretly hoping that the Baasians had done their end of the plan, while the others watched breathlessly from across the street as their new friend worked his magic. Then, jackpot: some whirring noise from the ATM's interior, and out slid 40 twenty-dollar bills. Charlie snatched the money, removed his bank card (he did NOT request a transaction receipt!), and walked nonchalantly to the others. As agreed, Charlie would accompany Iannis, since Iannis spoke no English and Taza paired up with Didier, who spoke barely passable English. Each person had $200, and it was stressed very clearly among them: SPEND WISELY.

Northwest Portland offered many temptations to forgo that advice. There were countless fashion boutiques, restaurants, gifts shops, and candy stores that seemed to bewitch the three blasts from the past, and Charlie had his hands full keeping them in line. "Don't buy more than you can carry," he told them repeatedly. Didier was fairly frugal, but Iannis wanted to sample every wine and beer in every wine shop and brewpub. Taza was the worst, since half the stores in Northwest Portland catered to women with discriminating taste in clothes. By the time they decided to break for lunch, Charlie had $102 left, Didier had $73, Iannis had $58 and Taza was down to $12. Most of the purchases were clothes for themselves and food for everyone back at the cistern. Lunch was held at the Cello Song Cafe, where Charlie bought them all deli sandwiches. Didier had discriminating tastes in food, and had eaten better, but he preferred it infinitely more than the food back at the soup kitchen.

By this time, all four of them were wearing new sets of clothes. Didier had found a used but tasteful suit and tie (which Charlie helped him knot properly) at a thrift store, while Iannis followed

Charlie's taste for jeans and flannel shirts. Taza, having taken mental notes of what other ladies her age were wearing, had a blouse and skirt ensemble with fishnet stockings in which she looked stunning—the male three-quarters of the party certainly didn't complain.

Refreshed with food, drink, and rest, they decided to make their way back to the cistern. Charlie announced a special treat: a bus ride, which would save them a great deal of walking. One of his purchases was a booklet of 20 bus tickets. He started explaining what a bus system was, but Iannis politely cut him off. "Actually, Charlie, we have spent years traveling in outer space surrounded by technology further advanced than yours." Charlie seemed to go into suspended animation with a dumbfounded expression on his face. Iannis laughed and continued, "We just need to know the details, my friend!"

"It's so hard to stop being a teacher," Charlie said. "Anyway, there is a bus route that stops very close to Forest Park."

"Excellent," Didier responded, "because my feet are getting very tired."

On the way to the nearest bus stop, they passed a coffee shop with sidewalk dining whose P.A. system was blasting electronic music with samples of Middle Eastern singing. Didier covered his ears. What horrible noise is this? he wondered. He wanted to get away as soon as possible—maybe find a store that played Haydn or Mozart. Iannis was bemused by the incessant 4/4 beat and odd sounds with next-to-no melody. Charlie and Taza seemed to enjoy it, though. Since the bus they wanted had just rolled by several minutes earlier, Charlie decided that they had some time to spare. Iannis and Didier chose to check out a Himalayan gift shop across the street while Charlie let Taza enjoy the music.

Unlike most of the other human guests of the Baasians, Taza considered herself a modern girl, and she wanted to embrace the present and future in reaction to her traumatic past. She found the techno beat hypnotic and intoxicating. She bobbed her head to the rhythm, then found herself starting to dance. She lapsed into a traditional dance of her people, which caught the attention of the patrons on the sidewalk, who started to nod, clap their hands to the beat, and cheer her on. Charlie stayed to the side, half-wanting to move on and not attract any attention, half-admiring Taza's skillful moves, and letting her enjoy herself for a change.

Two young men sitting farther inside the coffee shop, however, glared at her in contempt. They were Saudi Arabian exchange students enrolled at Portland State University, majoring in engineering. They saw an Arabian woman who had three strikes against her: no head covering, immodest clothing, and outrageous dancing. It was time for them to defend the honor of Islam.

Too late Charlie saw the two Saudi students threading their way through the crowd. Oh, shit, he said to himself. He recognized the look in their eyes from the two trials that altered his life permanently: True Believers on a Mission. Taza was in deep trouble, and he felt a sense of futility. Nonetheless, he tried to intervene. "Hey, guys," he reasoned with the students, "it's cool. She's not a Muslim."

"Shut up, infidel!" one of the students snapped, shoving him aside. He and his partner stormed to Taza, which started a rapid-fire exchange of Arabic tongues, pointing fingers, and shouting. Taza tried to remain calm at first, but the second student slapped her face. He was about to slap her again, but before Charlie could intervene, Taza grabbed the student's arm and delivered an expert kung fu kick to his ribs. The first student tried to grab her, but received a fist in his jaw for his efforts. Charlie watched in amazement as Taza became a combination of kick-boxer and Whirling Dervish. Fortunately, the fight was far away enough from the other patrons that no one else caught any blows, but they cheered Taza on even more. Before Charlie knew it, the fight was over, with Taza still standing, glowering in rage, and two very hurt Saudi Arabian exchange students lying on the sidewalk while the audience applauded enthusiastically. Charlie immediately escorted her from the scene. "You couldn't have attracted more attention if you fought them naked!" he admonished her sharply.

"I will not be treated like that at any time in history!" Taza shot back.

Iannis and Didier rushed out of the gift shop. "Good heavens!" Didier exclaimed. "What happened?"

"Two Muslim guys picked a fight with Taza," Charlie hurriedly explained, "and she beat the shit out of them."

Iannis' mouth gleefully widened. "They were that stupid?" He laughed. "Taza, you always amaze me!"

"There's a bus stop farther down the street," Charlie said, hustling everyone in that direction. "We really need to leave now!"

By the time they boarded the bus and sat all the way in back, they had calmed down enough for Taza to tell Charlie her story: her father had been killed by Abu Bakr's forces in Dibba during the Islamic conquest of her region, which now was the United Arab Emirates. Her mother was forced to marry one of Bakr's soldiers, and her family suffered terrible abuse from her stepfather, who was a raging drunk. After she was adopted by the Baasians, she met Wu Huong, a Chinese passenger who had fled the latest change of empire, and he had taught her some self-defense moves before returning to China on the previous trip. By the time they reached the cistern, around 6:30 that evening, Taza apologized for her behavior, and Charlie apologized for his outburst.

In another part of town, a Malaysian couple, also Muslim, also talked about the fight they had witnessed. The husband had caught both Taza's dance and the fight on the video function of his cell phone. The couple decided that they had to bring this to the attention of their imam.

CHAPTER NINE: CLOVER GETS CLOSER

"Look at the clothing!" Clodagh gasped when the City Party returned that evening. "I don't recognize any of you!"

Toochla was impressed. "Your plan worked flawlessly, Mister Schwitters. This food should last until our ship can retrieve us."

"Where's Clover?" Charlie asked. "I've brought a couple gifts for her."

"Xashan has taken her out walking," Drasher replied. "This time of day is fairly safe for her to be outside. There aren't as many people around."

Yehudi was sitting on a chair observing the revelry. He still felt unsure about using stolen money to alleviate their plight. Charlie's moral reasoning was fairly sound, he thought, but strategically risky. From the video he had seen of Rev. Graves back on the Mothership, he agreed that the powerful evangelist was a loathsome man. Such people, he knew, were not to be trifled with, regardless how small the slight. All he could do at the moment was pray that Charlie's plan would be effective long enough to ensure their safe escape from Earth.

Soon, Xashan and Clover returned. Again, Xashan was in her awkward human disguise. Clover's face lit up when she saw Charlie. She ran up to him, but stopped short of hugging him—still a little too shy.

Charlie beamed at her and dug into a grocery sack he was carrying. "I got a couple things for you." He held out a large T-shirt and a floppy, wide-brimmed hat. Clover accepted the gifts and looked at them curiously, not sure what to make of them. Charlie took the T-shirt and held it up to show her that it was the same kind of thing he was wearing. He motioned for her to put her arms, which she did obediently. He then gently slipped the shirt over her and pulled her head through the top hole. The front of the shirt had a flowery peace symbol silkscreened on it. The bottom of it barely covered her knees. Clover looked at the shirt, felt its cotton fabric, then smiled at Charlie. He gently placed the floppy hat on her head. He turned her to face the rest of the group and asked, "So what do you think?"

Taza looked at Clover. "She looks cute."

"And," Charlie added more expectantly, "more like a modern human?"

The others puzzled over the idea. Iannis asked," You're not thinking of taking her into town, are you? She is terrified of crowds in unfamiliar places."

"No, no. But I figure she could spend more time outside in the park without attracting too much attention."

"I see," Toochla said. "And I believe that you wish to spend more time with her yourself. Hence her disguise."

Charlie grinned. "I've been wanting to study her since I first saw her," he gushed. "I was hoping to do that tomorrow after our next visit to town. If that's okay with you, Toochla."

"You would have to stay close to the cistern. She is very precious to all of us. But I think you would make her very happy if you did spend some time with her."

"For a man of my training, this is the chance of a lifetime. There is no way I'd want to endanger her!"

"You have earned great trust from all of us, Mister Schwitters," Toochla declared. "For the duration of our stay here, you have total access to her."

"Fantastic!" He reached back into the shopping bag and pulled out two take-and-bake pizzas and two six-packs of locally-brewed ale. "Now, who's ready for dinner?"

Ever handy with her weapon, Xashan obligingly set it on "incinerate" and blew a low-level flame across the tops of the pizzas. Charlie produced his hunting knife and sliced the pizzas. It may not have been the most gourmet meal in the world, but it satisfied almost everyone. The holdout was Clover, who was wary about putting the hot melted cheese in her mouth. Charlie produced a bag of pepperoni sticks from another sack. He handed one to Clover. She sniffed it, then chewed on it. The spices it was cured with greatly appealed to her and she quickly devoured the rest of the stick. Delighted, Charlie handed her another. She grabbed it, then gave Charlie a big hug. "Whoa!" Charlie said, surprised. "I think she likes me." He didn't know the half of it. Clover remained by Charlie's side for the rest of the evening.

While dinner was being consumed, Charlie popped open the first bottle of ale and handed it to Iannis. Iannis took a big pull from the bottle, and exhaled mightily. "The brew here is heavenly. Watch the rest of it, because I might drink it all!"

Drasher was back at her job at the work station. While Charlie was in town with the others, she and Toochla had decided their system should cease reading the internet and concentrate on monitoring official communications. This proved to be a crucial decision, because Drasher now turned to Charlie and asked, "Mister Schwitters, do you know what a 'chopper' is?"

Charlie cautiously replied, "It's slang for several things. What's the context?"

"I am monitoring local police communications. They said they have sent one to Forest Park."

"Oh, shit," Charlie muttered. "It's a helicopter. They're probably using infrared to scan this area. Have you heard any news broadcasts from our radio or TV? Those guys Toochla zapped are probably the top story."

"It was mentioned earlier, yes, as we figured it would be."

"Infrared?" Toochla asked.

"It's a special system that uses infrared scanning to find heat sources," Charlie explained. Then it occurred to him: "Is your system connected to a transmitter or receiver outside of this cistern?"

"Xashan," Toochla ordered her partner, "bring in the antenna!"

"Yes, Leader," Xashan said as she scrambled to the door.

Toochla turned back to Charlie. "We use similar technology under a different name. Your people's technology has more in common with ours than we thought."

Xashan returned with the small, thin, metallic antenna. "I believe I heard a constant clipping noise coming from the south, about two miles away."

"That's the chopper," Charlie confirmed.

"What must we do?" Taza whispered.

"Everyone stay calm," Toochla answered. "Drasher, are you able to still hear any broadcast?"

Drasher looked at the controls. "Just low levels, Leader. I have put the work station on minimal function."

"Good," Toochla said as she dimmed the lamps. "The less heat we generate, the better we will be."

The helicopter's drone soon became audible. Clodagh held Yehudi's hand, Taza held Didier's hand, Clover held Charlie's torso, and Iannis held his beer. Not a word was spoken as the drone grew louder when the chopper flew over the cistern. Drasher fed the police radio broadcast directly to her ear translator, diligently listening for any sharp voices saying things like, "What's that?" Doppler-effect-like, the chopper's drone peaked in volume, then faded away as quickly as it had begun. Drasher reported, "A voice said, 'There's the cistern,' but they didn't detect us."

Everyone breathed a sigh of relief, except Charlie, who noted, "If they came here from the south, they'll probably pass by here on their way back to their base."

"Drasher," ordered Toochla, "keep monitoring the police broadcast until further notice."

"Yes, Leader."

"Damn," Charlie rued. "Had I known how severely those guys were damaged, I wouldn't have been so sure of my plans. The police aren't going to let this go that easily."

Xashan sat down and shook her head. "The earlier missions were so much easier," she said. "Now it seems like each solution we achieve yields yet another complication."

"Perhaps," Didier mused, "coming here was our biggest mistake."

"We all wanted to see Earth again," Iannis told him. "None of us could have predicted how far the technology would advance in such a short period. We should continue to find our options rather than mourn our fate."

"Iannis is right," Toochla declared. "That we have come this far without detection is reason enough for us to see this mission through. We cannot give up hope yet."

"The chopper is returning," Drasher alerted them.

"Stay calm, and don't talk," Toochla told the room. The chopper flew by again. Even though they were free to breathe easily, no one could bring themselves to do so. Eventually the chopper's drone faded away. Drasher held up a stern hand to the group while she strained to hear the chopper pilot's conversation. She relaxed and reported, "The operator of the chopper said, 'Nothing to report. We're heading in.' I assume he meant 'returning.'"

The tension in the room deflated. "Hot damn." Charlie sighed as he rubbed Clover's shoulder reassuringly.

Clodagh asked Toochla, "Does this alter our plans to go in to town tomorrow? I was so hoping to go."

"We will continue to monitor police broadcasts to assess our options for tomorrow," Toochla replied. "We have three days before we can safely leave."

"If you do go into town tomorrow," Charlie informed them, "you may have to go without me. The police will probably be looking for me, to ask me some questions. If they see you with me, they might start asking you questions as well. Questions like, 'Where are your passports,' or 'Do you have any I.D.?' None of you know what those are, do you?" The others shook their heads. "See? Today we were okay, because they weren't looking for me."

Iannis declared, "If you cannot go into town, we cannot go either."

Taza concurred. "And it was such a fun journey with you as our guide."

"Mister Schwitters has made a valid point," Toochla said. "It is, I'm sure, very disappointing for you humans, but staying near here may be our most prudent option. We do now have adequate provisions."

Seeing the looks of disappointment in their faces, Charlie tried to think of an alternate idea. Then it struck him: "Maybe I can send you to the Portland Saturday Market. It's very crowded this time of year. As long as none of you talk except for Didier, no one will pay much attention to you."

Thoughtful glances went around the room. Clover, of course, could only wonder what everyone was talking about. Toochla mulled it over. "That could be viable. How do you plan to get them there without you?"

"I can give written instructions to Didier. Which buses to take, what streets to look for, etc. If Xashan would be so kind, maybe she could arrange another donation from Rev. Graves for spending money. We could travel to the nearest bank on the bus route, make a quick withdrawal, then I can send them on their way and come back here."

"But what will you do back here, Charlie?" Clodagh asked.

Charlie looked at Clover, still clinging to him. He stroked her shoulder and replied, "Spend as much time with Clover as I could before you all leave."

Drasher immediately said, "You are invited to join us, Mister Schwitters. Have you given any thought to that?"

Charlie felt something fall within him. It finally dawned on him how close he had become these visitors. For the first time in years, he felt respected and needed. Seeing how quickly Clover took a shine to him made him lean closer to leaving with them. "It will depend," he finally replied, "on how well Clover and I get along tomorrow. If we can still stand each other, then I ... I will come with you."

A warm circle of friendship formed around Charlie and Clover. "That would be wonderful," Didier gushed. Iannis leaned down to Clover with a grin and told her half-seriously, "Don't you scare him away, young woman!"

Their plans thus affirmed, they decided to retire for the evening. Xashan was to stay up half the night to monitor the work station, with Toochla taking over early in the morning. Everyone retired to their tents. Clover followed Charlie to his tent. He stopped and looked at her, unsure of her intentions. Charlie asked Drasher, who was just about to enter her tent, "Um, doesn't Clover share your tent?"

Drasher smiled and replied, "Clover sleeps with whom she wants. She is very quiet company at night. She just doesn't like sleeping alone."

Charlie looked back at Clover. Clover had a hopeful expression on her round face. He thought for a bit, then shrugged and said, "Well, it's been a while since I've slept with a pretty lady." He opened the flap invitingly and Clover eagerly accepted.

Inside the tent Charlie stripped off his clothes down to his underwear. Clover stripped off her new hat and T-shirt, then undid her simple bodysuit, and stood before Charlie, smiling, in the buff. Charlie smiled sheepishly at her naked form; still some slight vestiges of lower primate in her, he thought, but I've seen much uglier modern women. "My intentions are honorable, m'lady," he told her half-jokingly. He crawled under his unzipped sleeping bag and lay down. Clover was a little timid at first, but then she crawled underneath the bag with him. Charlie rolled on his side facing away from her so she wouldn't feel pressured. Then Charlie felt her lay right next to him, facing away from him. Her body felt soft and warm and he started to feel aroused.

As the lamps shining through the tents dimmed, many thoughts raced through Charlie's mind: I'm really sharing a bed with a prehistoric woman; why am I starting to feel attracted to her? She knows no verbal language, yet she understands me, and I understand her. And everyone else in this group has bonded with me quickly as well. It still blows me away that, out so many millions of outcasts on this planet, they chose me to help them. I wonder if this is actually a strange, multidimensional cult. Weird, weird, weird ...

Snuggled up next him, Clover drifted off to sleep, thinking only happy thoughts.

*****

Farther south, in a quaint 1912 bungalow in southwest Portland, police Lt. Paul McLaughlin had just concluded a phone call he received while watching the 10:00 news. "Shit," he muttered.

"Was that work, Paul?" his wife, Bev, asked.

"Yep." He sighed. "They want me to come in tomorrow to meet some weapons expert from Seattle. It seems that the forensics folks are wracking their brains trying to figure out what nuked those two punks in Forest Park."

"Do you have any idea what could have done it?"

"Not a clue, myself. There are no exposed power lines in the area, and it sure as hell wasn't lightning. A taser would need a rack of 20 car batteries to generate such a charge. And the only known witnesses are the victims, and they're still in the hospital under heavy sedation."

"That is so bizarre," Bev said.

Those were nearly the exact words uttered by one of the forensics experts who examined the footprints at the crime scene when she finished her report for submission to Lt. McLaughlin the next morning. Her report included the following details:

2 sets of prints belonging to the attackers;

2 different sets of prints belonging to their potential victim: one set that stopped at the scene of the alleged attack, then led away farther into the woods; the other set entering the crime scene, then turning around and going back to Leif Erickson Drive;

2 sets of women's pumps entering the crime scene from the opposite end of the other prints, neither of which looked like suitable shoes for walking in the deep woods;

1 set of wading boots among the women's prints and the victim's first prints, showing a nearly impossible stride for an ordinary human;

4 sets of prints leaving the scene in the same direction: the alleged victim's, two women's shoes, and the wading boots. The trail of those tracks ended at the paved section of Leif Erickson Drive. They appeared to be headed northbound.

The expert's recommendation: find the homeless man who found the two assailants, who might lead to the mysterious weapon, its owner, and accomplices.

CHAPTER TEN: CONSEQUENCES

Early the next morning at Lovejoy Hospital, Travis Lawrence had finally awakened from heavy sedation, though it was hard for him to tell at first. He was now blind and his skin had no feeling at all. He vaguely remembered what had happened to him in the park. It was frightening, but he was now too tired to scream like he wanted to.

He heard a succession of voices. The first voices came from various doctors, nurses, and orderlies. Through them he learned that his partner, Daniel Bigby, was still unconscious, but had no sign of permanent brain damage. Next came his mother's quavering, teary voice, wondering why he ended up like this. Then there was Scott Eherly, council for the defense, instructing him and his mother to let Scott do the talking when the police lieutenant arrived. Finally came the police lieutenant's voice, the dulcet tones of Paul McLaughlin, wafting into Travis' ears with a serrated edge. After a brief introduction, Scott said, "Just to let you know up front, Paul; my client is under advisement to remain silent in the presence of the police until his hearing."

"You don't have to worry about the police, Scott," Paul replied with the thinnest veneer of amicability. "It looks like this case going to be taken out both of our hands."

"What do you mean? By who?"

"Homeland Security."

Travis' mother gasped. Scott cocked his head forward incredulously. "Homeland Security? Isn't that a bit overkill for what my client is accused of?"

"Wasn't my idea," Paul explained. "A weapons expert who I consulted with this morning has referred the case to them. He looked at what happened to the boys and the forensic evidence from the site. He said that the closest conclusion he could come to was that these boys were *microwaved*."

"Microwaved?!" Travis' mother wailed. "Oh, my god! No, no! That's not possible!"

Paul turned to her and said, "Mrs. Lawrence, I'm terribly sorry about all this, really. I know this is extremely hard on you. Maybe you should wait outside."

"I'm not leaving my son alone with you!"

"Okay." Paul sighed. "But I'm afraid that what I'm going to say is going to get ugly."

"I don't care."

"Say it to me," Scott demanded. "Why is Homeland Security getting involved?"

"The weapons expert had no idea what kind of weapon could inflict that kind of damage and be portable. None of us know who made it or what kind of technology he or they have on tap to build it, or whether they are friendly or unfriendly to this country. Nor do we know if the damned thing has higher settings!" Indicating Travis, he said, "As for your clients, they will be wanted for questioning about what they last saw that night."

"I told you that they are under advisement to remain silent—"

"—until their hearing," Paul chorused at the end of Scott's sentence. "Yes, you told me that. But if they do, they'll risk the federal charge of colluding with enemy forces."

"What?" Scott and Mrs. Lawrence cried together.

Paul was pure concrete. "If it turns out that the people behind that weapon are domestic or foreign terrorists, your clients' silence can be tantamount to collusion with hostile forces."

Scott was on guard. "What do you want, then?"

"First," Paul squared his shoulders, "since Daniel will be out for a while longer, I need to ask Travis for a physical description of the only other possible witness to this incident, the homeless man whom the evidence indicates they allegedly tried to assault that night."

Scott shook his head and declared, "No way. That's self-incrimination, and it flies in the face of constitutional law!"

"Well, consider this, Mr. Eherly," Paul growled, "further forensic evidence showed that the tire tracks from their bicycles match those found near the body of a murdered homeless man at Maclay Park a couple weeks ago—"

"Circumstantial, and totally irrelevant!"

"—AND that the curvature of one of the sawed-off golf clubs also found near them fit very neatly into the dents in the skull of former Army Corporal Jason Brown, disabled veteran of the Iraqi War!" He turned to Travis, pointed to himself and said, "To this *Gulf War veteran*, the unprovoked killing of a man who made such a great sacrifice for our country is treason enough. I'm sure the good folks at Homeland Security feel the same way! Do you still want to remain silent, Travis?"

Mrs. Lawrence burst into tears and fled the room. Scott's face grew pale, but he fought gamely. "Lieutenant," he declared, "this is clearly coercion by intimidation!"

"I'm relating facts here," Paul shot back.

"But-but it's totally outside of his constitutional rights! It's un-American!"

"If your clients don't talk," Paul said, turning back to Travis, "they won't be under the US Constitution anymore. They'll find themselves in some *Cuckoo-Land* that has its own set of principles and logic, which no sane human can comprehend! And its citizens are not going to give a shit about what shape the suspects are in when they interrogate them. THAT'S Homeland Security!" Turning back to Scott, he hissed, "Like I said at the beginning, Scott, this is going to be taken out of both our hands, and there ain't jack we can do about it!"

"We didn't know he was a veteran!" Travis suddenly blurted out.

The room fell silent. Scott put his hand over his pained face and shook his head. Paul looked at Travis, then knelt beside his bed and said more quietly, "I don't think you cared either. Travis Lawrence, you and your friend, Daniel Bigby, are officially under arrest for the murder of Corporal Jason Brown. If you cooperate with me, I'll see to it that you both go through due process in your prosecution. You may not be free men after this, but at least you'll know where you're at. Understand?"

Travis managed to choke out, "Yes."

Paul recited the suspect's Miranda Rights, then said, "Now, we believe that your alleged victim is the same person who discovered you in Forest Park yesterday morning. If we find him, then we have a better chance of finding the people who did this to you."

Travis gave his description of Charlie Schwitters, which Paul jotted down in his notebook. "Thank, you, Mr. Lawrence," Paul said softly, concluding the ordeal. "My apologies to your mother." He walked out, leaving both Scott Eherly and Travis Lawrence shattered and reeling.

*****

Meanwhile, in northeast Portland, Imam Ahmed al-Makhata sat in his office at the Parkrose Islamic Resource Center after concluding Saturday morning prayer service. He had many things on his mind that he would've preferred to take care of at that moment. Instead, he had to attend to two very insistent Saudis named Yusef and Muhammad, who had barged into his office. They had one very agitated demand, voiced by Yusef: "There is a blasphemous woman we want you to issue a fatwa on."

Ahmed immediately recognized them, but decided to let them talk more before revealing this. "A fatwa?" he asked calmly. "What has she done to deserve a fatwa?"

Muhammad repeated with barely contained anger, "What has she done? She seemed determined to violate all tenets of the Qur'an for women: uncovered head in public, extremely immodest dress, outrageous dancing in public—"

"All the while blaspheming the name of the Prophet and Allah while she danced!" continued Yusef. "We tried to stop her, but the infidels in the cafe overpowered us and let her get away."

"That woman must be stopped," insisted Muhammad. "She is a pox on Islam!"

Ahmed casually swished his finger on the touchpad of his laptop on his desk and tapped it twice. "Well, that sounds very serious," he said, turning the laptop so the boys could see the screen. "Before I consider issuing a fatwa on this woman, I want you to compare the story that you just told me with this video clip given to me by a couple of my parishioners last night."

The boys watched the clip. It was cell phone footage from the cafe. Ahmed could see Yusef and Mohammad deflating before his eyes. Shutting off the clip just after the bearded white guy pulled her away from the scene, Ahmed closed the laptop and looked directly at the Saudis. "There are some inconsistencies, don't you think?"

Flustered, the Saudis hemmed and hawed until Yusef managed to say, "Does it matter? The point is, she has blasphemed Islam, and so she must pay the price!"

"For the love of Allah," Mohammad begged, "will you please issue a fatwa on that woman?"

Ahmed arose from his chair, showing that he was almost as big as both visitors combined. "Gentlemen," he stated, "I have viewed this video several times. Yes, her behavior is very un-Islamic. But I don't think she deserves a fatwa at this time."

"How is that possible?" Yusef gasped.

"Back in Qatar," Ahmed explained, "I was a counsellor for troubled women in Do'ha for 12 years. That woman that you accosted had an edge in her voice that betrays great trauma in her past, and I think what she was doing was a reaction to that trauma, not a rational attack on Islam."

Yusef said, "But the Qur'an clearly states—"

"The Qur'an" Ahmed cut him off, "states that Allah will not punish the sick, but heal them."

"It clearly states," Yusef angrily continued his sentence, "that all who blaspheme the name of Allah Most High must be put to death! It is your duty to issue that woman a fatwa!"

Ahmed's eyes narrowed. "I am an imam," he snarled, "not a gangster! I also have a master's degree in Islamic studies from the University of Dubai, plus a Ph.D in psychology from Cambridge University in England. Tell me, O Wise Ones, what training do you have to tell me how to do my job?"

Yusef and Muhammad looked uneasily at each other, then Mohammad replied, "We are studying electronic engineering at PSU." Then the arrogance returned. "But we know blasphemy when we hear it!"

"And if you don't issue that woman a fatwa," Yusef threatened, "we will find a cleric who will. And we will have him issue YOU one as well!"

Ahmed stood his ground. "Then you will have to tell him a more convincing lie that you have told me!"

Indignant, the Saudi students left. Ahmed shook his head and muttered, "Idiots," under his breath. He sat back down and reopened the laptop, looking at the remainder of the footage that he purposely did not show the students.

The woman in question passed by the camera lens with three men. He kept re-running the footage, ever more puzzled. All four of them were conversing in four different languages: English, French, what he believed to be ancient Greek, and, to his astonishment, classical Arabic in an accent he did not recognize. I need to talk to this woman, he thought to himself. No one today speaks classical Arabic like that.

*****

The Portland Saturday Market was easy enough to find. Charlie had given Didier easy directions to follow. Arriving there, Didier,

Taza, Clodagh, and Iannis felt like they had died and gone to heaven. There were street musicians, great food, beautifully hand-crafted clothing, and every imaginable kind of art. There were many temptations to spend the $200 each of them got from Rev. Graves' secret Liechtenstein account, and Iannis was sternly advised by the others: No haggling! In turn, he and Didier advised Taza: No dancing! Being rather reserved by nature, Clodagh escaped admonishment. Thus with ground rules established and the meeting time and place determined, they temporarily went separate ways.

Iannis immediately found the beer garden. Falling in love with Portland's countless microbrews, he carefully listened to the man ahead of him order a beer and saw how much he paid. Then he simply repeated the name of the beer and placed a $20 bill on the counter of the cart. Didier, knowing Iannis too well, kept an eye on him while he himself ordered a polish sausage from a nearby food cart. Things went well until Iannis tried to carry his beer outside of the beer garden. The bartender called that he needed to stay in that area. Iannis gave this rule the strangest look, then shrugged and found a table and chair to sit at with Didier, who pointed out a Greek food cart with decadent-looking souvlaki. The two finally relaxed and marveled at how, despite all modern advances on their home planet, open-air markets still thrived. Iannis closed his eyes, happily remembering the agoras of his time in Greece. Didier saw tears leaking from behind those eyelids.

Taza loved jewelry, and kept adding up in her mind the amount she would spend on this or that. Not knowing any English, she was careful to simply hold up what she wanted to the artisan running the booth and pay for it. No one was the wiser. By the end of her time at the market, she had bought a pair of turquoise earrings (they complemented the color of her eyes), a silver bracelet with an intricate lacy pattern etched into it, a spectacular fused-glass pendant, and—she was so amused by it that she couldn't resist it— an insect mask fashioned out of old kitchen utensils.

Clodagh found interest in clothing and herbal products, and there was no shortage of either at the market. There were many varieties of soaps, bath salts, and herbal remedies, with lavender being the most common ingredient. She loved lavender, and her first purchase was a neck pillow filled with it. She then found a booth with clothing in the most spectacular arrays of color: it was tie-dye. She recognized how these clothes were made, but in her time showing the lines from the binding strings was a sign of an amateur's mistake. She was very impressed at how they turned this mistake into an art, and found a long-sleeved, purple and red-hued T-shirt for her husband Yehudi, and a beautiful long orange and pink skirt for herself.

Each of the four time-travelers wished that they could stay at this wonderful market—indeed, this wonderful city—for the rest of their lives. They were blissfully unaware of how forcefully that wish might come true.

By the time the others had reached the Market, Charlie had made his way back to the cistern to begin his quality time with Clover. He knew that he might soon be the most sought-after man in Portland. But in the interest of his science, he was determined to really get to know this hominid woman before anything tragic would happen. After today, he thought resolutely, he would let fate take its course.

CHAPTER ELEVEN: CHARSHWIT

When Charlie returned to the cistern, he found Clover waiting for him. He was flattered that she, without his prompting, was already wearing the T-shirt and floppy hat that he had bought for her yesterday. She looked adorable. Drasher was to accompany them from a safe distance. Her shift at the work station now over, she volunteered to be their look-out for any intruders that may be nearby. Warmly remembering their little walk the previous day, Charlie welcomed her along. He noticed that Drasher, normally the least outgoing of the Baasians, seemed to be more open around him.

Conditions couldn't be more idyllic. It was a warm late-August day in the Pacific Northwest, no clouds in the sky, the trees at their greenest and the flowers at their most colorful. Clover was very excited to be out with Charlie, and was eager to show him everywhere she had been so far. Charlie happily followed her around, taking mental notes of her behavior, but still infected with Clover's enthusiasm.

There was a large patch of blackberries in full ripeness that Clover had discovered on her first day out in the park. She ran to it, picked some berries, then ran back and carefully gave them to Charlie. It was an excellent year for berries, and Charlie ate them in one gulp. Clover grabbed Charlie's hand and hurriedly led him to the patch. Toochla had assured him earlier that she was approximately 27 years old, but Charlie could have sworn she acted only 10, so full of the thrill of discovery she seemed.

Farther up the vague trail, Clover led him to a small stream. Her enthusiasm came to a screeching halt as she crouched down and scanned the stream. Quick as a flash, she scooped up several tadpoles and let the water drain between her fingers. She picked out one tadpole and handed it to Charlie. Seeing the uncertainty in Charlie's eyes, she picked out another tadpole, held it up for him to see, then popped it into her mouth and swallowed it. Charlie watched the spectacle with revulsion, but he knew that Clover was demonstrating to him what was edible out here. Smiling bravely, he held up his tadpole, uttered "Cheers," then popped it in his mouth and swallowed it as fast as he could. He cringed at the thought of what he had just done.

Clover saw his reaction with bemused interest. She gobbled up the remaining tadpoles, then crouched back down to the stream and pulled out some very slimy algae. With a sly smirk on her face, she held it up very close-and-personal to Charlie's mouth. Charlie reared back and uttered with a laugh, "Wait a minute!" Clover relented, laughed and threw the horrid algae into the bushes. Charlie laughed with her. A sense of humor, he thought to himself; at this stage of evolution, hominids had a sense of humor!

Clover stopped laughing, purpose overtaking her expression. She again took Charlie's hand and led him to a clearing that was loaded with clover, roughly the same shade of purple as the Baasian bodysuit she still wore under her T-shirt. She sat down in it and had Charlie join her. They sat silently for a moment facing each other. Clover looked directly at Charlie and pointed to herself. Then, to Charlie's surprise, she uttered in a hoarse voice that was breath without intonation: "Ccco-fer"

Holy jumping-and-down-Martha! Charlie exclaimed to himself. She had picked up the English version of her name from him. He pointed to her and repeated, "Clover." Clover smiled and eagerly nodded her head. Charlie then pointed to himself and enunciated, "Char-lee Schwit-ters."

Clover leaned forward and struggled to repeat the name of the newcomer. "Cha ... Charshhh-wit ... Charshh ..."

Charlie gently put his right hand on her left shoulder and interrupted her efforts. He smiled and simplified his name for her sake. Again pointing to himself, he said, "Charshwit."

A glowing smile came into her round face. "Charshwit," she repeated warmly.

"That's it," Charlie said as he removed his hand from her shoulder. With great purpose, Clover seized Charlie's hand with both of hers. She looked anxiously at Charlie and held his hand up for him to see. Apparently there was something else she wanted to show him. Charlie didn't know what to expect, so he shrugged and relaxed his arm.

Closing her eyes and bowing her head, she gently pulled his hand onto her left breast and held it there firmly. Her breath seized up and she emitted a heartfelt sob. Tears streamed down her cheeks as she held his hand even tighter against her breast as if his hand were the most sacred object in her life. After a few more sobs and rivers more tears, she finally gazed up longingly at Charlie.

In her eyes was a longing, a hope, an unrequited expression of pure love, an instinctual desire for intimacy that spanned over 500,000 years to this modern man who was happy to see her at first sight. There was no other person in the world for her except Charshwit. He was her soulmate. He was her mate.

Too stunned to react, Charlie looked deeper into her eyes. From his perspective, she was no longer a living fossil, a surviving ancestor, an object of scientific observation. She was a woman; a woman who, by sheer happenstance, was the last of her kind. She didn't just want Charshwit—she *needed* him!

Through unthinking instinct of his own, Charlie took his free hand and wiped the tears from Clover's cheeks. Clover responded by embracing Charshwit tightly, a slight moan emitting from her throat. She began to caress him. Though Charlie had observed how coarse her mannerisms could be, her caress was soft, gentle, and radiated deep affection. Trancelike, he found himself reciprocating the caress, nestling his head on hers, kissing her forehead. Clover's caresses became more firm, then one of her legs wrapped around his lower back as she licked his cheeks and gave him crude kisses. They both lay on the ground, amid the clover that she found so intoxicating. Suddenly Clover sat upright, reached under her T-shirt, and pressed the button on her chest that undid the large flap of her bodysuit. She was ready to consummate.

Charlie was not. At least, his mind wasn't ready. It was happening too fast. He found himself resting on top of her. His desire was so great, she was so willing, it had been so long for him, he was about to undo his fly. He couldn't; his rationality had resurfaced. The moment withered away.

Clover spun around and looked at him in dismay. What was wrong? Why didn't they consummate their love? All Charlie could do was shake his head sadly and shrug.

Clover's expression imploded into anger and dismay. She let out a terrible cry of anguish, picked herself up and ran away, the flap of her bodysuit trailing behind her.

Sitting alone in the clover field, Charlie curled up, hugged his knees, and hid his head. He had absolutely know idea what was the right thing to do.

Moments later, Drasher, who had followed them from a respectful distance with her monitor, walked up. "I heard Clover cry out. Is something wrong?"

Charlie shook his head against his knees. "I didn't know it was going to go so far so fast," was all he could think of saying.

Drasher sat down next to him. "Please explain."

Charlie described as best he could the events that led up to such a reaction. Drasher sat patiently and listened. She asked, "Were you sexually aroused by Clover's actions?"

"I was overwhelmed. I've never had any woman give herself to me like that."

"You wanted to perform intercourse with her?"

"Desperately, yes. But my experiences with sex always end in disaster: I couldn't satisfy my wife, so she left me; one of my students accused me of molesting her because she knew she could get away with it..." He paused with a shudder, then said with a deep breath, "On my first night in prison, a gang of inmates..." He could not continue.

Drasher immediately knew the rest of his story. Too shy herself to put a sympathetic hand on his shoulder, she leaned closer and softly told him, "Do not blame yourself for what happened with Clover. It was unprecedented in your experience."

Straightening up, Charlie said, "I'll be okay. I just hope I didn't make her think I don't like her."

"If you show contrition, which she can detect in your speech cadences, I am sure she will forgive you." Drasher thought again, then wondered aloud, "It is still a mystery to us Baasians about human sexuality, since we are not a dual-gender species. There are so many instances of intelligent, strong people whose downfalls were rooted in sexual mishap."

Charlie leaned toward her and declared, "Take this case as a possible answer. To us humans, rationality inhibits our sex drive."

"That answer is quite consistent with my studies." Looking at her monitor, Drasher noticed that Clover was only a couple hundred yards away. "She has stopped running," she reported. "It is best if I approach her first. We don't want to stray too far from each other."

Alone among the evergreens, Clover sniffed back her runny nose and wiped her tears as she redid the buckle to her bodysuit. She didn't realize how close she was to Leif Erickson Drive. Suddenly she froze, hearing unfamiliar voices nearby. She hid behind a tree and sat motionless. Not far away, Drasher and Charlie were approaching but Drasher stopped and crouched low in the bushes. "Two humans are approaching from the main road," she whispered urgently.

He looked toward where Drasher was aiming her monitor: two chatting ladies had decided to venture off the main road for more scenery. They were approaching a spot in the trail where Clover could easily be seen. It was an "Aw, shit" moment that required quick thinking. Clover's white floppy hat could be seen through the ferns, which reminded him of why he had bought Clover those clothes. Straightening himself into Casual Respectability, he boldly walked toward the ladies, calling, "Clover? Clover! Quit playing around and come here!"

Though still mad at Charlie, Clover didn't feel safe with these unfamiliar people coming toward her. Gathering her courage, she bolted from her hiding spot and into Charshwit's protective arms, startling the hikers.

"Hello, ladies," Charlie greeted them with polite cheeriness. "Sorry about that. Don't want to get too lost out here."

"That's okay," the blond woman replied. "Is this your daughter?"

Yeah," Charlie said, thankful that Clover's face was mostly hidden by the hat. "She's a little autistic; shy around strangers and such."

"Oh, sorry," said the slightly heavier brunette. "I have a nephew who is autistic—Asperger's, I think. Which counseling service does she go to?"

Just my luck, thought Charlie. He decided to go out on a limb: "The Mercer Center," he replied, recalling a real autism facility he had heard about from a school counsellor he worked with in happier times. "It's a place in Topeka, Kansas. We're visiting my sister here for a couple weeks."

"Well, we won't trouble you any further. Have a nice day." The ladies left them in peace, taking a fork in the trail that led away from where Drasher was hiding. So help me, Charlie thought, if either of them were from Topeka...

Reunited, Drasher smiled admiringly at Charlie. "You are a brilliant man, Mr. Schwitters," she said.

"I've just picked up some 'street smarts' since I've been homeless," he replied modestly. "Maybe we should head back to the cistern. That was a little too close."

"Agreed," Drasher replied. The sense of relief was spoiled by Clover, who remembered that she was angry with Charshwit, and walked beside the Baasian instead. Drasher reassured Charlie, "Just give her time."

*****

At about 5:00 PM that day, Jim Tucker, one of park maintenance staff, was hosing down a public restroom near the south end of Leif Erickson Drive when he was visited by two very official-looking men who flashed Homeland Security badges. They gave a description of a homeless man wanted for questioning. "That may be Charlie Schwitters," Jim answered. "He's a regular here. Does this have to do with guys who were found in the gully?"

"Yes," replied one of the men, who sported a shaved head. "We just need more information from him."

Jim liked Charlie and was aware of the circumstances behind his homelessness. Nonetheless, when it came to police or legal matters, Jim and the other park employees would not cover for him; Charlie understood that as well. Jim told the men, "I can't tell you where he is at the moment. You might walk down the Drive until you come across yellow tape and a sign that says, 'Caution: Spraying for garlic mustard.' He puts that up sometimes when he wants some privacy. We're not spraying for garlic mustard at this time."

The men thanked Jim and started their hike north. It was a dead heat as to which party would make it to the cistern first, the Homeland Security officers or Charlie Schwitters and his new friends.

CHAPTER TWELVE: THE ARREST

Back at the cistern a half hour later, Xashan was minding the work station. She kept a close eye on the foot traffic on Leif Erickson Drive, particularly at the entrance to the path to the cistern. This had become rather tedious work, until Xashan noticed two dots on the satellite monitor had stopped at the entrance. After a brief hesitation, both dots began their detour straight toward the cistern. "Leader," she blurted to Toochla, "two unrecognized humans are approaching!"

Toochla bolted to Xashan's side and gazed at the monitor. She saw the two foreign dots and noted where Drasher, Charlie, and Clover were. The situation required a decision that Toochla dreaded. She activated the Translator Intercom and said, "Attention, all in Landing Party. This is Toochla. Unrecognized intruders are approaching the cistern. Repeat, unrecognized intruders are approaching the cistern. Drasher, take Clover and hide as best as you can. Charlie Schwitters, get back here immediately, and try to distract them. Those of you at the market, stay together but do not return to the cistern until further notice. Repeat, DO NOT return to the cistern until further notice. Toochla out."

Toochla and Xashan looked at the monitor. The dot representing Charlie had accelerated its pace toward the cistern while the dots representing Drasher and Clover stopped, then flitted to one side.

Charlie ran as fast as he could through the woods to intercept the intruders. Shit on a stick, he thought to himself, I'll bet they're cops! He formulated what he was going to say when he got there. Charlie was not a member of the Landing Party, and could have chosen to cover his own butt and flee the scene instead of taking orders from Toochla. But he owed them his life, and it was now time to pay up.

Charlie reached the cistern first. He was a little winded. Thinking quickly, he decided to use it. "Whoa, hello!" he called to the strangers, who were a mere 42 yards from the cistern. "Saw a couple coyotes back there. Didn't want to get too close. How's it goin'?"

The strangers weren't there to make friends. "Are you Charles Andrew Schwitters?" one of them asked.

They used my real name, Charlie thought to himself. Not good. "Yes," he replied, still Mister Amiable. "What's up?"

The strangers flashed their badges. "Ed Harper and Tom Machenski," Ed Harper, the bald one, said coldly, "Homeland Security. We need to ask you some questions about the two young men you discovered in the gully near here yesterday morning,"

"All I know about them," Charlie politely insisted, "was that they were really bad shape when I found them."

"And you thought they were muggers," Ed continued Charlie's sentence for him.

"That's right, yeah."

"Are you sure," Tom asked, "that you didn't encounter them before? Like, did they chase you into the woods and beat on you?"

It was clear that these men knew what had really happened that evening. These men could also tell that Charlie knew as well. All Charlie could do is tell as much truth as he dared to. "Look," he pleaded, "after all the shit I've been through been through these past years, I really—"

"Take it easy," Ed interrupted him with an assurance that wasn't real. "We just want you to lead us to whoever used their weapon on your assailants. Then you'll be free to go."

Bullshit, Charlie thought. He could sense a bait-and-switch tactic here. "I wish I could," he replied with resignation, "but whoever-it-was dropped me off on the Drive, then split somewhere into the hills. It was a very traumatic night for me, and I don't know what else to tell you!"

"Well," Tom said, "maybe a night in a nice safe place with an indoor toilet and electricity could set your mind at ease and you could remember things better. Will you please come with us?"

Charlie's spirit plummeted. "Translated: 'come with us if you ever want to go outdoors again.' Is that right?"

Ed smirked and said, "Glad we speak the same language, Charlie."

Then what's Homeland-ese for "Go fuck yourselves?" Charlie bitterly thought.

Suddenly out of nowhere, a golfball-sized rock beaned Ed Harper on the side of the head, temporarily dazing him. Charlie yelled, "Clover, NO!" Tom Machenski spun to see to a girl—no, a chimp—no, he didn't know what it was. It stood several yards away, glowering and hissing. Tom reached for his gun, but Charlie wrapped his arms firmly around him. "Don't shoot her! Don't shoot!" Charlie cried. "Clover, get out of here! RUN!"

Ed recovered enough to start chasing the hominid back into the woods. Tom used his martial arts training to give Charlie a sharp elbow to the ribs. Tom aimed his revolver at Charlie's chest. Charlie held his hands above his head and begged, "Don't shoot anyone! You don't what could happen if you did!"

Tom wasn't interested in Charlie's plea. "What the hell was that thing?" he demanded.

Charlie knew that he'd run out of options. "She's 500,000 years old, believe it not." he hurriedly tried to explain. "She's a *homo antecessor*, an ancestor of the human race. If you could just knock off the 'Men In Black' shit, I'll give you the whole story! Just don't kill her!"

Tom didn't listen. His free hand dug out his two-way radio. "This is King Snake," he said, "requesting back-up. Repeat, requesting back-up." Replacing the radio, he said to Charlie, "Looks like you'll have a whole class to lecture to, Mister Schwitters. We have orders to take all involved parties alive, but we have our limits. Got it?" Then he spotted a dark-complected man hobbling toward them with a cane who looked too-warmly dressed for summer. "You there," he called to him. "Stop right there and put your hands up!"

Charlie looked back. It was Yehudi, who looked alarmed and confused at what he was seeing. "Yehudi," Charlie told him cautiously, "we're being arrested. Just do as he says."

Yehudi braced his feet, dropped his cane and raised his arms. He asked, "Clover?" Charlie could only shrug.

Through the woods, Clover ran as fast as she could, losing her new hat along the way. Ed Harper was in hot pursuit, wondering what he was chasing. Whatever it was, he was amazed at its speed and agility.

The shirt Clover was wearing had proven effective as a disguise, but it was also very loose-fitting. As she bounded down a small slope, the shirt caught on the branch of a fallen tree. Her momentum stretched and tore the shirt, flipping it over her face and arms, yanking her to the ground. Too stunned to think, she cried and struggled to free herself. Then she felt nearly 200 pounds of modern man descend upon her and roll face down. Two strong hands seized her wrists and bound them behind her back with a plastic strap. Ed Harper had made his bust.

Clover's piercing cries reverberated through the park all the way back to Charlie, Yehudi, and Tom. "Clover!" Charlie gasped. To Tom, he growled, "So help me, if anything bad happens to her ..."

"I told you, we have orders to take you alive," Tom grudgingly reassured Charlie. "What would you do anyway?" He held out the hunting knife he had confiscated from Charlie. "You know that old saying about bringing a knife to a gun fight!" Charlie could only look at him.

Moments later, Ed returned with a still-struggling, still screaming Clover firmly in his grip. He carefully tore the remains of the T-shirt from her face. Clover saw Charlie, and cried, "Charshwit! Charshwit!"

"Damn, Charlie," muttered Tom. "Where in hell did you dig her up from?"

"Look, guys," Charlie pleaded to his captors, "she'll be easier to deal with if I held her. There's no way we can escape anyway."

"Hell, you can have her," Ed said as he shoved Clover to Charlie. She trembled and cried within Charshwit's firm embrace, but as he'd predicted, she became more docile.

"Okay," Ed announced sarcastically. "Thank you all for coming. I now call this meeting to order. First on the agenda, Mr. Schwitters," he looked at Charlie, "I would like you to tell me where we can find the weapon that nuked those two bike punks last Thursday evening."

Charlie looked beseechingly at Yehudi. Yehudi could only sadly shake his head. Charlie turned back to Ed and replied, "Let me say this: the owner of that weapon is not an enemy to the United States. But for me to divulge where that person is would be like opening Pandora's box."

Ed was skeptical. "Pandora's box, huh?"

"The shit will hit the fan," Charlie clarified.

"In other words, you don't trust Homeland Security to do the right thing."

Charlie's response sailed out of his mouth faster than he could think about it: "With the way you're treating us, no."

"Whoa-ho!" Tom crowed. "You've balls, I'll give you that!"

Clover heard the exchange. Charshwit was at least holding these enemies at bay. She wished her hands were free so she could fight alongside him. Despite his wimp-out back at the clover patch, she still had faith in him. She stopped trembling.

Ed stalked up to Yehudi. "You've been awful quiet. The victims of the weapon in question said that the deployer of that weapon was dressed from head to toe in shabby clothes and had a strange walk. You seem to fit that description quite well."

"It wasn't him," Charlie pointed out.

"I'm addressing this gentleman here," Ed rebuked Charlie. Turning back to Yehudi, he said, "Please state your full name for me."

Yehudi hesitated, then reluctantly answered, "Yeshua bar Yusef bar Nazareth."

Ed blinked. "So why does Charlie call you Yehudi?"

Through his translator, Yehudi (né Yeshua) understood the question. But he knew that he could not answer in modern English. Charlie tried to cover for him. "His English isn't too good," he offered.

Again, Ed shot Charlie a direct look. He ordered Yeshua, "Please remove your hat." Yeshua shrugged and shook his head. "Then allow me," Ed said, and pulled off Yeshua's stocking cap. Yeshua closed his eyes and winced. Everyone, except Clover, gazed at what the cap was hiding: a ring of scars that resembled multiple puncture wounds .... from thorns.

Tom, gun still pointed at Charlie and Clover, gawked at Yeshua's wounds. "What the hell happened to you?"

Charlie gawked as well. He had his suspicions before, but now those suspicions looked like they were being confirmed. "Uh, fun fact, guys," he muttered timidly: "'Yeshua' is the original Aramaic pronunciation of 'Jesus.'"

Out of impatience and disbelief, Ed snarled, "Bullshit!" and yanked off Yeshua's left glove, then gawked even harder—on both sides of his hand were the entrance and exit wounds of a large nail. Obligingly, Yeshua pulled off the other glove and revealed a matched set of perforated palms. He then slipped off one of the worn-out loafers on his feet—another nail hole.

Tom's gun hand dropped to his side, his eyes wide and unblinking. "This isn't right," he gasped.

Ed glared at Yeshua, not knowing how to respond. He turned, glassy-eyed, back to Charlie, and said, "Okay, Charlie. We're ready to hear your explanation."

Now the man of the hour, Charlie said, "I'll admit that this is news to me as well. I only met him a couple days ago."

Pointing to Clover, who cringed at his meaty finger, Ed asked, "And what did you say she was?"

Glad to be back in more familiar intellectual territory, Charlie explained, "She's of the species *homo antecessor*, an early species of human that was around just before the Neanderthals."

Ed and Tom took a closer look at Clover. Finding herself the center of their attention, she huddled even closer to Charlie. Tom said, "I thought she was some aborigine or something."

"We're getting away from the main purpose here," a flustered Ed declared. To Charlie, he demanded, "You still haven't led us to the weapon that fried those bikers. If you don't cooperate NOW, you and your freak show here are going to be 'warehoused' until who-knows-when!"

"Stop!" called a muted-trumpet-like voice from the thick of the woods. Charlie froze: that was Drasher's voice, and she actually used an English word. Through the trees, the others could see Clover's white hat waving back and forth. "Stop! No weapon!" Drasher's voice said.

Charlie figured that the jig was up. To prevent Tom and Ed from firing their guns in panic, he volunteered, "Mister Harper and Mister Machenski: meet Drasher, a very nice lady from the planet Baas."

Drasher carefully stepped into the open where she could be fully seen. She still waved Clover's hat and pleaded, "No weapon. Stop please."

Ed was closest to the approaching alien, and almost jumped out of his skin. "Jesus Christ!" he yelled. Charlie felt the compulsion to correct him and point to Yeshua, but he refrained from doing so.

Tom aimed his gun at Drasher. "Wha-wha-what the fuck is THAT THING?" he shrieked.

Charlie told him, "Her name is Drasher, and she is surrendering. Please don't shoot her!"

Drasher dropped Clover's hat, knelt down on all four knees and spread out all four arms. "No weapon," she repeated.

Ed calmed down enough to ask her, "Are you the one who fired your weapon at those boys two days ago?"

"Weapon mine," Drasher replied with a nod of her head.

"Okay," Ed said, desperately trying to stay focused on his job. "Now we're getting somewhere. Where is your weapon?"

Drasher pointed the opposite way from the cistern. Ed ordered, "Then lead us to it."

Drasher held one halting hand forward. "Stop." She looked toward where she'd just pointed. Suddenly, a muted explosion with a blue and orange ball of fire emerged from just over the knoll. Drasher turned back to Ed and said with a smile, "No weapon."

Ed ran toward the explosion. Tom led the others at gunpoint, following him. The explosion left a charred area about six yards in diameter, but no flames. Ed came across what was left of Drasher's weapon. It looked like a turbo-sized cattle prod, as his information had described it. But it was now burnt, melted, and useless. Ed looked at Drasher in bewilderment. "Why?" he asked, shaking his head.

Reaching the limits of her command of English, Drasher gave her to reply to Charlie, who relayed to Ed, "She says the technology of that weapon is too dangerous for us humans to handle. Can't say that I blame her."

Ed marched up to Charlie and grabbed him by the front of his shirt. "What the fuck do you have to do with this alien invader, traitor?"

Clover snarled and tried to bite Ed on the arm. Ed was quick enough to avoid her bite, then backhanded her across the face. Clover staggered a bit, and Charlie held her protectively. "They've been visiting us for the last 500,000 years, goddammit!" Charlie hurriedly explained. "They could have easily taken us out millennia ago! Just keep your cool."

"Trust me, Schwitters," Ed growled, "this IS keeping my cool!" Spinning back to Drasher, he demanded, "Obviously, there are more of you here. Now where are the rest hiding?"

Beyond the frenzy surrounding her, Drasher could barely see a familiar bluish-white glow from near the cistern. Then the glow ceased. Drasher smiled and pointed at the sky. "There now," she said. "Was in .... cistern."

Tom's shoulders slumped. "The old cistern!" he gasped. "Shit, we were so close to it! Come on!" The group followed him back to the Baasians' hideout. When they got there, the access door was wide open. Peeking inside, all Ed could find were some old clothes and some dome-like tents. He went back outside and confronted Drasher. "You were a diversion, weren't you?" he hissed furiously. He pointed his gun between her eyes. "MY weapon still works, bitch!"

Charlie blurted out in horror, "Shooting her would be an act of war!" This was pure bluff, but he didn't want Drasher murdered before his eyes.

Tom seconded the motion, saying, "Take it easy, Ed. Let's take them to the Nest and interrogate them there."

Ed grudgingly lowered his gun. He demanded of Tom, "Where's our back-up?"

"They should be here any time."

"Let's get these people under wraps before they get here! How many more wrist straps have you got?"

"Two."

"Strap Schwitters and—" he froze when he looked at Yeshua— "and this guy too. I'll take care of the spider woman here."

Firmly bound, Charlie, Yeshua, and Clover sat together on a nearby fallen tree. Drasher sat in a Baasian version of the lotus position on the ground while Ed bound all four of her wrists behind her back with Tom's wrist straps. Except for Clover's whimpering, all were soon quiet. Drasher spoke to her fellow travelers in her native tongue. "This was my idea. Toochla will not abandon us. We will see this through."

Ed looked at Charlie and demanded, "What did she say?"

"She told us to just keep cool and cooperate, and we'll be okay."

Ed scowled, "Don't bet on it!"

Charlie and Yeshua exchanged concerned glances. Clover huddled close to Charlie. The only thing that kept them from breaking down was Drasher's serene composure.

CHAPTER THIRTEEN: THE GHOST FROM DIBBA

It was now 7:30 PM, two and a half hours after the Portland Saturday Market had closed for the day. Several blocks away, under the Steel Bridge near the banks of the Willamette River, Iannis, Taza, Didier, and Clodagh stood brooding about their next move. Or rather, their lack of a next move. They had received Toochla's message through their ear translators just before the Market vendors started packing up their wares. Iannis tried to contact Toochla with his communicator, but there was too much interference from competing signals in the downtown area. They all really, really wished that Charlie Schwitters was with them; perhaps he would have another trick up his sleeve. At the moment, the four of them were stranded with valid bus tickets, but nowhere to safely spend the night.

"Apparently," Taza commented bitterly, "Mister Schwitters underestimated how much time he had bought for us."

"In matters of police enforcement," Iannis replied, "it is hard for non-police people to know how fast authorities will respond. Perhaps those boys' injuries were so novel that they captured the authorities' attention more quickly."

Didier added nervously, "Well, we are four novelties in their midst right now! It will only be a matter of time before we are discovered."

"Maybe the cistern will safe by the time we get there," Clodagh suggested.

"From what I understand of their modern methods," Iannis noted, "they will be searching the whole of Forest Park for the next several days. None of our friends will stand a chance of avoiding detection."

"Then they will put them on display like captured animals," Taza fretted, "and they'll be seen all over the planet!"

Clodagh asked, "What if they realize Yeshua's true identity? There will total chaos!"

"Not to mention what they may do to Drasher and Clover," Taza said.

Iannis put up a silencing hand. "They may not reveal them so quickly. Didier, remember that odd paper you noticed when we first got into town? That paper in the market?"

"Yes, that paper that made me think that we had been discovered," Didier replied.

"And we were so concerned until you read the story and realized it was pure drivel?"

"Yes," Didier said, "and so were all of its other stories."

Iannis nodded. "I think that mass panic about our presence may be the least of our worries right now."

"It is small comfort." Taza snorted. "We still need to know how we are going to survive tonight!"

A fifth voice from several yards away joined the conversation, in stilted classical Arabic. "May I be of help to you?"

All four turned toward the voice. He was a large Arabic man in his late forties, wearing casual slacks and a long-sleeved striped shirt. He approached them cautiously. "My name is Ahmed," he introduced himself, mainly to Taza. "I am an imam in this area. I wish you no harm."

Taza's eyes widened in alarm. She started to tremble. The last person she wanted to meet then was an Islamic leader. She could barely say, "This is none of your concern."

Ahmed held up a peaceful hand. "Please hear me. Two members of my congregation showed me video of the boys who attacked you yesterday. On behalf of the local Muslim community, I wish to apologize for how they behaved toward you. It was totally inappropriate."

Though Ahmed's words translated fluently in all their earpieces, the non-Arab three allowed Taza to do all the talking to this stranger. At first, Taza was unsure how to respond to this apology. Finally, she said, "So everyone can make video these days, huh? Why should my fate concern you? I am not a Muslim!"

"So I understand," Ahmed replied. "I used to be a counsellor for troubled women in my old country, Qatar. I could hear in your voice that you are in some trouble." He looked apologetically to the others and said, "I also noticed how well you speak old Arabic, and that you and your friends were conversing in four different languages. It seems that all of you are in some trouble. I have much experience in immigration matters."

The impression all four of them received from Ahmed was that he would not believe any protest that all was rosy with them. Didier answered diplomatically, "I speak some English, *monsieur*. We appreciate your concern. But there is little you may do for us."

"Perhaps," Ahmed replied equally diplomatically. He then noticed Clodagh and commented, "Yesterday you were with an American man. Where is he?"

All four looked dejectedly away from Ahmed. Didier replied, "Let us say he is in the same problem as we are. We do wish he were with us now."

"He was your guide, I assume? Perhaps I can help you find him."

"First, Imam," Taza asked, still suspicious of Ahmed's intentions, "how did you find us in such a big city?"

"Coincidence. My oldest daughter was shopping at the Saturday Market, and recognized you from the video. She called me."

"It is impossible to hide on Earth any more," Iannis lamented in his native tongue.

Ahmed pointed at Iannis and observed, "That is ancient Greek you speak, isn't it?"

Clodagh said urgently to her friends, "We really must go now!"

"Enough of this!" Iannis suddenly announced with a raise of his hands. "I want to talk directly to him. Taza, lend him your earpiece."

Taza was aghast. "Are you mad?" she demanded.

Iannis impaled her with his piercing gaze. "We are out of options. We now must risk! Please lend him your earpiece."

Taza looked at Didier and Clodagh, and saw that she was outvoted. Flustered, she carefully pulled her translator out of her right ear and handed it to Ahmed. Ahmed wiped it with his handkerchief, examined it, then inserted it into his right ear. It felt like a foam ear plug used for hearing protection. Iannis looked directly at him and said, "I am still speaking my language. Do you understand me now?"

Ahmed's eyes widened. "I can hear your voice," he gasped, "but I now hear it in classical Arabic! That is amazing! So this is how you all can communicate."

"But don't attract any attention!" Iannis shushed him. "These devices are not man's technology."

Ahmed's amazement turned to concern. "Then who made these?"

Clodagh begged, "Iannis, please!"

"We have no other choice, Clodagh," Iannis told her. To Ahmed, he pleaded, "Sir, there is so much to explain about us. But our most immediate concern is a place to stay the night. Please swear that you will keep our meeting a secret!"

"In the name of Allah, Most Merciful," Ahmed avowed, "I swear I will not divulge your secrets." He handed back Taza her translator then started to walk west. "I have a mini-van parked four blocks this way. My daughter is waiting for us. I will drive you to the place where I work. You will be safe there tonight."

Iannis, Clodagh, and Didier started to follow him, noticing that Taza stood still. Iannis came back and whispered to her, "Do you have a better option for us?" Taza looked down silently. Iannis put his arm around her and said, "I will see to it that nothing bad happens to you. Now, come." Reluctantly, she complied.

Ahmed's mini-van was large and comfortable. His daughter, Jazari, waited in the front passenger's seat. She was barely twenty years old with a thin body and beautiful smile. She wore designer jeans, a loose-fitting cotton blouse, and a pink and purple scarf on her head. Seeing her father return with the mysterious strangers, she obligingly exited the van and invited them into the back seats. Ahmed said to Didier, "This is my daughter, Jazari, who found you. She will be going to Paris this October with some of her college friends. Perhaps you could tell her about it."

Didier gulped as he climbed into the farthest back seat. "I will try, monsieur," he said with trepidation, "but it has been many years since I have been there myself."

"No pressure," Ahmed reassured him. "Her French is quite good."

Clodagh got in the back seat with Didier. Iannis had to give Taza an extra nudge to get her in the middle seat before he climbed in. With all seated, Ahmed started the van, but a repeating chime from the dashboard indicated that they were not ready. Ahmed asked, "Are all of you buckled in?" They looked at him quizzically. "I cannot drive until you are wearing your safety belts."

The four looked around the van. Acting on the word "belt," Clodagh was the first to notice hers; she gave it a gentle pull, then found its corresponding buckle and shoved it in. The others saw this and clumsily imitated her with their own belts. Ahmed and Jazari exchanged puzzled glances. Ahmed shrugged and put the van into gear and maneuvered out of the parking space.

There was silence at first except for the car stereo set on a local news station at low volume. "That is the news?" Didier asked Ahmed.

"Yes."

The Frenchman leaned forward and asked in English, "Has your radio said any news about Forest Park today?"

Jazari looked back and answered, "I heard it while I was waiting for you. They said there was a major drug bust up there."

All four faces in the back fell. None of them knew what a "drug bust" was, but it sounded serious. "Do you mean," Didier asked her, "an arrest?"

"Yes," Jazari replied. "Some people had a meth lab in some old water reservoir—"

"NO!" Didier cried mournfully. The others in back silently registered the same emotion. Ahmed immediately pulled the van over into an empty parking lot. "You are involved in a meth lab?" he asked urgently.

"We do not know what a meth lab is," Iannis insisted. "But we were staying in the old cistern there with those who returned us to —" he then realized what he was about to blurt out—"Earth."

Ahmed shut off the engine. He looked at his passengers with a mixture of suspicion and confusion. Remaining calm, he told them, "Before we go any farther, you need to explain who you are."

There was a reluctant silence before Iannis spoke up. "I am Iannis Phalodopidos. I was born in Greece in 339 BC, according to your modern calendar."

Ahmed looked at Iannis with astonishment. Jazari nervously asked, "You can understand him, Father?" He slowly nodded.

Clodagh followed suit. "Clodagh the Midwife, born in England in 1047."

"But," Ahmed said, "you do not speak English!"

"My village spoke mostly Saxon. English was not yet a language in my time."

Didier then announced, "I am Didier Bouléz, born in Lyon, France, 1750." To Jazari, he confessed in French, "My apologies, *mademoiselle.* But when I returned, I was the only living Frenchman who had never heard of Napoleon Bonaparte!"

Jazari's jaw dropped in astonishment. Taza sat silently. Iannis nudged her and said, "It's your turn to say who you are."

Taza kept her head lowered. She finally muttered, "Taza Q'tab."

Ahmed asked her gently, "Where—and when—are you from?"

Taza looked up and glared at Ahmed. She was holding back tears. "Dibba," she choked, "in the year 621." Then she dropped her head in her hands and wept. Iannis tried to put a comforting arm around her, but she flung it off and burrowed into the side of the van.

Jazari, who had also studied classical Arabic, put her hand over her mouth. "Oh, my God!" she blurted. In what she knew of Taza's language, she asked, "You were in the battle of Dibba?"

Ahmed turned slowly forward and stared blankly through the windshield. "We have a ghost in our van," he whispered in dread.

"She is not a ghost," Iannis corrected him. "We are all alive!" Taza was now sobbing audibly. Jazari, who became emotional when she saw others cry, grabbed some tissue from the glove compartment and offered it to the Ghost of Dibba.

A long silence ensued. Finally, Ahmed asked as diplomatically as he could, "So how did you arrive at this place and time?"

Didier, to save translating time, told their story in French. He told of the Baasians and their visits to Earth, of Clover the Ancient Hominid, of the circumstances of their latest mission to Earth. Ahmed and Jazari listened intently. Finally, Jazari volunteered, "My younger brother is into astronomy. He said other astronomers at NASA found mysterious streaks across the latest pictures from our space telescopes. Could that have been your ship?"

Didier nodded and said, "If they were pointed toward the Pleiades, yes."

"I think they were," Jazari confirmed, wide-eyed.

Ahmed said, "Didier, I was going to ask earlier: who was the American man with you yesterday, and what does he have to do with you?"

"We needed to find someone who could guide us down here Someone like us who had been unfairly rejected by his or her society, as each of us was. Searching your internet system, we decided that he was our best candidate. His name is Charlie Schwitters."

"That was Charlie Schwitters?" Ahmed asked suddenly.

"What is this about Charlie Schwitters?" Taza, who could only understand Ahmed's end of the conversation. "You know of him?"

"I *admire* him!" Ahmed exulted. "He took such a brave stand again Fellowship America and Rev. Graves."

Iannis was surprised. "You do not like Rev. Graves either?"

"Ugh, he's a horrible man!" Ahmed spat. "The way he speaks of Muslim Americans is a disgrace!"

Deciding to cement this new bond further, Iannis interjected, "If you are curious about where we got money to spend at the market, it was Charlie Schwitters who took it from Rev. Graves' secret bank."

This dirt was too good for Ahmed to resist. He asked conspiratorially, "How did he get it?" Iannis explained, and Ahmed's eyes squinted as he blew air out of his mouth. "Allah forgive me, I love it!" To all his passengers, he proclaimed, "My guests, I am your ally. You may stay in my care as long as you need!"

"We will try not to be too much trouble," offered Clodagh.

Ahmed pulled the translator out of his ear, wiped it clean with a tissue, and handed it back to Taza. In old Arabic, he assured her, "I still wish to talk with you in private later. Not as a Muslim, but as a friend. You and your friends are still my guests."

Drying her tears, Taza could only look at Ahmed and his daughter as she slipped her translator back into her ear. Iannis rested his hand on her shoulder and gave her a reassuring wink.

CHAPTER FOURTEEN: PENDING NEXT MOVES

Toochla and Xashan sat silently, remorsefully, in the decontamination chamber aboard the Reconnaissance ship. It had been a terrible decision to make. Their top priority was to keep their weapons and work station from falling into the hands of the humans. Toochla, officially, had made the right decision to call for immediate retrieval, even though it was still too early to use the Gate without risk of detection. But leaving everyone else behind, especially Drasher and Clover, was very hard for Toochla and Xashan to accept. It was a sick thought, but Toochla felt that if her weapon been set to "atomize" instead of "stun" Charlie Schwitters' assailants that day, they could have safely completed their mission and left with everyone at once.

Xashan kept looking at the workstation monitor that shared the chamber with them, scanning the Portland police radio frequencies, trying desperately to find out who had been captured and what was going to happen to them. She threw up her hands in frustration. "Nothing!" she cried. "Nothing at all about them! One would think that the police radio signals would be *dominated* by talk of such a capture!"

Toochla sat still in deep thought. "Perhaps," she suggested, "it was not the police who captured them."

Xashan agitatedly tapped on a neutral area of the workstation control board. Then she rechecked the scans of the tracking particles embedded in Drasher, Clover, and Yeshua (Charlie's had not yet been embedded within him). She could see on the electronic map where they were being taken. She had anticipated that they would be taken to one of the local police facilities in the downtown area. To her surprise, the map showed them being driven away from downtown Portland. "I think you are right, Leader," she said. "They are going on a major road called State Highway 26."

"That means," Toochla conjectured, "that high levels of their government are aware of our presence, but wish to keep it secret. They won't expose us to the main populace ... yet."

"I wonder how the High Council will react to this," Xashan said.

Toochla slumped even more. "Let us just hope that calmer minds will prevail." Noticing through the chamber window the ship's captain approaching, she added, "I believe we're about to find out. We are almost done in here."

The hermetically-sealed door to the chamber slid open. Toochla and Xashan stepped out and greeted Capt. Mrovinta with a bow. Mrovinta returned the bow and said, "This has been a very ignominious end to your mission on Earth. I'm very sorry."

Toochla blinked in disbelief. "End?" she asked incredulously. "Captain, it was interrupted by intruders. If we could reestablish our base, we could—"

"Again, I am sorry," Mrovinta cut her off as compassionately as she could. "But the High Council has declared that the Earth has become too dangerous for us to explore as we have in the past."

Toochla and Xashan bowed their heads. "We understand," Toochla said with a slight choke. "But what of those we had to leave behind?"

"The mission has been turned over to the Security Force. It is no longer a scientific endeavor. They will do everything they can to rescue them. Your expertise will be consulted, but I must insist that you remain on this ship until this problem is resolved. Now please follow me to my private quarters. There is much more to discuss."

Inside Mrovinta's room, the captain poured the two scientists some of her fine wine. After a sip from her own cup, Mrovinta said, "Everyone on the Mothership was hoping to establish formal ties with the humans when we saw how much their technology had grown. Their communication technology almost rivals ours." She sighed, then continued, "Yet there is so much irresponsibility and outright savagery in how they use it."

"As there was in our species' adolescence," Xashan pointed out.

"So noted," Mrovinta replied. "As circumstances currently stand, one of our own people and some of our technology are in their possession. Relations between our two species are at a dangerous crossroads. Indications are not good in the way Drasher and the others were forcibly taken."

"Maybe it is time for us to reveal ourselves to the humans," Toochla proposed.

"But in what way?" Mrovinta asked. "The High Council doesn't trust any of the humans' high-level governments. As for their media, our experts are absolutely dumbfounded at how much misinformation is disseminated in their airwaves, as well as how much banal entertainment."

"Drasher felt the same way," Xashan commented. "She became very upset and flustered at how it kept overloading our workstation."

"That is worrisome," Mrovinta muttered. "If she succumbed to the stress of monitoring the media, she may be permanently traumatized by her current ordeal."

"Perhaps not," Toochla said thoughtfully. "Drasher often amazes us with her resiliency. Also, she has been captured with our new human contact, Charlie Schwitters, who has proven himself quite savvy in dealing with authorities. Drasher and Clover have developed a close rapport with him. As long as none of them are separated, there is some hope." The captain's monitor received a call from the ship's Information Dissemination Department. It was from its head, Leetanula, and it was Top Priority. "Yes, Leetanula?" Mrovinta responded.

"We have identified the human agents who captured our people," Leetanula reported. "The vehicle they operate has a license number that indicates ownership by the United States Homeland Security Department, a high-level national protection agency."

"Very good. Have you been able to monitor their audio conversations?"

"Yes, Captain, but much of their talk is in code words that we have yet to decipher."

"Play me what you've recorded," Mrovinta ordered.

"Yes, Captain."

The voice played was that of Agent Ed Harper: "Caterpillar, this is Cherry-picker. We've picked up Cradle-Robber plus three, uh, other suspects at site. Over."

The next voice was from "Caterpillar": "Good job, Cherry-picker. Did you pick up the brass ring?"

"Affirmative. Brass ring has been rendered inoperable by, uh, suspect we will refer to as 'Tarantula.'"

"Inoperable, huh?"

"Yes, sir. There is enough left to analyze. It's charred all to hell, but it still has some shape to it."

"Well, we'll take what we can get. What about these other suspects?"

"Uhhh, well, it's about as motley a crew as you can imagine. We'll show them on video conference when we arrive at the Nest. They've got to be seen to be believed!"

"I can hardly wait. Anything else confiscated?"

"Affirmative. Three of the four suspects had these communication devices worn like hearing-aids. They are instantaneous translators with several languages. They're really amazing."

"Anything else?"

"We have the others scouring the site for more evidence, but they haven't reported any significant findings. We'll let you know if they do."

"Okay, Cherry-picker. Caterpillar out."

Leetanula's voice resumed. "That was the whole conversation, Captain."

Mrovinta shook her head. "Thank you, specialist. I'll relay this to the High Council. Keep monitoring as before." Turning back to Toochla and Xashan, she said heavily, "My impression from that conversation is that these agents have great interest in our weaponry. The High Council will consider this as a potential future danger to both ourselves and to the human species."

Another message arrived on the captain's monitor. It was Iannis. Toochla and Xashan almost jumped out of their chairs. Mrovinta answered it: "Iannis! We have been waiting to hear from you! Are you and your party safe?"

"Great fortune!" Iannis replied. "A local religious leader has taken us in for the night. He is very sympathetic to us."

"How much about you does he know?" the captain asked suspiciously.

"Only what he has already suspected of us. The same with his daughter. They both seem very levelheaded."

Mrovinta looked at Toochla for assurance in the Greek's decisions. Toochla nodded. The captain checked another window in her monitor. "According to our map," she said to Iannis, "you are at the Parkrose Islamic Resource Center. What is that?"

"A place where local people of the Islamic faith gather. Do you know what has happened to Drasher and the others?"

"They are in custody of something called Homeland Security. We are unsure how they will be treated."

Iannis paused. "I understand. How long until the Gate is prepared again?"

"Tomorrow evening in your region. It is imperative that we find a secluded location to open the Gate for you. It is bad enough that three of the Landing Party have been captured. We will search for areas with little or no signal interference."

"Understood. I will call you again when I need to."

"Very good," Mrovinta concluded. "Captain out."

Xashan had a worried hand up to her forehead. "Oh, Taza," she lamented softly. "Of all things, she had to be rescued by Muslims."

"Any shelter in a storm," Toochla commented.

*****

Instinctively, Iannis did not mention Taza's reaction to her temporary shelter when he spoke to the Baasians. She had refused to enter it. She stood near the shrubbery that flanked its front doors, arms folded and head down. Clodagh stayed beside her, trying to coax her in. Ahmed, after getting bedding arrangements finalized with Didier, came outside to talk to Taza. "I understand you have quite a story to tell," he said tactfully. "I will not force Islam upon you, but I at least want to understand you."

Taza glared at him. "Why?" she demanded.

"I read about the Battle of Dibba in my school days. It was Islamic authors who wrote the history of that. As the old saying goes, it is the victors who write the history books. If you were harmed by the conquest of Dibba, I should, as a Muslim, do what I can to ease your pain."

Taza still glared at him. "Why?" she demanded again. "The Muslims won, my people lost. Why should you not enjoy that benefit?"

Clodagh, in turn, glared at Taza. "He wants to hear your story," she said. "He is being very kind to us. Let us not have a poisonous air this night." She then went inside.

Taza stood silently while Ahmed waited. Finally, Taza said to him, "You love your daughter, don't you?"

"Yes," Ahmed replied emphatically. "I love both my daughters."

"Then how would you react if someone broke into your house and raped them? You would try to defend them, right?"

Already, Ahmed could sense the darkness in Taza's story. "I would defend them to the death."

Taza nodded agitatedly. "That is what my father did," she said, "to his death! When Hudayfa's army sacked my town, they killed my father when they broke into my house."

Ahmed's eyes reflected genuine sorrow. "I'm so very sorry," he whispered. "Did the soldiers violate you and your family?"

"That came later." Taza snorted bitterly. "After the fighting was over, all the women and children who had lost their fathers and husbands were rounded up and distributed among willing soldiers. My mother, myself, and my siblings were handed over to a soldier who declared himself my mother's new husband, and then declared my whole family to be under Islam." She fell silent, then added, "I was only thirteen at the time. My sister was ten. My brother was only seven."

"And then ..." Ahmed hesitated in his next question.

Taza nodded. "My mother tried to make the best of it, learning about the Prophet and his laws. My siblings and I were obliged to follow her example." She shuddered. "But our new father only wanted power over us. 'Allah is merciful,' you say; 'Allah is just!' My family received neither mercy or justice from that man! I was forced to stay in a house with a man who would beat us at the slightest provocation, or for no reason at all! When my mother complained to the Islamic authorities in our region, they wouldn't help us! In fact, my stepfather would beat us even worse after these complaints—no help at all from our new authorities, never!" After another shudder, she continued, seemingly away from Ahmed, "It was the raping that drove me mad. He would get drunk on wine, then no female in our home was safe! One night, he raped both me and my sister in front of our mother. It was bad enough what he did to me, but to my younger sister ... I was too hurt to help her when he did it. At that moment, my sanity disappeared. I could no longer cry, I could no longer think. Every element in my body screamed for revenge." She paused to compose herself. "It was then that I realized that his heavy drinking was an advantage for me. Late that night, when everyone else was asleep, I arose from my bed and went to his room. He slept with his sword, but he was too drunk to hold onto it while he slept." Another pause, and a deep breath: "I picked it up, raised it up over my head ... and brought it down upon his neck ..."

Ahmed gawked in horror. "You cut off his head?" he gasped.

Taza grunted and said, "I tried to, to be honest. But his sword was heavier than I had anticipated. But it cut deep enough to kill him .... then I ran away, and never saw my mother or siblings again ..." Her voice trailed off and tears started streaming down her cheeks.

After a respectful pause, Ahmed asked, "How were you rescued?"

Taza struggled to answer coherently, "I ran as fast as I could out of town. A couple miles into the desert, I came across a camp. I snuck up closer to see who was there. I heard foreign voices, so I assumed it was safe for me to ask them for help. One of the people there was Iannis." She closed her eyes and went into a full-fledged cry. She pointed into the Resource Center and sobbed. "Iannis and these others have been so kind to me! They will be my family for the rest of my life! Now you see why I hate Islam!"

After another respectful pause, Ahmed said, "I cannot blame you for your anger toward the Muslims who mistreated you. I can only say that every religious culture surviving today has blood on its hands. Islam, Christianity, Judaism, Hinduism—we all have much atrocity we must answer for."

"How?" Taza exploded. "How can someone like you answer for so much horror?"

"By getting people away from it indulging in it," Ahmed stoutly declared. "Several years ago, some devout Muslims flew large airplanes into two tall towers in New York City, killing themselves and thousands of people. This country is still in shock from it to this day. In this city, many people came to me as a representative of the Muslim community to try to heal bad feelings and misunderstandings between Muslims and non-Muslims. All the time I tell my people the folly of being controlled by fear and anger. I have seen firsthand that it only leads to ruin in one's own life." He looked into her eyes and said, "I cannot tell you to forget your anger at what happened to you and your family. But how is lashing out at me, thinking that I condone such atrocities, helping you? How would throwing me away help you and your friends? I could have just as easily turned you all in to the authorities."

Taza cried bitterly. "I suppose," she choked, "that you think I'm a hopeless infidel who can't control her own life!"

"No," Ahmed replied soothingly. "At heart, I believe you are a righteous woman, whatever your belief in a higher power might be. But if you continue to be bitter toward all Muslims about what your stepfather did to you, then I'm afraid that his victory over you continues to this day. All I ask is that you don't unfairly condemn all of us. There are millions more Muslims like myself who could be your allies if you just realize that none of them are your stepfather."

Taza's crying subsided when Ahmed mentioned continuing the enemy's victory—it was identical to how Cossakki had advised her fellow Baasians to react to the legacy of the Frachetor Alliance's atrocities. Softening considerably to her host, Taza asked, "What do you think about those boys who attacked me yesterday?"

Ahmed stiffened and declared, "I feel pity for any women who would be forced to marry them!"

The humor behind that slam sank in. Finally, Taza smiled, wiping tears from her eyes. At her host's invitation, she joined her adoptive family inside the Resource Center. Inside, Iannis was talking with Clodagh, and Jazari was smothering Didier with questions about France.

Wisely, the subject of women's head-covering never came up.

CHAPTER FIFTEEN: IN THE NEST

It was at least a two-hour ride in back of the almost windowless van that was transporting the Forest Park Four to "the Nest." Drasher, both sets of arms bound behind her back and both sets of legs bound to each other, sat next to Yeshua. Facing opposite them were Charlie and Clover. Conversation was almost nonexistent because their captors had confiscated all the earpieces. Clover spent the trip huddled next to Charlie.

About a half hour into the trip, Yeshua softly sang an old song in Hebrew. That helped break the monotony, so when he had finished, Charlie in turn sang a ballad from King Crimson, "I Talk To The Wind." Before he had finished the song's first chorus, he felt Clover's head rest gently against his shoulder. He kissed the top of her head, then started the second verse. After he finished, there started a very unusual drone—it sounded like two, maybe three bassoons in a harmony that somehow made sense on its own terms. It was Drasher, whom none of the others had heard sing before. Yeshua and Clover recognized the style if not content of the Baasian tune. Though not a musicologist, Charlie was very impressed. Knowing that Drasher knew a little English, he simply said, "Good, Drasher."

"Good, Charlie," she replied in English.

Half-kidding, Charlie nudged Clover and asked, "Know any Joni Mitchell tunes?" All were silent for a moment. Then Clover emitted a gruff, yet soft, atonal, nasal vocalization. It was all improvised, but it was just as eloquent an expression of quiet desperation as the others' more formal efforts. In return, Charlie rested his head on top of hers.

Hearing things quieting down in the back, Ed Harper, riding shotgun upfront, slid the small window in the wall and peered in. They all looked peaceful enough, so he slid the window closed. He nudged Tom Machenski, and said with a smirk, "Charlie Schwitters and that Neanderthal girl seem to be really tight. I wonder if he's doing her?"

Tom was not amused. "Get your mind out of the gutter, Ed," he replied, negotiating rural Highway 26 in twilight.

"Wouldn't surprise me. You know how the Big Guy described him. Shit, it wouldn't surprise me if he tried that alien thing."

It was obvious that Tom was ready to freak out. "Damn it, Ed! We might have just busted the real Jesus Christ! Doesn't that bother you?"

"That's not the real Jesus," Ed firmly stated. "He may come from that time, but that's not him."

"How are you so sure?"

"Last I heard, the second coming of Jesus was supposed to have a bit more fanfare," Ed confidently replied. "Why would He come back accompanied by a child molester, a cavewoman, and a four-armed alien? Yeah, it's weird. But there's a lot we don't know yet. So relax."

"But suppose that he IS the real Jesus," Tom nervously conjectured, "and the atheists were correct—he is just an ordinary man? Then all of Christianity is screwed! We're sitting on a nuclear bomb, Ed!"

"That's why we're coming out here instead of going to a TV station," Ed answered matter-of-factly. "Besides, it's the alien and Charlie Schwitters we need to interrogate, not him. We're a couple of miles from the turnoff. Better keep an eye out for it."

Soon, the captives felt the smooth pavement of Highway 26 give way to a bumpy gravel road. The bumps continued for five very long miles. Finally, one big turn, a shift into reverse, and suddenly the van engine fell silent. The rear doors flew open. Charlie, led first out of the van, looked at the new scenery by the light of the half-moon. In contrast to the lush evergreen forest they last saw, there was now vast sagebrush and stunted pines, with the Cascade

Range in the distance. Under better circumstances, the captives might have enjoyed the isolation of the place.

Ed and Tom led them into a solitary, weathered ranch-style house and inserted Drasher and Yeshua's translators into their ears while keeping Charlie's in his own ear. "Get a good night sleep," Ed told them. "We've got a busy day tomorrow. Oh, and if your people try to rescue you," he told Drasher, "the 26th Infantry of the US Army is located only five minutes from here. If they see or hear anything they cannot immediately identify in this area, they are going to spring into action, and Tom's and my guns will be aimed point-blank at your heads. You may have superior weapons, but weapons aren't the only things that win wars."

Led into a musty basement, the captives saw two jail cells, each with a toilet and two bunks. Charlie and Yeshua were put in one, Clover and Drasher in the other. The men's wrist straps were cut once they were secured in their cell. The females however, remained strapped. "Come on, guys!" Charlie implored Ed and Tom. "They're behind bars. Give them some dignity!"

Ed was unmoved. "You guys are normal enough to predict what you can do," he explained icily. "We don't know about these two. And don't think I've forgotten what the cave girl did to me back at the park!"

"Well, you guys didn't exactly make the best first impression either," Charlie retorted.

Ed marched up to the cage. "Want me to bind your hands again to show them your solidarity?"

Charlie calmed down. "I've known them longer than you. Not much longer, but I've gained their trust simply by talking to them. You want a smoother investigation? Fine, we'll do what we can for you. I know how odd this all this is."

Ed pretended to soften. "Okay, I like smooth investigations. You get your spider-lizard friend to tell us about the weapon that almost killed those punks who attacked you, and we'll all live happily ever after." He then looked at Drasher, who sat uncomfortably on the built-in bench against the far wall. She seemed to be breathing a little heavier than before. "What, is our air not good for you?"

"Too much nitrogen," she replied. "I need more oxygen."

"Fine," Ed replied. "I can send Tom out to the nearest hospital and scare up an oxygen tank for you. Can you wait until tomorrow morning?"

"Yes, thank you," Drasher panted. She sat back on the bench.

Charlie addressed Ed, "If I said, 'pretty-please, with sugar on it,' may I have my translator back? I want to at least talk to my friends again."

"Nope. Need 'em all back. It's a security thing." He held out his hand to Yeshua, who obediently relinquished his. To Drasher, he ordered, "Hey, Miss Universe. Get over here so I can get yours." Drasher carefully arose and walked to the bars. As Ed reached to pull out her earpiece, Clover suddenly sprang up and tried to bite him. Ed instinctively grabbed his heavy police flashlight and jabbed her in the stomach, sending her to the floor, writhing in pain. Removing Drasher's earpiece, he angrily said to a distressed Charlie, "If that animal attacks me again, I'm calling in a taxidermist! Got it?" He stormed out of the basement.

Charlie got on his knees at the bars of his cell and carefully reached his hand around to the other cell. "Clover?" he called softly. "Charshwit is here." He waited patiently until he felt Clover's cheek against his open palm. He could feel her tears moistening his fingers. "I hope they find someone better to deal with us," he muttered in a soothing voice laced with frustration. "That thug has no clue." After a few moments of comforting, Charlie gently removed his hand and pointed at Drasher, saying, "You need to sleep with Drasher tonight. Go to her." As if on cue, Drasher called her by her Baasian name. Clover reluctantly slunk over to Drasher's bunk and lay down beside her.

Charlie found himself sitting on his bunk glumly facing Yeshua. Yeshua looked back at him, equally glum. Finally, on a whim,

Charlie decided to find out if Yeshua understood Latin. He said, "*E pluribus unum.*"

Yeshua's eyes brightened a little. "*Bene velle,*" he replied with a smile.

Charlie tried to remember more Latin phrases. He knew "*quo vadis?*" and "*ecce homo*" would be rather tacky if Yeshua turned out to be the historical Jesus. The only other Latin words he used on a regular basis were scientific names. His knowledge of ancient Greek was next to nonexistent. Finally, he asked with a twirl of his finger before his mouth, "English?" Yeshua could only shake his head. Heaving a heavy sigh, Charlie lay back on his bunk and tried to fall asleep. Glancing through his cell's bars he noticed a round analog clock on the far wall of the lobby. It read 11:17 PM. He lay down, eyes wide open. After several minutes of contemplation, he regretfully said to his fellow captives, "I'm sorry that I didn't buy you enough time to escape this planet. Guess I just made your bad situation worse."

"You are good, Charlie," he heard Drasher say in English.

Charlie felt a lump in his throat. "Well," he said, "I try my best."

*****

Upstairs, Tom Machenski was engaged in an urgent phone call as Ed reached the top of the stairs. Tom was holding the remains of Drasher's destroyed weapon as he spoke nervously, "We can discern what the casing is made of and what was shot out of it. But there are no surviving moving parts ... Uh, well, its owner is in our custody ... She's not putting up a fight, but she won't talk ... Yes, Charlie Schwitters is one of the captives, but I doubt that he could tell us anything about the weapon ... The other two? One doesn't speak at all; the other—" he exhaled heavily "—to be honest, chief, I'm very wary about asking him anything ... No, he's not violent. But, I ... well ..."

Ed snapped his fingers expectantly and reached for the phone, which Tom was relieved to give him. "Harper here," Ed said into the phone. "To save time, here's the straight shit: the owner of that weapon is not from this planet ... That's right, Chief. It sounds weird, but there's no other way to explain it ... an eight-limbed lizard with hair. When you see her, you'll see that I'm not on drugs ... According to Charlie Schwitters, they came in peace and only fired the weapon in defense ... From what little information we can get out of him, these aliens have been visiting the Earth for thousands of years ... They've got two other humans with them. One's this nasty little shit cave woman who's sweet on Schwitters ... Yeah, that figures with him, don't it? Anyway, she don't talk. The guy who Tom is so intimidated by claims to be the real Jesus Christ ... Well, he speaks what Charlie says is Aramaic, and he does have the same wounds ... I checked them—they are real ... I don't think he's the real Jesus. Considering the company he's keeping, I think he'd be the Antichrist ... Sure, I'll hold."

"Is he taking our story seriously?" Tom asked.

"Very seriously. There's been some talk about that weird streak in that NASA photo being an omen. Our prisoners may have something to do with it. The chief said he's making an emergency phone call to the Big Guy."

"But the Big Guy's at the Fellowship America Convention. He won't have the time to—"

Ed cut Tom off with a raised hand as the phone call resumed. Ed's eyes widened as he listened. "No kidding," he said. "Okay. We'll have them ready for you tomorrow morning. Bye." Ed hung up and turned to his colleague. "First thing tomorrow morning, go to Madras and pick up an oxygen tank for Miss Universe. We have to get them ready to fly to Colorado Springs. The Big Guy wants to see them for himself."

Tom gawked. "Can't he just send someone here? Why do we have to drag them over there?"

"Because the Big Guy told us to," Ed replied directly. "For something this potentially big, he wants to act on it ASAP. The chief says that the Big Guy has been obsessing over that NASA photo ever since it was announced. He says timing is extremely important, especially with one more day of the convention to go."

Tom shook his head nervously. "We'd better say some very heavy prayers tonight."

Ed nudged Tom amiably. "Hey, you should be excited, not scared. For all we know, we may have in our custody the False Prophet and the Antichrist—plus two weird women!"

*****

Somewhere in the twilight area of the moon, Mrovinta's crew pinpointed the van's stopping point about 20 miles south of the town of Madras. Xashan suggested that they aim the Gate near the Nest and free the hostages, a maneuver rejected by Mrovinta. "They are too close to a military installation, and they are securely incarcerated and closely monitored," she reasoned. "Unless they are ready to run through the Gate mere seconds after it is opened, we would only be endangering more of our lives and complicating our mission even further. This Ed Harper seems prone to rash action with little provocation, and such a rescue under these circumstances may have dire and unnecessary consequences. Do you understand me, Xashan?"

Toochla was sitting next to her life-mate. She put two arms over her shoulder and said, "All we can do is wait, love. Let us set up an alert for when we can communicate with them, then get some rest."

"So help me," Xashan growled, "if those authorities do any harm to our people—"

"Our response needs to be rational, not emotional. A rash action on our part would prompt a rash reaction on their part. As long as our friends remain alive, there is hope we can end this crisis with their return. Now, let us retire to our quarters."

The two life-mates made their way to their suite on the Reconnaissance Ship.

Meanwhile, Captain Mrovinta was in contact with Fretta of the High Council on the Mothership. Reflecting the mood of the rest of the Baasians, Fretta was very upset at the news about the capture of half of the Landing Party. "This excursion was ill-fated from the start," Fretta stated sadly. "We may have stumbled into a military confrontation with the humans. What do you know of the authority who has captured them?"

"It is difficult to confirm," Mrovinta replied hesitantly. "From our new contact's translator, we were able to obtain the names of their captors and the agency they represent. The agency is 'United States Department of Homeland Security,' which battles foreign insurgent warriors. The agents' names are Ed Harper and Tom Machenski."

Fretta shook her head. "That seems rather clear," she said. "Where is the confusion?"

"According to the data we obtained from the computers at Homeland Security," Mrovinta explained, "the agents are not under their authority—they only have security clearance as visiting help. They are minions of a business called Teller Munitions, a private enterprise that brokers weapons for various government agencies, including Homeland Security."

"What?" Fretta exclaimed. "They are impersonating authorities?"

"They are deputies of authorities," Mrovinta said. "Apparently, their only objective was to obtain our weapon that was used to fend off two attackers. It seems that Drasher's presence was a shocking surprise to them. Clover and Yeshua were additional surprises. Our new contact, Charlie Schwitters, tried his best to keep the agents from using their own weapons. Until last transmission, the agents still seemed fixated on learning about our weapons."

Fretta stiffened. "Was there any attempt from the agents to learn about our people?" she asked.

"Not from what we observed. Their training seems to be in combat and enforcement rather than diplomacy."

"Greed seems to also be a factor in their motives," Fretta growled. "Access to our technology would fetch an extremely high monetary price on Earth!"

"Apparently so, Leader."

"Prepare your ship for immediate mobility," Fretta ordered. "I'm afraid that a confrontation is inevitable. How we shall respond to this depends on how our people are treated by these dubious authorities. That is all for now."

"Yes, Fretta," Mrovinta replied before signing off. Sitting back in her chair, she pondered how her people were going to respond. The thought of killing innocent humans along with the guilty sickened her. But she also knew the danger of exposing such an unpredictable species to such powerful technology. The most disturbing sentence she heard from the agents was, "There is enough left of the weapon to analyze." Though the alloys would be extremely difficult to synthesize on Earth, the humans were born strivers—and aggressive colonizers. At their worst, the humans seemed oblivious to destroying their own planet to achieve selfish, petty goals, just like the Frachetor Alliance back on Baas. Mrovinta knew Drasher to be a very gentle soul. If those aggressive agents mistreat her in any way, she decided to herself, drastic action would be taken against them. Defeating those agents and rescuing the captives in itself wouldn't be that difficult; the real battle would dealing with the aftermath.

CHAPTER SIXTEEN: INTERROGATIONS

Ed Harper trotted down the basement stairs to wake his captives. He enjoyed this part of his job, because he could be creative in how he did it. This morning's wake-up call came in the form of a two-gallon aluminum pot, which he hurled at the bars of Drasher and Clover's cell. The resulting clang and clatter jolted three of the captives out of their bunks, especially scaring Clover. Only Drasher stayed on her bunk, having heard Ed's approaching footsteps.

"Wakey wakey, campers," Ed called mockingly. "We have a big day ahead of us!" Looking at the two females, he was startled to notice that both of their bodysuits were undone. "How the hell did you get undressed?"

Deducing his question, Drasher calmly pointed her left, dexterous toes at the toilet. That eloquently answered Ed's question, though it didn't exactly please him. Seeing Clover cowering in the corner, however, did. He handed Yeshua his earpiece and inserted Drasher's earpiece in her ear. Addressing all the captives, he clapped his hands together and announced, "Well, you'll all be happy to know that you get a free, all-expenses-paid trip to Colorado Springs, where the Fellowship America Convention is currently taking place. You are all so blessed!"

Drasher and Yeshua were puzzled by this news. Charlie was anything but amused. Clover was just scared. "So," Charlie groused, "are we to be the final event in the festivities? Say, like a public waterboarding or something? Wouldn't it make more sense to torture us here?"

Ed glared at Charlie. "Now, why do think we're going to use torture?" he smoothly asked. "My boss said to learn as much as we can about that amazing weapon of yours. As soon as Miss Universe tells us the details of how it works, I'll turn you all over to the authorities, and you will be treated properly."

"I take it that these 'authorities' happen to be at the Fellowship America gig?" Charlie asked suspiciously.

Ed smiled and pointed at him. "Bingo," he answered. "My boss has close ties with Reverend Graves." He nodded at Yeshua and said, "When my partner described to our boss who we have in custody, he immediately contacted Graves, who was so impressed that he sent his own private jet to the Madras Airport to take you to Colorado Springs." He looked at Drasher and said, "Now if you tell me what I want to know, your treatment will improve dramatically."

Drasher looked at Ed calmly and stated, "Mister Harper, you would not give a troubled adolescent a weapon, would you? So be it with you and our weapons. I cannot divulge to you."

Ed's jovial demeanor fell away. "It's obvious that your people are still nearby," he said with increasing menace. "Well, guess what? We humans have every right to defend our planet from invaders," he pointed at Clover, "their *pets,*" then he pointed at Charlie and Yeshua, "and any *TRAITORS of our own people* that they use! You used that thing of yours against MY people. Yes, we're going to assume hostile intent! You think we're so immature, bitch? So why have your people been sneaking around instead of talking to us directly?"

Drasher was completely unruffled. "You are demonstrating my answer," she replied.

Ed knew that he couldn't go any further with his inquiry for now. "I am under orders from my boss," he declared, "to extract information about your weapons. I admit, I'm no diplomat. But that's how it is right now. My country needs the best technology it can use against its enemies to ensure world peace, and that's what I intend to get." He reached into a plastic grocery bag and threw some apples into the cells. "There's your fucking breakfast! We leave in ten minutes." He stomped up the stairs.

Charlie picked up a bruised apple and wiped it off. "He's a real charmer, isn't he?" he muttered to Yeshua before taking a bite.

Yeshua's eyes suddenly widened. He excitedly patted Charlie's shoulder, pointed at his earpiece then pointed up. Charlie leaned his ear next Yeshua's ear. A Baasian voice was coming through: "Toochla!" Yeshua whispered.

Drasher started whispering in response. She was describing their current situation. Without his own earpiece, Charlie could only sit and listen. Clover leaned her ear up to Drasher's; just hearing Toochla's voice was a balm to her.

Yeshua said something in Aramaic, then pulled out his earpiece and handed it to Charlie, gesturing for him to plug it in. Wiping off the earpiece with his shirt, Charlie inserted the earpiece and heard Toochla's voice. "Be calm," she said. We will try to resolve this as peacefully as we can. You have done extremely well for us, and we will amply reward you for your efforts, Charlie Schwitters."

"Toochla," Charlie whispered, keeping an ear toward the basement stairs, "I hate to say this, but the word 'peacefully' is not in these agents' vocabulary. They want your weapons more than your friendship! I also think they are operating outside of the law."

"Yes," Toochla replied, "our experts have confirmed that."

"So what are you going to do, and when will you do it?"

"We hope to take action in the evening in your current region. What we will do depends on the circumstances."

Through gritted teeth, Charlie said, "Frankly, I don't see circumstances improving at this time!"

Ed's footsteps thundered down the stairs. "Shit!" he hissed. "I forgot to take back the earpieces!" He saw Charlie pulling Yeshua's earpiece out of his ear. "What the hell are you listening to?" Ed demanded.

Feigning innocence, Charlie responded, "The Blazers are up by four points."

Ed held out his hand. Charlie obligingly handed him the earpiece. Instead of accepting the earpiece, Ed grabbed Charlie's hand and yanked with full force, smashing Charlie's face into the bars. Charlie cried in pain.

"Charshwit!" Clover cried. "Charshwit!"

"Shut up, you monkey!" Ed yelled at the frightened hominid. To Charlie, he growled, "The only thing keeping your ass out of a body bag right now is that meeting at Colorado Springs! I suggest you watch your fucking mouth!"

Yeshua stooped down and helped Charlie to his bunk. He glared at Ed but said nothing. Tom Machenski ran down the stairs yelling, "What the hell's going on down here?" Seeing Charlie rocking back and forth holding his bruised head and the two females partially clad, with Clover frantically jumping up and down and crying, he cried, "Ed, we were told to lay off the rough stuff!"

Suddenly Mister Professional, Ed replied plainly, "No rough stuff unless necessary. I think those earpieces are sending signals back to their ship, so I had to force them away."

"He handed you the earpiece, and you hurt him," Yeshua suddenly cried.

Ed glared at Yeshua. But knowing that Tom couldn't understand Aramaic, he ignored the outburst. He asked Tom, "Do you have the oxygen tank for the alien?"

"It's upstairs," Tom replied nervously.

Ed opened Clover and Drasher's cell door and said, "Let's make them a little more presentable. We'll have to knock out the cave girl. There should be some chloroform in the van."

"Goddammit!" Charlie cried. "For the last time, she's calmer with me or Drasher holding her! *You're* the ones making her harder to deal with!"

"Shut up, Schwitters!" barked Ed.

A female voice called from the top of the stairs, "Is everything all right? We need to get moving."

Ed exhaled in exasperation. "Everything's fine," he answered in his best all-is-right-with-the-world voice. "We just need to get everyone ready." He stepped up to the males' cage, gave Yeshua his earpiece and said in a low voice, "That's one of Rev. Graves' top assistants. We are going to cover all of you with blankets so she and the flight crew don't have to see you. Cooperate fully with us, and we'll cuff all your hands in front instead of behind your backs for this trip." He turned to Drasher and asked, "Do you understand what I'm saying?"

"Yes," Drasher replied. "Yeshua, Charlie, and I can keep Clover calm."

"Cover me, Tom," he said as he unlocked the males' cage door. Tom had his pistol ready. Charlie and Yeshua carefully walked out. Upon seeing Charlie, Clover screamed, "Charshwit!" and ran up to her cage door, crying uncontrollably. Ed said to Drasher, "Come over here so I can cut you loose. I want you to hold her when I cut her loose." Drasher politely obeyed and presented both sets of wrists to her captor. After Ed cut her free with his hunting knife, she placed all four of her hands firmly on Clover's shoulders and made soothing sounds. She then redid Clover's bodysuit before doing up her own. True to Charlie's prediction, Clover started to regain her composure. Hugging Clover from behind, Drasher said to her captors, "She is not bad. She is scared."

"She's still an animal in my book," Ed sneered as he cut Clover's hands free.

"She is one of God's children," Yeshua admonished.

Her hands free, Clover nearly collapsed in a storm of tears. Charlie came up and hugged her as strongly as he dared. Yeshua completed the group hug.

The woman from Rev. Graves' jet came down the stairs faster than Ed or Tom could stop her. She was a stocky and attractive Filipino woman in her mid-thirties. Her blue business dress and pumps were less-than-practical attire for the central Oregon terrain. "We need to be in Colorado Springs—" was all she said before she caught a glimpse of Drasher and froze in her tracks. She was about to fall over backward when Tom caught her with one hand while awkwardly aiming his pistol at the captives with the other. A terrified scream managed to squeeze out of her vocal cords. Clover's head popped up from the group hug, startled at this.

Through her tears she looked at the new visitor with fleeting curiosity.

"Ah, shit!" Ed spat. "That's one more person who's seen 'em!"

Sensing more chaos on the horizon, Charlie designated himself the captives' spokesman. Keeping a protective arm around Clover, he formally announced to the woman, "Madam, my name is Charlie Schwitters. I am the liaison for this group of visitors." Cocking his head toward the four-armed extraterrestrial, he explained, "To answer your first question: this is Drasher, an anthropologist from the planet Baas. She is very civilized and pleasant to talk to."

Calmed somewhat by Charlie's formal demeanor, the woman composed herself enough to reply, "I'm Marilee Navidad, personal assistant to Rev. Graves." She shook her head in disbelief and gasped, "What are you doing with these—people?"

"Long story," Charlie replied. "We can tell you on the flight."

Ed was fuming. HE was in charge here, not this pedophile atheist! Trouble was, Miss Navidad, a representative of one of the most powerful men in America, was not someone to offend. "Look," was all he could say, "the fewer people who see these things the better. We've got blankets in the bedrooms."

All four captives were handcuffed, swaddled in blankets, then herded into the van. Half an hour later, they were led to the waiting Lear jet. Charlie immediately recognized the numbers: it was Rev. Graves' Niger-to-Zurich shuttle. Inside were eight seats arranged around a small table, conference-style. The captives were allowed to remove their blankets and choose a seat. On one side sat the captives, with Clover safely seated between Drasher and Charlie, and Yeshua on the other side of Charlie. On the other side were Marilee and Ed. Tom Machenski was left to drive the van back to Portland.

Once airborne, Drasher was supplied with an oxygen tank to help her breathe. Clover and Yeshua began to feel a little nauseous. Charlie noticed this and felt under his seat, producing an airsickness bag for Clover. Charlie then directed Yeshua to the bag under his own seat, making a barfing gesture. Yeshua accepted it gratefully, nearly gagging at Charlie's gesture.

Marilee could not take her eyes off the captives. None of them seemed particularly violent. The oxygen tank made the alien look especially harmless. The hominid girl stared back suspiciously at her, but held on to Charlie for security. Disturbing her most now were the scars on Yeshua's large hands and forehead. Charlie tried to break the ice by observing with a slight grin, "Kind of takes 'diversity' to a whole new level, doesn't it?"

Marilee remembered her task and stated, "I need some information to prepare Rev. Graves for his meeting with all of you." She dug out her laptop computer and booted it up. She said to Charlie, "First of all, Mr. Schwitters, what is your connection with ... uh, these people?"

"The Baasians," Charlie replied, pointing to Drasher, "have been studying humans and Earth for around 500,000 years. To get more intimate details, they adopt individuals who had been unfairly screwed and rejected by their society." His voice grew pitch-dark. "In my case, by your boss' society."

"I'm not at liberty to discuss that," Marilee answered evasively, but politely, as she typed. She had been briefed about Charlie Schwitters beforehand, but was relieved that he was at least cooperating. "I take it that these others with you," she continued, "were rejected by their respective societies?"

"This woman," Charlie nodded toward Clover, "is over 500,000 years old, and was rejected by her tribe." Noticing the small crucifix hanging around Marilee's neck, he looked at Yeshua and hesitantly said, "I haven't known Yeshua long enough to catch his story, but I think the scars he has tell quite a lot of it."

"F.Y.I.," Ed sternly said to Marilee, "Yeshua is not who you think he is! Let's just let it go at that."

"A suggestion?" Charlie offered to her. "Mr. Harper here has my translating device in his ear. If you want to converse with Yeshua—"

"No," Ed said abruptly.

"I think that would help," Marilee agreed.

"Not at this time!" Ed replied abruptly.

There was a pause. Finally, Charlie looked Ed straight in the eye and stoutly uttered, "Yeshua!"

Marilee now looked very confused. Ed looked murderously at Charlie. Charlie sat back in his chair with a half-smirk on his face: he knew that the translator kept translating "Yeshua" to "Jesus."

CHAPTER SEVENTEEN: THE FATWA, AS PROMISED

There was a large kitchen at the Parkrose Islamic Resource Center. Clodagh was the first of the guests awake, so she took it upon herself to prepare breakfast. Although her father had gone home, Jazari had spent the night with the guests, and was pressed into service to help Clodagh. Didier, in turn, was awakened to translate Clodagh's Saxon into French for Jazari. After being tutored in the use of the modern human appliances, Clodagh was given access to the kitchen's impressive inventory of herbs and spices. She cracked a dozen eggs into a large frying pan, then appeared almost possessed as she chose, measured, and mixed various spices into the eggs, all without using any measuring spoons or cups. Jazari observed her cooking with mounting esteem; a good cook herself, the young Muslim woman saw combinations of ingredients she never dreamed of using together. "It smells delicious," she complimented the chef. Clodagh smiled as she carefully stirred the eggs.

Iannis was the last to awaken. He stretched, then arose to follow the wonderful aroma emanating from the kitchen. He saw Taza standing in a hallway, looking at crayon drawings on the walls made by children who attended the Islamic day care program during the week. "Are you ready for breakfast?" he asked her gently.

As if being snapped out of hypnosis, Taza smiled and replied, "Yes."

After all were seated in the dining area, orange juice was served with the scrambled eggs. Conversation was sporadic, mostly speculating on what the Baasians were going to do for both halves of the Landing Party. Jazari sat and listened to the four languages interacting, sometimes asking Didier for a translation—she could just barely understand Taza. Breakfast was almost finished when the Reconnaissance Ship contacted the guests through their earpieces. It was Toochla. "Is everyone in your party still well?" she asked.

"We are all well," Iannis answered. "Our host and his daughter are treating us very kindly. Is there any news on the others?"

"A new development, and it is not good. They are being taken to a city called Colorado Springs at the behest of Reverend Graves."

"*Mon dieu!*" Didier cried.

Clodagh was stricken. "Does he want to see Yeshua?" she asked timidly.

"From what we could gather, he has an interest in seeing all four of them. From our observations of how Rev. Graves operates, this is of great concern to us."

Taza volunteered, "Perhaps Rev. Graves found out we stole his money."

"We have no indication that he has noticed that yet," Toochla said. "Their main captor, Ed Harper, is a malevolent person who currently wears Charlie's earpiece." All four guests gasped in horror. "This is actually a boon to us, for we can get more information about how they are being treated. He is especially malicious to Charlie and Clover."

"They are in danger?" cried Clodagh.

"Not at the moment. They are in the company of a personal assistant to Rev. Graves. In her presence, Ed Harper is behaving more civilized."

"What is your plan?" asked Iannis.

"We are hoping to rescue them in Colorado Springs' evening time, to minimize witnesses to the event. However, at the first sign that their lives are in danger, we will have to rescue them regardless of circumstances."

"What shall we do until then?" asked Iannis.

"Do not stray far from each other. Have everything you plan to bring within easy reach. Search for a secluded, open space for our rendezvous. Be as discreet about your leisure activities as you can. Any further questions?"

"Our hosts," said Didier, who had been quietly translating for Jazari, "have been most kind to us. We wish to compensate them. Perhaps you could help provide them with something?"

"I will," Taza answered. She walked over to Jazari and handed her a small metal bracelet. "This is made from part of the Mothership, which is a converted moon," she explained. "It is an alloy not found on Earth. You may have it. The Baasians can make me another."

Jazari accepted the bracelet and admired it. It had the feel of silver mesh, but the look of turquoise. "It's beautiful," she gushed. Taza smiled warmly in return.

Between the closed front window curtains, Didier noticed a shiny red vehicle (a new Audi sports coupe, to modern eyes) pull into the Resource Center's empty parking lot. He saw two disturbingly familiar young Arab men emerge from it. "It is the men who attacked Taza!" he exclaimed.

"Everyone hide," Iannis urged. Taza and Clodagh ran into the kitchen and grabbed the biggest knives they could find. Iannis and Didier shoved a large sofa in front of the doors. Jazari ran to the building's alarm system and hurriedly keyed in the "armed" code. The two Arab men stalked up to the front doors, found them locked tight, and pounded on them. "We know the apostate woman is in there!" one them yelled in modern Arabic. "Surrender her now, and no one will get hurt!"

Jazari cautiously walked closer to the doors and called through them, "If you don't go away now, I'm calling the police."

"Let the police come!" the other Arab man replied. "We are here to defend the honor of Islam!"

Jazari's concern grew. These boys may be fools, she thought, but fools can make deadly decisions. Taza boldly returned to the front room brandishing a huge carving knife. "I will take care of them," she snarled. "Let them come in!"

The shadow of one of the Arabs appeared at the front window. One of the arms disappeared into the body of the shadow. There was a pause, then suddenly three loud, sharp explosions ripped through the extra-heavy glass. Jazari screamed and grabbed the startled Taza, both scrambling back to the kitchen. "What was that?" cried Taza.

"They have guns!" Jazari cried. "Guns" didn't quite translate in Taza's earpiece, but she knew she was out-armed.

The alarm system screamed to life. Everyone in the Center desperately covered their ears. The Arab men, though wincing from the siren's blare, were committed to their cause, and one stuck a leg through the jagged hole in the window, intending to climb into the room.

Iannis, displaying an almost superhuman presence of mind, was crouched just underneath the front window. As soon as the leg poked through the window, he grabbed it, then fell to the floor, hugging the leg for dear life. The sharp remaining glass underneath tore into the Arab man's crotch, making him scream as loud as the siren. The victim grabbed his bleeding crotch with both hands, forgetting about his pistol. Iannis, sensing that it was a weapon, grabbed the pistol and ran out of the room.

The other man struggled through the broken window and saw his partner bleeding profusely from between the legs. He was too late to see Clodagh rush in to throw a big handful of hot curry powder into his face. Temporarily blinded and deafened, he was now an easier target for Taza, who eschewed the knife in favor of her knee applied sharply to his groin. Didier, the only visitor who knew what a gun was, confiscated the second man's pistol. All five Center dwellers exited the loud, messy building.

Toochla's voice came through the earpieces. "What is that horrible noise? Are you under attack?"

"They have an alert system," Iannis explained assuredly. "We were able to subdue both attackers. Our host's daughter said the police are on their way to deal with them."

"Another complication!" Toochla muttered in frustration. She then ordered, "Leave there at once. The police will detain you for questioning!"

Iannis looked around and saw neighbors gawking. He then realized that the Resource Center was in the middle of a mostly residential area. "Toochla," he said forlornly, "that would be our worst move. There are too many witnesses!"

Just then, Didier saw the two suspects stagger out the front door and was seized by an idea. He strode up to the two men with as mean a scowl as his eighteenth-century academic face could muster. He held their pistol at their startled faces and they froze in their painful tracks. The Frenchman waved the pistol toward their car and coldly ordered them, "Go. Now!"

The two scrambled into the Audi coupe. The man wearing the curry powder was able to see enough to drive while his partner tried to stem his own bleeding. Soon, the Audi was peeling out of the parking lot and onto the boulevard. The timing was almost too perfect: Didier saw a car marked "Portland Police" roll up to the intersection several houses away. Slipping the gun quickly (and carefully!) into his pants pocket, he waved at the officers and pointed frantically in the direction of the fleeing Audi. Taking the hint, the police drove past and turned on their sirens.

When the police were out of sight, the others looked at Didier with amazement. "Fiendishly clever!" Taza gasped, using of one of Didier's favorite exclamations.

"There is no time for congratulations," Iannis warned. "We must leave immediately."

Ahmed's minivan pulled up. Jazari was finishing her phone call to the police, and she ran to her father as he emerged from the vehicle. "Those boys who attacked Taza," Jazari hurriedly explained, "shot out the front window and tried to attack us!"

"Argh!" Ahmed exclaimed with hands on his face. "Those stupid fools! Is anybody hurt?"

"Just the attackers. They drove off and a police car took off after them, but there will be more police coming here! I just know it."

Iannis was again talking to Toochla. "When is the earliest time you can retrieve us?" he asked desperately.

"Not for several hours. The moon is not in position yet. The High Council will not let us move from our position until further notice."

Taza hung her head. "This is all my fault," she muttered with a catch in her throat. "I should never have fought with those boys." The tears started to flow. "I'm sorry!"

Didier put a comforting arm around Taza's shoulder. "You did not teach those boys to be dunderheads," he reassured her. He then turned to Ahmed and pleaded, "*Monsieur*, we do not wish to place you or your daughter in our own peril. Could you at least convince the authorities not to separate us?"

Ahmed saw the concern in his guests' eyes. Everyone knew that things were going to get worse before they got better. Another patrol car pulled into the parking lot, followed by emergency vehicles. Inspiration came to him. "All of you," he ordered, "get back into the building."

They did as told. As she shut off the alarm, Jazari told Didier and Iannis to get the pistols out of their pockets and lay them inside of the broken window. Ahmed said, "Jazari, just tell them exactly what happened. Let me explain our guests to the police."

"Yes, Father."

As the police officers approached, Ahmed recognized Paul McLaughlin. "Wish we could meet under more pleasant circumstances for a change, Ahmed," the Lieutenant greeted him with a shake of hands. "So, what's the story?"

Bearing in mind the story the attackers were eventually going to tell, Ahmed explained, "I have under my care a Saudi woman seeking asylum in this country. Two Saudi men saw her in public without head-covering, and accosted her forcefully. She fought them off, and they somehow found that she was here."

Lt. McLaughlin nodded. "And they came looking for revenge?"

"First they had come to my office asking me to issue a fatwa on her."

"Was she the only one fighting them here?"

Ahmed let Jazari explain what transpired. Lt. McLaughlin regarded the mixture of glass, blood, and curry powder on the floor. He also saw the two guns. "Wow," he said with a grin. "Helluva team effort. We'll need to question the other participants."

This was expected, and Ahmed responded, "You may question them here. However, I must insist that they remain in this building for temporary political asylum."

McLaughlin cocked his head. "Political asylum? Do any of them have proper documentation or I.D.?"

"Not with them, no."

Suspicions mounting, McLaughlin asked, "Then how can we confirm who they really are?"

"Permit me to explain, *Monsieur*," Didier unexpectedly volunteered. "We are traveling under the auspices of ... Amnesty International. The ... human rights group?"

"Oh, yes, I've heard of them."

"Yes. Well, it is the most unfortunate thing. When we arrived at the ... airport, a man claiming to be our ride tricked us into his ... minivan. He drove us to ... an abandoned building, where he and another man robbed us of everything: money, luggage, passports, everything! They locked us in the building, and then they drove off."

"Oh, man!" the lieutenant winced. "I've heard of that kind of shit happening. Did you get a good look at the men?"

"One was bald and wore a gray suit and tie. The other was dressed, er, in a dark blue jacket, brown hair. Both wore dark glasses."

McLaughlin turned to Ahmed and Jazari and muttered, "Sorry, but I need to ask this next question." Back to Didier, he asked, "What color was their skin?"

"They were both Caucasian, officer."

"Could you identify the van they drove?"

"White, with no back windows."

"That should have tipped you off that something was wrong," McLaughlin said sympathetically.

"It was a long flight, *monsieur*."

"What about the building they took you to? Can you identify it?"

Didier thought for a moment. "It was a very old business building in the ... northwest industrial district," he said. "After we escaped, we felt we had to hide ourselves until we could contact our host, *Monsieur* Ahmed."

"Yes," Ahmed agreed, improvising. "They were to stay with me anyway. It was fortunate that my daughter discovered them downtown."

Paul asked Didier, "Do you remember where this building is? Is it, like near a bridge or an intersection?"

Didier thought for a moment. "There is a bridge somewhere north of it. It is just off of the main road ... It is in back of a storage place."

Paul raised his eyebrows. "The old tool and die place. Yeah, we've had to deal with drug activity there several times. Well, we'll get on it. In the meantime, I hope you get replacement passports as soon as possible."

Ahmed again improvised. "I was contacting Immigration when my daughter called me about this. I will need to call them back when we're done."

"Okay," Paul said. "I agree that you folks should not leave this building until your replacement passports arrive."

"Absolutely, *monsieur*," Didier agreed. "Thank you so much for your help."

"My pleasure," Paul smiled as he and his officers walked toward the door. "I hope the rest of your visit goes better."

"I think it will, *monsieur*."

After the police departed, Iannis burst out laughing. The rest of the guests weren't as loud, but they were just as relieved. Ahmed and Jazari were confused. "How did you come up with that story?" Ahmed asked in amazement.

Didier grinned and pointed at his earpiece. "Toochla told it to me. Those men I described are the captors of our friends! Drasher was able to relay the information to her fellow Baasians before she surrendered to the men. As for the building, the Baasians scanned police files for recent criminal activities in that section of town. All they had to do was relay the information for me to repeat to the police."

Ahmed slowly shook his head, grinning. "I want to meet these Baasians," he said mock-pleadingly.

Didier shrugged and said, "Perhaps this afternoon?" That suggestion triggered a barrage of questions about the Baasians from the hosts.

CHAPTER EIGHTEEN: REVEREND GRAVES MEETS HIS SAVIOR

One couldn't meet a more inviting, cordial man than Rev. Allen Graves. Hefty but still youthful-looking in his late 60s, with a slightly receding hairline bordering blond hair gracefully turning gray, along with a voice that could go from the gentlest murmur to an earth-shaking thunderclap in one sentence, he had a commanding presence. In the political arena, those qualities enhanced his ferocious debating style. There were four topics that brought the lion out of his lamb: abortion, homosexuality, evolution, and atheism. Charlie Schwitters represented the latter two, and supported the rights of the former two. He had also brought out the inner sociopath in Rev. Graves, via hard questioning in a venue that Graves did not control—district court. If Graves' candidates won enough elections that year, many of those venues would soon become his as well.

At present, Graves was taking a break from hosting the Fellowship America Convention to attend to an urgent matter involving Schwitters at a conference room in the basement of the Colorado Springs Airport. Since there were many political candidates attending his convention looking for his blessing and support, the last thing he wanted was a National Security crisis upstaging his event.

The sight of the group that awaited him in the conference room put a strain on his composure: an atheist, an extraterrestrial, an ape woman, and—most disconcerting—a man claiming to be the historical Jesus. They had all been fed, bathed, potty-breaked and handcuffed hands-front, in preparation for this historic moment. Ed Harper stood by the prisoners, looking as pleasant as a large, burly man holding a police flashlight could look, patiently awaiting the end of this formality.

Rev. Graves' personal assistant Marilee was there to greet him. "Everything's ready. We have their English translator thing pointed at a microphone that's fed through a portable P.A. system. The room also has a signal-scrambler to prevent outside electronic surveillance."

"Good girl," Rev. Graves replied, a ray of warmth escaping through his apprehension. Turning to his old nemesis, he said sorrowfully, "Mr. Schwitters, I really wish you had reconsidered my offer back then. Look where your lack of faith has gotten you."

"And you said that with a straight face," Charlie shot back sarcastically.

Brushing off the retort, Rev. Graves motioned for everyone to be seated at the table. Charlie's earpiece had been placed on top of a plate microphone that could pick up all sound in the room. The P.A. system was basically an amplifier with two small speakers set up at opposite corners of the room. Graves said to Drasher, who was still breathing from the oxygen tank, "I'm curious as to what an alien would say. Could you please say something to make sure this set-up works?"

Drasher took a breath, removed the mask and said, "There is much I can say to you, Reverend Graves. But I doubt that you would listen." She then replaced the mask and kept steadily breathing.

Not exactly the "We come in peace" spiel he was hoping for, Graves leaned forward and said amicably to Drasher, "Look, I don't know what Mr. Schwitters has told you about me, but I am willing to listen to you. I want to know what you are doing on this planet."

Drasher took another breath from the tank and answered, "We have been waiting for another planet to be terraformed. Our home planet is now uninhabitable for us."

"That's terrible," Graves responded. "What happened?"

"Look at the people who make war on this planet," Drasher told him sternly, "and you will have your answer about my planet's fate."

Graves, Marilee, and Ed looked at each other. Drasher continued, "My people's impression of you, Reverend Graves, was made by listening to your speeches several weeks before we met

Charlie Schwitters. They are nearly identical to speeches by the leaders who destroyed my planet."

"You think that I'm a warmonger?" he asked, hurt. "My speeches are about defending our values, our freedom, our country —"

Charlie dropped his cuffed wrists on the table. "MY freedom, Reverend?" he snarled. Clover, who stayed close to Charlie, bared her teeth in sympathy with Charshwit's anger.

Ed brandished the heavy flashlight. "Watch it!" he warned.

Graves looked at Clover, then eyed Charlie suspiciously. "How old is this girl?"

"Well within the age of consent," Charlie replied. "She's over 500,000 years old."

"She looks not older than 13," Graves retorted. "That's why you're not a free man, Charlie."

"When we first adopted her," Drasher explained, "she was about that age. She is now approximately 27."

"You adopted her?" Graves asked with an edge. "For what purpose?"

Drasher took more gulps of oxygen. "She was banished from the tribe we were observing on our first excursion to your planet over 500,000 linear years ago."

"Linear years?"

"Years measured in regular time," Drasher explained. "When our Mothership's speed reaches the speed of light, we inside the Mothership enter a state we call 'Slow Time.'"

"Slow time?! Isn't that the opposite of what you just described?"

"On our ship," Drasher clarified, "time stays linear. We have aged only 20 years since our journey began. Time on our ship slows down."

"But you still haven't answered my original question: Why have you been visiting Earth?"

After another breath, Drasher replied, "For plant and animal samples to add to our new planet."

Graves eyed her suspiciously. "That's it? We have a perfectly livable planet right here. Why don't you just take us over?"

Drasher tapped the oxygen tank with her fingers. "We cannot breathe your air for long. Too much nitrogen."

More insistently, Graves asked, "So why didn't you try to terraform our planet to suit your needs?"

Drasher looked straight at him and declared, "Tampering with your air would kill off most life on Earth. It would be pointless to do so."

Graves was not convinced. "And those two boys whom you nearly killed with your weapon—wasn't that extreme? Couldn't you have just stunned them without blinding them and destroying most of their nerve endings?"

"They attacked our contact, Charlie Schwitters, for no plausible reason. We defended him."

"But couldn't you have done so without harming those boys so badly?"

"Not under the circumstances of that time," Drasher replied.

Jumping quickly to another topic, Graves inquired, "So what is so special about Charlie Schwitters to you? Of the billions of people on this planet, why did your people choose to contact a convicted child molester?"

"We choose people who have been unjustly rejected by their societies, Reverend. Charlie was convicted by innuendo and politics, not by your laws."

"Because these rejects are easier for you to manipulate?"

"We simply ask them to give us more intimate knowledge about their planet, not divulge secret information," Drasher said. She frowned and added, "You are not one to accuse others of manipulation, Reverend Graves."

Graves' shoulders slumped. "You are really determined to hate me, aren't you?"

"Hatred of you would be an irrational reaction. My distrust of you and your minions is very rational."

It was increasingly evident in Drasher's demeanor that she didn't want to talk to Rev. Graves. He turned to Clover and said, "So you are both 27 and 500,000 years old, eh?"

"She only speaks peoples' names," Charlie muttered. "Her tribe had no complex verbal language."

Clover glared at the reverend. Seeing how her beloved friend Drasher was reacting to him, she knew that he was no friend of hers. A small growl rumbled in her throat. Graves told Charlie, "She seems very attached to you. Have you had relations with her?"

Charlie looked at Clover, then defiantly said to Graves, "I'd rather have her than Monica Ludlake!"

Graves's eyes almost burst through his glasses. "You are a very sick man! She can't be more than 13 years old, and she's a wild animal!"

Seeing Charshwit under attack, Clover jumped up and gave a warning bark at Graves. Graves was ready to vacate the room, but Charlie was able to coax Clover back into her chair before Ed Harper intervened. Charlie looked disdainfully at Graves and calmly stated, "She's adult, she's sane, and she doesn't like you!"

Graves clutched at his chest, but remained seated. Marilee cowered in a far corner of the conference room, not knowing what kind of violence Clover was capable of. Graves gasped in horror, "Lilith!"

Charlie caught the reference to the legendary, pre-Eve wife of Adam. "Oh, come on, Graves!" he cried in exasperation. "She had a mother and father like everyone else!"

"We can show you our notes on her," Drasher offered.

Graves regained his composure, but his fear and anger remained. "With your technology," he said accusingly to Drasher, "you can manufacture any evidence you want! You give me no reason to believe what you say about that creature—" he then pointed at Yeshua—"or who HE really is."

"And yet," Yeshua suddenly spoke, "you expect others to believe that everything YOU say is true."

Everyone turned to him. Yeshua had uttered almost nothing the entire trip from Portland to Colorado Springs. He held up his scarred hands and stoutly declared, "I have proof to show who I am. Where is your proof that God speaks directly to you?"

Graves glared icily at Yeshua. "I will NOT be persuaded by a false Jesus,"

"And what," Yeshua inquired, "is your TRUE Jesus like?"

Stiffening up again, Graves replied, "For one thing, he wouldn't return to Earth as a pathetically-dressed bum accompanied by people like this. The Book of Revelations spells out how he would return to Earth. Him coming back in a spaceship with an ape girl and four-armed alien is absurd!"

"But what is your true Jesus like?" Yeshua insisted. "I do not need to hear what he is not."

To Marilee, it seemed like such a simple question. She thought her boss would easily answer it,yet she saw him hesitate. She wanted to offer an answer, but found herself hesitating as well.

Reverend Graves finally said, "Jesus is the savior of all those who believe in him. He is the one who washes away the sin that is inherent in all people, if only they would ask him. He is the ultimate judge of who goes to heaven and who goes to hell!" He grabbed the Bible he had brought in with him and held it in Yeshua's face. "If you want more information, you can read this!" he growled.

Yeshua looked unimpressed. "There are many different men in that book with the name of Jesus. There is the Jesus who taught his people to love their enemies, and the Jesus who said to kill all his enemies. Which Jesus do you think is the real Jesus, Reverend Graves?"

Graves started to tremble in rage. "I know YOU'RE not the real Jesus!"

Yeshua grinned knowingly. "You avoid my question."

Graves gripped the edge of the table and leaned in menacingly. "Apparently you think you already know the answer yourself, smart guy."

"Apparently," Yeshua calmly retorted, "the Jesus you worship is a merciless warlord who wants his followers to curry his favor."

This answer flummoxed the powerful reverend. Trying not to stammer, Graves clarified through gritted teeth, "I meant who YOU think the real Jesus is!"

"A good man. A man living under an oppressive regime who did his best to help his people find inner strength. A man who finds goodness in people outside of the religion he was raised in." His gaze and his voice hardened. "A man whose favor is not bought by fawning sycophants!"

"So," Graves crowed, "anyone who prays to the Real Jesus is a sycophant; is that what you are saying?" Before Yeshua could answer, Graves stood and rushed over to Marilee and put a protective arm around her. "Marilee here prays every day to Jesus. Are you saying SHE is a sycophant?"

Yeshua looked at Marilee, who was on the verge of tears. His voice softened for her sake. "If all she prays for is happiness in her life and for her family, no, she is not."

Graves released his arm from his assistant and again confronted Yeshua. "Then what about those people who work in charities in Jesus' name?" he demanded. "Do you think they're just currying your favor?"

"Those who help others in my name are my blessing. Those who *harm* others in my name are my curse!"

Marilee burst into tears. Graves stopped short of punching Yeshua in the nose. "Congratulations, Mister False Jesus," he snarled, nearly on the verge of hysteria himself. "You just shattered that woman's faith into a million pieces! Is that why you came back? To invalidate the Christian faith of billions of people?"

Yeshua shook his head sadly. "I only want to destroy the legends about me."

"You are an anonymous impostor," Graves declared. "There are no legends about you!"

Charlie blurted out, "Then probe the wounds, Doubting Thomas!"

Graves froze at Charlie's biblical reference. Ed Harper needed just one more provocation to cold-cock Charlie with his flashlight. The others looked at Charlie, fearing more for his life than did Charlie. He looked unblinkingly at Graves. Graves appeared to calm down. He turned to Charlie and asked, "So you believe that this man is the historical Jesus?"

"Yes."

"So why do you believe him and not the Gospels?"

"He stumped you in the same way that he stumped the religious leaders of his time. His answers are also fresh and not derivative of what the Gospels say. Not to mention the wounds on his body that correspond to how he was executed. So what's stopping you from believing him? Are you expecting him to pull out his driver's license?"

"So," Reverend Graves sneered, "you believe that he is the original Jesus, and yet, you remain an atheist?"

"I'm more interested in his philosophy than whether or not he performs miracles."

Ed Harper grumbled, "You're going to be wishing he *could* perform miracles!"

Graves pointed at Charlie and asked Yeshua, "And how do YOU feel about this atheist denying your divinity? Doesn't that bother you?"

Yeshua shook his head. "He has committed no crime against me. If he wants my philosophy, I am happy to share it with him. If you demand miracles and rewards from me, you will only be disappointed."

Charlie leaned back in his chair. "So, if Jesus doesn't give you everything you want, Graves, are you gonna become an atheist? Or are you just going to keep marketing his name for personal gain?"

Clover had been quietly studying everyone's faces and voices. She kept an eye on the hairless man with the large, black stick who had hit her in the stomach the night before. She was ready to duck at the first move he made. To her surprise, however, it was the old man with the glasses on his face who struck a blow. She saw Reverend Graves take a swing at Charlie. Pure instinct kicking in, she bolted across the table with a shriek to fend off the elderly attacker, even though her hands were still bound together. Charlie was able to block the blow with his cuffed hands, but he was too late to restrain Clover. She clipped Graves' head, knocking off his glasses. As Ed raised his baton to strike Clover, Yeshua stood between them, only to be forcefully shoved to the floor. Charlie used his body to protect Clover from Ed's blows while covering his head with his arms.

Drasher tried to shy away from the fray, but was knocked off her chair when Ed shoved Charlie into her, the oxygen tank escaping her grip. With all the captives on the floor and momentarily subdued, Drasher started to gasp horribly for air.

Marilee, cowering in the corner, was astonished at what she saw: Clover screamed "Drasha!" and crawled over to her, grabbing the oxygen mask and shoving it onto her face. Charlie and Yeshua scrambled to assist her back into her chair. Yeshua asked if she was okay; Drasher barely nodded. Charlie, smarting from the flashlight blows, kept his body between his friends and the sadistic Ed Harper.

Rev. Graves, visibly shaken, immediately composed himself when he saw that the situation was under control. Ed hovered over the captives like a funnel cloud waiting to touch down as a tornado. Replacing his glasses, Graves announced to the room, "Well, I believe this meeting is over. I've heard enough." He quickly trotted out of the conference room with Marilee in tow. He was silent as he strode into the elevator to the main floor on his way back to his waiting limo. Even though she had worked for him for little over a year, Marilee had never seen him out of control of a situation. This encounter seemed to have shaken him to his foundation. Finally, after they stepped out of the elevator, Graves turned to Marilee and said in hushed, urgent tones, "That was a genuinely satanic experience in there!"

Marilee was confused. The sight of the savage ape girl suddenly helping the alien woman with her oxygen mask was freshly seared into her mind. "Satanic" wasn't the word she would have used. Strange and unnerving, yes. "They didn't seem like evil people," she hesitantly mentioned.

"Are you that gullible?" Graves snarled at her. "Satan has sent them to distract us from preparing for the Apocalypse. Their very existence threatens all of humanity!"

In her years of education at missionary schools in Luzon, Marilee had never heard of anything remotely like what her boss was describing. Nonetheless, he was the Great Reverend Allen Graves, the savior of America. "I understand," she mustered. "But what will we do about them?"

"Go back to the conference room," Graves ordered in a low voice, "tell Ed that he and his people need to take the alien and extract any information they can from her. As for the other three—I never want to see them again."

As Graves was about to leave, Marilee asked anxiously, "What about the other three?"

Graves turned and impaled her with a direct look. "*I never want to see them again!*" he repeated in carefully measured words. "Ed will understand. Meet me back at the convention center when you're done." He strode down the hallway toward his limousine. His mind became occupied by the next speech he was to give at the convention: it required a quick, extensive rewrite.

CHAPTER NINETEEN: NO MORE SECRETS

Earlier that day, Captain Mrovinta's surveillance team had made a discovery that led to a turning point in the Reconnaissance Ship's mission. After easily locating the whereabouts of Reverend Graves, they were amazed to discover that he himself wore an earpiece—a hearing aid, to be precise (even though he had once claimed that Jesus had healed him of his deafness in that ear). With their pinpoint-accurate instruments utilizing Earth's own communication satellites, the team was able to easily monitor Graves' conversations. There was a moment of frustration when the captives were led into the surveillance-proof room that blocked all electronic communication. But Graves himself had provided the Baasians the incentive to make their next, fateful move: he had stepped *outside of the room* and uttered unmistakably, " ... take the alien and extract any information they can ... as for the other three, I never want to see them again."

Mrovinta's face froze upon hearing those final words repeated with such cold resolution. Toochla and Xashan were sitting next to the captain. Protocol had kept them quiet while the team did their job, but Toochla just had to speak up. "They are going to kill them!"

One of Mrovinta's hands shot up in a stifling gesture. She ordered one of the team, "Send this emergency missive to the Mothership: 'High Council: Earth leaders incarcerating our people show hostile, lethal intent toward them. We respectfully, but urgently, request aggressive rescue efforts. As captain of the Reconnaissance Ship under your command, and as informed by the most knowledgeable people of the human species in our ranks, I feel that we must risk open contact with them. We will respect your decision on this dire matter. Captain Mrovinta.'"

"Message sent with intercepted communications, Captain," one of the team replied.

Mrovinta's shoulders slumped. "And so," she mumbled, "we await their response."

"What about Iannis and the others?" Xashan asked.

"We will rescue them when our position permits use of the Gate. Once they are safe, we can concentrate on rescuing Drasher and the others without worrying about further abductions."

From the far side of the sun several eons-long moments later came the response from the High Council on the Mothership: "With reluctance, we deny you permission to carry out aggressive rescue efforts. As hostile leaders wish to keep their captives' existence secret, our anonymity will not be compromised. We still have 2 months until we leave for New Baas. We may have to sacrifice our people for the sake of our mission, but hope that the situation does not deteriorate to such a point. We trust your judgment in this matter, Captain, as do the human guests on the Mothership, to do what is best for us all. Good luck to you."

"That is outrageous!" Toochla cried. "No sentient life is worth discarding for the sake of secrecy!"

Mrovinta glared at Toochla. "I will do everything in my power to rescue Drasher and the others," she declared sternly. "But sentiment cannot override duty. I am afraid you both must go to your quarters for now so I can concentrate on avoiding having to make such a sacrifice. Dismissed." She solemnly went back to her duty.

Toochla and Xashan turned slowly and exited the helm. As they entered the hallway to their private quarters, Xashan broke down and wept. All Toochla could do was comfort her and fight back her own emotions.

*****

As she dutifully made her way back to the conference room, Marilee felt that she was becoming an accessory to a terrible crime. None of the captives seemed evil to her. Even Charlie Schwitters, her boss' old nemesis, seemed more angry than hateful. In fact, there was a stark contrast between him and her boss at that meeting: Charlie had been straightforward in his answers and probing in his questions, whereas Graves was evasive and accusatory. She recalled some rumors among her fellow employees about why her predecessor resigned from Graves' ministry: allegedly, Graves' previous personal assistant had been sickened by how he'd handled the whole Monica Ludlake affair, prompting her to resign, claiming family concerns. Before today, Marilee had simply brushed off such talk as scuttlebutt. Now she had nagging suspicions.

Nonetheless, she arrived as ordered back to the conference room. She knocked on the door, and Ed opened it. The captives were back in their seats, looking subdued. Ed Harper stood over them, easily the scariest person in that room to Marilee. "So," Ed asked, "What's the plan?"

Marilee entered the room and mechanically relayed Reverend Graves' message, word for word. Ed cocked his head and trilled, "Consider it done."

Charlie's head dropped in despair. "The man's a cold-blooded fucking murderer," he muttered bitterly. Yeshua and Drasher looked at Marilee in shock. Clover saw how the others reacted to what the brown lady said, and instinctively feared for her life. Marilee looked miserably at the captives and barely squeaked, "I'm sorry!"

"Oh, come now," Ed admonished mock-soothingly. "What makes you think that I'm going to kill you nice people? We're just going to go for a nice little ride out in the countryside so Reverend Graves never has to see you again." To Marilee, he said more seriously, "Go round up the rest of our guys, will you?"

Past Ed, Marilee gasped as she saw Drasher take the mask away from her mouth and twist the knob to stop the oxygen flow. Ed rushed over and force the mask back onto her. "Oh, no!" he demanded. "We need you alive!"

Seizing the opportunity, Charlie leapt up and threw his cuffed arms around Ed's neck and started to strangle him. Clover bit down hard on Ed's right arm as he struggled to free himself. Drasher, who was holding her breath, got up, hefted the oxygen tank, and brought it down onto Ed's bald head, knocking him cold.

Working quickly, Charlie searched Ed's pockets and produced the key to the handcuffs. He freed Drasher's hands first, then Yeshua's, and finally Clover's. Clover gave Charshwit a big hug as Yeshua freed him. Charlie reached down and picked up his translator earpiece and held it to Ed's unconscious face. "Mine!" he snapped as he inserted it into his own ear. He commanded Yeshua, "Help me cuff him to the table!"

Marilee was about to flee the room, but Clover darted to the doorway, glowering and growling as she blocked her exit. Marilee was too frightened to scream. Yeshua and Charlie intervened after Ed was securely cuffed to the struts under the heavy oak conference table. Charlie got between the two women while Yeshua put a protective arm around the frightened Filipino woman and grabbed her hand. Charlie told Marilee, "If you want to get on her good side, shake his hand!"

Obediently, she did just that. Clover saw this, and grudgingly abandoned her aggressive pose. Marilee, apparently out of danger, looked up at Yeshua and realized who she was shaking hands with. Then she fainted in his arms. Yeshua looked at Charlie with dismay and remarked, "Let us hope that our next move has more thought behind it!"

Charlie brought over a chair and Yeshua sat Marilee down in it. Fortunately, she was soon moaning weakly. Charlie knelt down next to her and put a reassuring hand on her shoulder. "Miss Navidad," he said gently but earnestly, "don't worry. None of us are going to hurt you. But we desperately need your help!"

Marilee flinched when she saw Charlie's face so close. "What do you want from me?"

"Just a safe way out of here. Drasher's people are coming back for her. If she is harmed in any way, the whole human species could be in danger."

Marilee looked at Drasher, who said in simple English, "We not want war."

Ed regained consciousness and started to struggle. "You're all traitors," he grunted weakly, "if you help that alien escape!"

Clover growled and slowly approached with Ed's police flashlight. Ed looked at her in alarm, which only made her more bold. Charlie kept an arm between the two and told Ed, "Either you cooperate with us, or I step out of her way!"

Ed did his best not to show fear, but he knew that there was considerable power in Clover's arms. "So what?" he asked defiantly. "After you beat me, where will you go? There is no way you can sneak out of this airport unnoticed. And my people know this place better than you do!"

Charlie hesitated. He knew that Ed was right. But his face hardened in resolve. "Miss Navidad, take us to the baggage claim area."

That demand surprised both Ed and Marilee. "But that's a very public place!" Marilee gasped.

"If we can't leave this airport unnoticed," Charlie replied as he tore a strip off of his hiding blanket and gagged Ed with it, "then we will leave it *extremely* noticed!"

"Are you mad?" Yeshua gasped.

"No. I am tired of hiding. If enough of a crowd sees us, the authorities are going to be careful how they deal with us!"

Drasher told Charlie, "But that will breach my mission's protocol! It is the High Council's decision to announce ourselves to your world when they decide the time! It is better that I die than defy the High Council!"

Softening his voice, Charlie said to Drasher, "You Baasians told me when we first met about how unprepared you were for today's human society. My argument to your High Council is that your protocol needs revision. I also argue that we humans are mature enough to meet you now. My third argument is that I don't want you to die. Okay?"

Drasher looked deep into Charlie's eyes. Again, in this unlikely setting, she found feelings for him surging within her. Suddenly, her mission's protocol was pointless. She turned to Marilee and asked her in English, "Miss Navidad, do you fear me?"

For the first time, Marilee looked directly at the Baasian. She was afraid, but when she saw a sympathetic fear in Drasher's eyes, she shook her head slightly and answered, "No, I don't."

Uncertainty drained out of Drasher's expression. "I need to inform Toochla," she softly said and reached deeply under her bodysuit with her two bottom hands. Carefully, and to the astonishment of her friends and the revulsion of Ed and Marilee, she pulled out a slime-covered plastic shopping bag that had been held within her cavernous Baasian vagina. From that, she produced her hand-held monitor.

Charlie gawked. "I wondered what you did with that!" he cried delightedly.

Drasher wiped off her monitor with her blanket then used the monitor's "sterilize" ray on the blanket and the slimy shopping bag. Marilee could not help but marvel at the device. Ed cringed, wondering what that device could do to him. Yeshua nervously shook his head and muttered, "We will be caught again, Drasher."

"I believe," Drasher calmly replied, "that Charlie has the better plan." Turning on the "communicate" function, she said, "The door needs to be open."

Carefully, Charlie cracked the door to the conference room. When the monitor registered a connection to the Reconnaissance Ship, Drasher, said into it, "Leader, it is Drasher."

Toochla's voice suddenly bolted from the monitor's speaker. "Drasher!" she cried with delight, giving Marilee a jolt. "Joyous to hear from you! Are you and the others okay?"

"My lung filter has worn off and I have been supplied with a tank of pure oxygen. But we are all well."

"Are you able to go to a secluded area where we can open the Gate?"

"No. We have overpowered our captor and removed our bonds. But we cannot leave this air-flight facility undetected. Charlie Schwitters is going to lead us to a public part of the facility."

Toochla's voice hesitated. Then she asked, "What is his reasoning?"

"May I?" Charlie asked. Drasher aimed the monitor toward him. "I know it sounds insane, Toochla," he said. "But our captors thrive in secrecy. Since they already know of your presence on our planet, it's best that the rest of my world knows about you as well."

Another hesitation on Toochla's end. "That goes directly against our security protocol. The High Council will disapprove."

"The High Council is not down here dealing with this mess," Charlie retorted.

"Leader," Drasher said pressingly, "Rev. Graves' assistant, Miss Navidad, has agreed to help us escape. I believe that indicates that our people can finally reveal ourselves to all humans"

Toochla sighed. "Go. I will explain it to the Captain. Good fortune to all of you."

Smiling nervously, Charlie asked Marilee, "Miss Navidad, will you please take us to the baggage claim area?"

"Yes," Marilee heard herself answer. She then looked down and shook her head. "I can't believe I'm going along with this!"

Charlie smiled. "We'll do our best to make sure that you don't regret it."

As the group exited the secret conference room, Clover stopped and looked back at Ed Harper. Scowling with contempt, she carefully picked up the Drasher-slimed plastic bag and flopped it into Ed's face, much to his screaming revulsion, before storming out of the room.

"Naughty-naughty," Charlie gently admonished as he followed her out the door.

CHAPTER TWENTY: HISTORY, READY OR NOT

"Has Charlie Schwitters gone mad?" Captain Mrovinta exclaimed toToochla. "Did you not tell him of our need to stay hidden?"

"I did. He reasoned that our covertness could be used against us by Reverend Graves and his minions, who thrive in secrecy."

Mrovinta resisted pounding the armrest of her captain's chair in frustration. "Drasher and Yeshua also approved of this decision?"

"They trust him deeply. He has kept them alive so far. They are best informed of their current situation."

Slumping in her chair, Mrovinta sighed and ordered the Communications team, "Keep monitoring Drasher's group as best you can." To Toochla, she said, "I will recommend to the High Council that we prepare for both diplomatic and defensive maneuvers. Tell Mister Schwitters that the High Council will hold him personally responsible how this confrontation plays out."

"You may also inform the High Council," Toochla recommended, "that one of Graves' assistants is helping them to escape. I personally believe that Charlie Schwitters' reasoning behind his actions is sound. As Iannis' group were able to find assistance as well, perhaps the human species is finally mature enough to meet us."

"But if the humans who accept us are far outnumbered by those who fear us ..." Mrovinta said before she caught herself, "then those who fear us may turn more humans against us ... Toochla, you and Xashan prepare diplomatic statements for public broadcast over Earth's media. If no one on the High Council can think of a better time to announce our presence, then perhaps it is we Baasians who are not mature enough to contact the human species!"

"Thank you, Captain," Toochla replied enthusiastically.

*****

The four guests at the Parkrose Islamic Resource Center suddenly became very excited. Toochla had just called them. Didier turned to their curious hosts, Ahmed and Jazari, and said, "The Reconnaissance Ship is departing from the moon. They are going to reveal themselves when they rescue us!"

"What?" Ahmed cried. "I thought you said they were trying to avoid detection."

"The lives of our colleagues have been threatened," Didier explained. "The decision has been made in order to save them."

"Are we going to war?" Jazari fearfully asked.

"Heavens, no!" Didier reassured her. Showing uncertainty himself, he said, "I am only hoping that your world leaders do not declare war against them!"

"When will they be here?" Ahmed asked breathlessly.

"About one hour."

Ahmed's eyes bugged out. "*One hour?* Your ship can travel that fast?"

"Even faster." Didier smiled. "But they do not want to shoot past the Earth!"

Ahmed and Jazari gawked at each other. "Which direction will they come from?" Ahmed asked.

"West, I believe."

Ahmed whipped out his cell phone and hit the call button to his home line. As he spoke excitedly in Arabic, Taza asked, "Who are you talking to?"

Ahmed interrupted his conversation long enough to reply, "My son. I'm telling him to point his telescope to the west!" Then he resumed his animated conversation.

Taza asked Jazari, "What is a telescope?"

"A device that looks at far away places," Jazari replied with contained glee. "Father wants my brother to be among the first to see your ship!"

Iannis laughed and remarked in ancient Greek. Didier translated, "Your brother may be jealous of you. For you will see us enter the ship."

Ahmed overheard the translation. "Your ship isn't going to land here, is it?"

Didier waved his hands reassuringly. "Oh, heavens no. It is almost three miles long!"

"Then," Ahmed asked, "how will you board the ship?"

Didier grinned. "We simply walk onto it, of course!"

Ahmed and Jazari's faces registered confusion. Didier explained, "The Baasians are able to bend space and time to create small passageways between two distant places—"

Jazari gasped. "Oh, wormholes!"

Didier blinked. "You have a term for it?"

"Our top scientists have theories about bending space and time," Jazari answered. "I watch science shows all the time. How far can they go?"

"From the Earth to the moon is close to the farthest limit. The closer they are to the destination, the safer the journey. It takes enormous energy to achieve this."

Ahmed nodded wide-eyed. "I can imagine."

Clodagh was seated on the couch, contemplating her reunion with Yeshua. She would not rest until everyone was reunited on the Mothership. Her contemplation was interrupted by an increasing crowd noise from the streets. Peering out the window between the curtains, she saw people rushing from their houses and into the street. All eyes were fixed westward. She turned to her friends and announced, "Word has gotten out about the ship. There are people everywhere!"

Iannis bolted to the window and peered out. "Shit! We need a secluded area to enter the Gate! That is impossible now!"

Ahmed grabbed a remote control and turned on the wall-mounted TV. On Central News, the anchorwoman was in the middle of a breaking story: "—appears to be an artificial object, not, repeat, NOT an asteroid or comet. It is heading toward Earth at a breathtaking speed of 1800 miles an hour, and accelerating. All nonmilitary aircraft have been ordered to land at the nearest airfield."

Taza asked her hosts, "Isn't there anywhere you can take us to get away from this crowd?"

Eyes still watching the TV, Ahmed replied, "We can't take the chance of you leaving this building. The roads will be clogged, and the police will be everywhere."

"Our playground has a fence around it," Jazari offered reluctantly. "But I don't know how well its gate can hold back a crowd."

"We won't need much time," Didier assured her. "Once they give us the signal we will run out there and be gone. We just need to be keep ourselves hidden for one hour until then."

Clodagh's arms were folded in worry. "So much could happen in an hour."

"As long as the neighbors keep looking at the sky and away from us," Iannis told her optimistically, "we will be fine."

*****

"I wanted to reveal myself to our world under better conditions," Yeshua griped nervously as the fugitives rode the elevator to their questionable freedom. "I should have stayed on the Mothership."

Charlie turned to him curiously. "I've been meaning to ask you, in your condition, why did you join the Landing Party down here?"

Yeshua shrugged and admitted, "I was tired of being on the Mothership."

Upon reaching the third floor, the elevator doors slid open. "It's show time, people," Charlie said with a deep breath. "Just keep calm and we'll get through this okay."

The west end of the Colorado Springs Airport baggage claim area was relatively unpopulated, since the next arrival was not due for twenty minutes. Bob Nagakami, an information guide, was relaxing for a moment at his station, reading his copy of the *Daily Yomiuri*, thinking of his parents back in Tokyo. Out of the corner of his eye, he spotted some people led by a Filipino woman. Since they weren't walking toward him, he went back to his reading. Moments later, he heard a woman gasp, "Oh, my god!" He looked up again. This time he saw a middle-aged couple gawking at the Filipino's group. Though they were at a distance, he could see that one of the group had four hands and purple skin; another looked like Jesus Christ in thrift store clothes; yet another looked like Miss Aborigine in the swimsuit competition. Tossing aside his paper, he hit a button on his station's phone and hissed, "Security to Baggage Claim A! We have some strange-looking people here. Come quickly!" He trotted over to the strange-looking people. The fifth one in the party, who looked like a roughed-up Peace Corps volunteer, saw him approaching as they found seats, waved and said a tired, "Hello. Don't mind us. We're just waiting for our flight."

Bob couldn't answer until his eyes drank in the sight before him. His lips moved silently and his finger shook as it pointed. "What's ... what's all this?" he gasped.

"I know," Charlie said with casual resignation. "This isn't something you see every day, is it? We're willing to explain." Clover looked at Bob with suspicion and huddled closer to Charshwit.

"I—I—I don't think you should be here," Bob stammered.

"Couldn't agree with you more, dude," Charlie said amiably. "We were shanghaied yesterday from Portland, Oregon by Reverend Allen Graves' people and were flown here in his private jet this morning."

Bob gawked at them. "YOU were the 'High Level' meeting they were talking about? What are you doing out here?"

"Fleeing for our lives, pretty much."

Marilee felt it was time for her to intervene. "I'm Marilee Navidad, personal assistant to Rev. Graves," she flashed her high-clearance Fellowship America Convention ID badge. "In the name of world security, we need to return this—" she pointed at Drasher and tried to find the most appropriate pronoun "—*extraterrestrial* to her people."

Bob Nagakami was well on the way to hysteria now. "You mean, *more* of those things are coming?" he shrieked. "We're being *invaded?*"

Drasher shook her head and pointed to herself. "Get me," she said in English, then waved her hand. "Not invade."

More people had gathered around them. A collective gasp arose when Drasher spoke. One woman's voice in the throng asked, "Is that the real Jesus?"

Yeshua gave Charlie a desperate glance. Charlie raised his hand and stood up. "Please calm down, folks. We have no weapons or special magic powers. There has been an amazing run of events and circumstances that have brought us all here, and we are happy to explain them."

"Is that the real Jesus?" A man's voice repeated the woman's question.

Well, this is it Charshwit, Charlie said to himself. "If you mean a miracle worker who will give you eternal life in Heaven," he answered, "no, he is not. If you mean the man whose life and teachings inspired the books of the New Testament ... then, yes."

The gathering audience reared back in awe. Each of the five individuals at the center of this attention wondered what was going to happen next. Their answer came in the form of four armed airport security guards rushing through the crowd, guns and tasers drawn. The lead guard, Brad Aronson, cried, "Freeze! Put your hands— *what—the—fuck?!*"

Clover screamed in terror and clamped her arms tightly around Charshwit, burrowing her head into his chest. Keeping calm,

Charlie politely completed Brad's line: "Hands in the air? We're cool." He raised one hand while keeping a comforting hand on Clover's shoulder. Yeshua raised both his hands, exposing the scars in his palms. Drasher raised one set of arms while holding her breathing apparatus with the other set. Marilee raised her arms as well, saying a silent prayer.

Brad Aronson and his guards got a better look at the people they were aiming their guns at. "Okay," Brad drawled, keeping his gun cautiously drawn. "Would all of you please come with us?"

Charlie's demeanor switched from cooperative to commanding. "With all due respect for the important job you do," he answered in carefully chosen words, "you can check us for weapons and interrogate us right here. We will cooperate, but we will not be held prisoner without formal charge again! And if you don't want us here, then you can talk to the man who brought us here: Reverend Allen Graves!"

The guards' eyes lit up. Marilee flashed her ID to them. "I work for Rev. Graves," she said. In recognition of her current status, her voice lowered, "Though probably not for much longer. It's true. They were captured by agents from a weapons contractor, which Rev. Graves is connected to. When he was told that one of them seemed to be the real Jesus, Graves had them flown here to meet them himself."

Bob Nagakami pointed at them and confirmed, "They were that high level meeting we were briefed on!"

Coming clean on an important matter, Charlie added, "The main agent who kidnapped us, Ed Harper, is down in the secured conference room on the SB2 floor, handcuffed to the table. When we were told that Graves wanted us eliminated, we had a little kerfuffle. I have the key to the cuffs in my shirt pocket if you'd like fetch him and get his side of the story."

Brad and the guards still had their guns drawn, but would have been hard-pressed to remember how to use them. "Bev," Brad asked the guard nearest to him, "are you seeing and hearing the same things I am?"

Bev nodded her head slowly and answered,"Yeah."

Brad said to the group of strangers tactfully, "For your safety, I strongly urge you to come with us. We're not going to harm you."

Charlie replied equally tactfully, "Please tell us what we are being arrested for, sir, for the public record. Then we'll come quietly."

The guards looked at each other. None of them could think of a charge beyond Causing a Disturbance. "We have an office of Homeland Security downstairs," Brad said. "That's the most I could tell you."

"Well, here's the least I can tell you," Charlie said directly, "there is going to be an extremely huge spaceship coming to Earth looking for these people. How we are treated by Homeland Security, or whoever you're going throw us to, will effect how that ship arrives. The *goons* who captured us could end up getting our planet torn a new asshole if we're busted again! Am I making sense to you?"

The whole thing didn't make sense to the guards or anyone else. Brad looked at Drasher and ordered, "You with the oxygen tank. Could you please stand up and walk toward me? I want to see who we're dealing with."

Drasher obliged. She rose from the seat with the tank and cautiously walked up to Brad. She took a breath from the tank, then briefly removed the mask to show Brad her face and say in English, "Hello. My name is Drasher." Then she replaced the mask.

The crowd and the personnel were transfixed by this simple action. Brad stared intently at Drasher, then said, "Damned if you're not real! You may sit down."

Drasher bowed her head politely, then went back to her seat. Charlie glanced at the pressure gauge at the top of the tank and said to Brad, "She's got about another twenty minutes of air. Could we scare up another oxygen tank?"

"We've got plenty," Brad replied, dropping his aggressive posture. "Look, I'm sorry, folks. But your presence is causing a disruption in the crowd flow here. We need to move you to a more private area."

Just then, two soothing tones chimed throughout the airport. "Attention all passengers and airport personnel," a calm but commanding male voice announced. "It has been confirmed by top astronomers at the Mauna Loa Observatory that a large object has ejected from the far side of the moon and is headed straight toward the Earth."

The collective gasps throughout the airport nearly created a vacuum. Charlie announced emphatically, "Don't panic, folks! That's our ride!"

The announcement continued: "The object has been confirmed as being of artificial, but unknown origin. The President of the United States has issued orders for all nonmilitary aircraft to be grounded, or land as soon as safely possible. Based on the speed of the object, interception with Earth may occur in approximately one hour. The President also insists that all people, with the exception of military and emergency personnel, remain where they are until further notice. Above all, please remain calm and alert for further information."

The crowd in the baggage claim area became restless. The security guards turned their attention and their guns from the Unusual Five to the Uneasy Five Hundred (estimated). Marilee started to panic; Charlie's radical idea was about to get them lynched. Indeed, one fifty-ish man burst away from the crowd and ran angrily toward Charlie. Fortunately, two of the guards restrained him. "Traitor!" he screamed in a blind rage. "You sold out your own planet, you fucking traitor!"

"He is not a traitor," a soft, oboe-like voice came over the same P.A. speakers, stopping everyone, including the would-be rioter, in their tracks.

Drasher stood up, speaking into her monitor. "My people have no intention of invading your planet. We are scientists who have been studying Earth while we wait for a new planet of our own to be terraformed. Observe," she held up her oxygen mask then put it back over her face, "we cannot breathe your air because of its high nitrogen content. We kept ourselves hidden from you to avoid causing mass panic and strife. On behalf of my people, I wish to apologize for any misunderstanding of our mission. For our sake as well as your own, I beg you to be calm."

Brad looked at the device Drasher was talking into. "Whoa," he muttered. "That's one helluva cell phone!"

As everyone settled into restrained anticipation, Clover started to moan and rock uneasily. Charlie grew concerned and tried to comfort her. Drasher, however, knew better. "She needs to relieve herself," she explained.

Immediately, Charlie turned to Brad and said, "Clover here really needs the ladies' room." Bev stepped forward and said, "I can take her there." Clover growled in warning, but stepped behind Charshwit. "She's still pretty insecure," Charlie explained. "I'd better come along. I could use a pitstop anyway."

"Does she know how to use a toilet?" Bev asked, unsure of Clover's intelligence.

Drasher answered, "Fecal disposal is one of the first things my people taught her." The statement came through the P.A. speakers, to Drasher's slight embarrassment.

Marilee stepped forward. "I could use it too!" .

Charlie looked at Drasher and Yeshua. "Do either of you need relief?" he asked politely. Both shook their heads.

The restrooms were fortuitously located near the elevator they'd arrived in. It took some pantomimic convincing of Clover that Charshwit had to use the room opposite where she had to go, but there was no incident. Bev patiently waited outside the door.

Marilee cautiously opened a door to one of the stalls for Clover. Immediately sensing that that was the right place to do business, Clover undid her bodysuit buckle and sat down. Quickly, Marilee took the next stall over and shut the door securely. She didn't really need to use the toilet. She sat down on it, then shuddered uncontrollably, emitting a deep sob. She buried her head in her hands as she wept, overwhelmed by the situation she found herself in and the potential consequences of her betrayal of her boss, the powerful Reverend Allen Graves.

After the outburst subsided, Marilee heard Clover tear off toilet paper, then a flush—the toilets were motion-activated. She shakily rose, daubed her eyes, and blew her nose on a wad of toilet paper, then exited the stall. Standing next to the sinks was Clover, hands folded in front of her. Marilee looked at her. Clover's expression had softened considerably as she looked back. Not knowing what else to do, Clover started to walk out. Strangely enough, Marilee's sense of hygiene emerged and she politely stopped Clover and pointed at the sink. She then demonstrated washing her hands. Clover studied what she did, then carefully imitated her moves. As she started to rub dispensed soap foam on her hands, Clover stopped, then took a deep whiff of the suds. She exhaled luxuriously and looked at Marilee. To Marilee's amazement, Clover gave her a smile, then casually rubbed the suds all the way up her arms. Marilee was about to stop her from that faux pas, but then thought better of it. Mutually relieved, they both exited the restroom.

Waiting for them outside, Charlie noticed the white, eucalyptus-smelling streaks on Clover's arms and ascertained the explanation. "You nut!" he laughed as he put his arm around her and walked back to their seats. He noticed that Marilee was finally smiling. "She really is a person!" she gasped. Her expression of wonderment infected the crowd as the strangers took their seats.

CHAPTER TWENTY-ONE: THE SERMON AT BAGGAGE CLAIM "A"

Under ordinary traffic conditions, it would have been a 20 minute drive from the airport to the Colorado Springs Convention Center. Rev. Graves sat in the back of his limousine diligently reworking his next speech, which he was due to deliver in half an hour. Seated with him was another personal assistant, Tim Dunn. They had been on the freeway for about ten minutes when Tim glanced out the tinted windows. "That's weird," he muttered.

"What's weird?" Graves asked distractedly.

"A lot of vehicles have pulled over into the emergency lane. I wonder what's going on?"

Graves buzzed the limo driver. "Any idea what's going on out there, Rich?"

Rich replied, "Reverend, they just announced on the radio that some UFO from the moon is heading toward the Earth."

Graves' eyes lit up as his face fell. "Oh, Lord Jesus!" he muttered.

"Uh, Reverend," Rich added, "the President has ordered all roads cleared except for emergency vehicles. What should I do?"

Before Graves could answer, his cell phone rang. It was Ed Harper. "Keep driving," he told Rich as he answered the call. "Yeah, Ed. What's going ... you can't be serious ..." His face turned red. "You dumb SHIT! How'd you let that happen? ... Yes, I've just been told ... It's too damned late. Just get your ass out of there! ... Let Airport Security handle them for now. Where's Marilee?" The answer added a new shade of red to the reverend's pallor. He threw his free hand over his head and groaned in exasperation. "That stupid, gullible *twat*," he grumbled. "Listen, Ed: you lie low and deny everything until further notice. I've got a shit-load of damage control to do myself right now ... Just get out!

Goodbye!" He slapped the cell phone onto the empty seat next to him.

"Reverend," Rich called back, "Airport Security is on my line. They're requesting that you return to the airport."

Graves fell silent in agitated thought. "Keep going to the Convention Center," he ordered.

"But Reverend—"

"Keeping driving, Rich! I've got more pressing concerns rights now!" Graves turned to Tim and ordered, "Tell Justin to gas up the plane and get ready to fly me to Zurich! General Livingstone can give me military clearance."

Rich and Tim did as ordered. Each was mystified about what concerned Graves, since neither knew whom Graves met with back at the airport.

*****

For many people at the airport, the shock of meeting Drasher and Clover had died away. Yeshua, however, was a different matter. Charlie Schwitters now realized an important point he had failed to consider in his getaway plan: that the majority of travelers that day were people attending the Fellowship America Convention. It seemed that every person with two ears in the whole airport was crowded into the baggage claim area to hear the latest thing Jesus had to say. Drasher allowed him to use her device to speak. The modern people waited breathlessly to hear their savior give his first sermon in English. His first words through the P.A. speakers: "May we get something to eat first, please?"

Seemingly out of thin air poured several workers from the terminal restaurants eagerly waiting to cater to them all, free of charge. Yeshua ordered fish and wine (to the shock of some of the more puritanical travelers), Charlie decided on a chicken sandwich, fries and an India Pale Ale, Marilee ordered a chef's salad and diet soda, Drasher said she could tolerate nuts, raw vegetables, and water, while Clover would eat anything but didn't like hot foods—she got a rare marinated teriyaki steak, mixed vegetables, and a glass of apple juice. The crowd waited patiently while snacking on their own foods.

His mood improved considerably after the delicious meal, Yeshua picked up Drasher's device and began to speak:

"Back in my time and place, I shocked many people with my words. Those shocked had blindly followed traditional teachings and customs that caused unnecessary strife among us peoples under Roman subjugation. You people of this time and place, if you were taught to look to me to solve all your problems through miracles and blessings, I am afraid that you will be equally shocked. For I have returned to Earth not to fulfill prophecies, but to erase them! Through my experience and travels, I have learned that it is folly to base one's philosophy on prophecies. Anyone with a mouth can prophesy, but no one can predict which prophecies will come to pass." He indicated Drasher and said, "I never prophesied that I would meet the Baasians!"

"Are you saying that the Bible is all wrong?" a man's voice suddenly asked. Many annoyed hushes descended upon the question.

Yeshua was not annoyed. But he was prepared to answer. "There are many great philosophies in the Bible, but they are in common with great philosophies in all cultures. The needs and desires of all people are born within us; I did not invent them." He limped over to Clover, took her gently by the hand and proclaimed to the crowd, "This young woman was born hundreds of thousands of years ago. Yet her needs and desires are the same as all people throughout all history."

"What needs and desires are you talking about?" another man's question arose.

"In sum," Yeshua replied patiently, "to be alive, and to be happy. Back in my time, I saw much misery among my people. I felt it was another Roman victory that their spirits were so broken. So I started talking to those whom I felt were most miserable: those whom my own society shunned. Lepers, madmen, widows, hemorrhaging women, tax collectors—it is an experience I will never forget. The healings that the Bible claims I did? Those are silly magic tricks compared to what I accomplished with the people I had spoken with. Their spirits started to mend, simply because I spoke with them as a friend! That's all that so many needed— someone to talk to. I helped make them feel like people again. What good is turning water into wine when a friendly conversation could accomplish so much more good?" His lower lip disappeared between his teeth, then he added longingly, "If only the Bible had recorded my talks with those people instead of spinning all this miracle nonsense, how much better I would feel about Christianity!"

Anxious murmurs reverberated throughout the airport. "Are you saying," a trembly woman's voice called out, "that you reject your own religion?"

"I have never rejected belief in God," Yeshua responded sternly. "I reject folly. I reject hypocrisy. I reject ignorance. How one prays to God is not my concern. But if you see folly, hypocrisy, and ignorance in your religion, then you must first destroy those evils within yourselves before you can rid them from others. I saw those evils within my own religion and the harm it caused others as well as ourselves, and I tried to eliminate them." His gaze grew more distant as his voice softened. "At first, I thought my mission was succeeding. My following grew by leaps and bounds. I was so pleased by this that I began adding more bold prophecies to my sermons about how our movement would bring about the Kingdom of God in our lifetimes. When people started hailing me as the Messiah, I started to believe it myself." He shook his head sadly. "I was seduced by my own fame. Only when I was dying on the cross did I realize that my best work had been done on an intimate scale: talking to the sick and rejected, person-to-person. When more and more people demanded my attention, that intimacy became impossible."

One woman's concerned voice called out, "If this how you feel about the religion you inspired, what are all of us Christians supposed to do? I mean, what's the point in believing in you if you won't deliver us from evil?"

Now Yeshua was annoyed. This woman, and he was sure there were many others in the audience, did not absorb what he had just said. "In other words, dear woman," he responded, "you wish a reward in Paradise for your piety?"

"Well, yes," the woman replied reluctantly.

"Then you will not be delivered from evil, regardless of whether I am the Messiah or not," Yeshua told her sternly. "The idea of heavenly reward attracts the greedy and the gullible! In my travels through history, I learned of a saying by Kung Fu Tsu of China that I wish I would have thought of: 'If you cannot serve people properly, how can you serve God?' I ask the same of anyone who needs to be *paid* to be righteous! I say to you, a just and merciful god would not foster competition for his favor. If you wish your rewards for your virtue to be justice and mercy, then you must demonstrate those virtues yourself in your lifetime!"

"I've been following the Bible all my life," a southern-accented voice called out testily. "That is the revealed word of God Almighty. If you're the real Jesus tryin' to rewrite the Bible, then show me a miracle. If you can't, then I'm stickin' to what the Bible says to earn my place in heaven, and if you don't trust the Bible, then you could just burn in hell!"

Yeshua shook his head in frustration. "Suppose you went to heaven," he conjectured, "and you found people you despise living there? And God told you that you had to accept them if you wanted to stay there because he knew what was in their hearts better than you knew?"

"If God says they can be there," the southerner declared, "then I'll accept them."

"Because you had a genuine change of heart?" Charlie pushed the subject. "Or because you'd just be covering your butt to stay in heaven?"

The southerner stepped to the front of the crowd. He was well-dressed, in his early thirties, and built like a linebacker for the Dallas Cowboys. He was definitely not pleased with that comment. The guards held him at bay. He glared at the motley group and growled, "I don't know what you expect to gain from this blasphemous shit, Charlie Schwitters! But I think all of you are a buncha frauds!" He pointed at Yeshua. "Especially you! Any o' them wounds on your body can be done with cosmetic surgery!" Then he pointed at Clover and proclaimed, "And that retarded girl should be in an institution instead of travelin' with this freak show!" To Drasher he said, "As for you ... well, that's one helluva costume!"

The large room became very quiet. Nonplussed, Drasher looked at the large heckler. Patiently, she took a big hit of air from her oxygen tank and rose to face the southerner. She did some slow-motion dance moves to demonstrate her authenticity. She did two stepping-somersaults, several pirouettes on each foot and touched her back with all four hands. The audience found her moves surprisingly graceful, and some people even applauded as she exhaled and briskly retrieved the oxygen tank. She calmly walked up to the heckler. With a free hand, she pointed at her face. The heckler looked her in the eyes warily. Then Drasher removed the oxygen mask, opened her mouth (which could comfortably accommodate a whole pineapple) as wide as she could and said, "Ahh."

"Gagh!!" the southerner shrieked in fright as he broke away and ran back into the crowd. Clover broke out in laughter. Her own dignity intact, Drasher walked back and reclaimed her seat. Charlie sat back down next Marilee, who gazed in astonishment at the improvised prank, and wiggled his eyebrows.

Yeshua, suppressing his own laughter, announced to the crowd, "That was my reaction when I first saw the Baasians."

"Your attention, please," a professional-sounding man's voice announced over the PA when Yeshua provided a long-enough pause. "It has been confirmed that the object heading toward the Earth has begun to decelerate and maneuver into a trajectory that will bring it into Earth's orbit. Therefore it is under intelligent control. The object will not, repeat, NOT impact our planet. Scientists at NASA are trying to establish contact with its occupants to determine the intention of this visit. All military personnel throughout the world are on high alert. All nonmilitary air travel has been suspended. We at the Colorado Springs Airport will do our best to keep all our visitors comfortable until the government permits commercial flights to resume. Thank you for your patience.

It became apparent that the crowd now had other things demanding their attention, so Yeshua returned the device to Drasher, then said something in Aramaic to Charlie. Brad the security guard asked Charlie, "What did he say?"

Unable to resist the temptation, Charlie pointed at the restrooms and muttered politely, "Holy shit."

Brad put his hand over his face and shook his head. "Please don't do that to me!" he said with a pained, stifled giggle as he led Yeshua away.

Not to be outdone, Yeshua call back to Charlie another Aramaic phrase that made Charlie laugh. Marilee asked him, "What did he say?"

Charlie quoted him verbatim: "I will soon have something from myself that Reverend Graves can worship!"

CHAPTER TWENTY-TWO: REVEREND GRAVES DECLARES WAR

At the approximate time that Yeshua had concluded his sermon, Rev. Graves had returned to the Convention Center. When he was hurriedly ushered to the Main Stage, he was chagrined to see that the attention of the 5,000-strong audience—*his* audience—was transfixed on the giant big-screen monitors suspended around the stage. Central News Corporation was showing live coverage of the incoming spacecraft, which was now identifiable by any amateur's telescope. The governor of Colorado and a close ally of the Great Reverend, Erica Leeching, ran up to him and confided, "The convention is over now, Allen. This story is just too huge."

"I have one more speech to give," he replied.

Gov. Leeching blinked in disbelief. "Allen, all the media people have left to go to the airport! There's a report that an extraterrestrial is there—"

"Believe it or not," Graves cut her off, "my story is even bigger." Without further ado, he made his way to the podium and tapped the microphone to make sure it was on. "Can you mute the TV, please?" he called to the sound engineer. When it was apparent that the engineer was engrossed in the new top news story, Graves barked agitatedly, "I said mute the TV!" All eyes were now on Graves, many expressing dismay at this interruption of such a historic event. Graves sensed that dismay, and launched boldly into his speech: "My friends, I'm sorry to interrupt this story. I know it's very important. But I have information about this alien visit that our government does not yet know: the alien race aboard that ship has delivered unto us—the Antichrist!"

Gasps of shock and murmurs of disbelief rippled throughout the Convention Center. Graves continued, "Some of my people who work for Homeland Security had captured an alien being in Portland, Oregon, yesterday, and the Antichrist was captured with it. This no joke or delusion on my part, I swear to Almighty God! I saw them myself at the airport under heavy security. In their company was an animal-like woman who I think is the demon, Lilith, the disobedient first mate of Adam. She tried to physically attack me." More gasps from the crowd. Graves' eyes narrowed as he added, "And the man who is their human agent was also captured: the child-molesting evolutionist Charlie Schwitters!"

Even more expressions of shock emanated from the crowd, as Graves expected. Noticing Governor Leeching backstage shaking her head, flabbergasted, Graves elaborated (i.e., embellished) even more. "I was just as shocked as you, even more so, when I first laid eyes on this unholy foursome. They all saw me as a man of God, and they hated me. Especially the Antichrist! On the outside, he appears to have the same wounds inflicted upon the real Jesus from His crucifixion, from the nail holes to the Crown of Thorns, and speaks the same language as our Lord. But what he says is a dead giveaway of what he truly is: he denies the holiness of the Bible! He has befriended Lilith and the child molester! He says he hates Christianity and all Christians! He told me—and this is a direct quote—'I want to destroy what people think about me'!

"You think this is ludicrous? Do you think he is just crazy? I wish I could dismiss him as another kook. But my personal assistant, Marilee Navidad, was seduced by him. As faithful and innocent a Christian woman as I have ever met, Marilee has betrayed me and her entire faith. Soon after I left to return here, I got a call from one of the Homeland Security agents, saying that Marilee helped the Antichrist and his minions overpower him and escape to the baggage claim area of the airport. As I speak, the Antichrist is spreading his own terrible religion to everyone in the airport, and they are under his spell. Most of the people he is talking to came from this very convention! You will see it on TV shortly. You will see how seductive he truly is!

"The Great Tribulation is upon us, O faithful! The Apocalypse is truly here! We must rise up in the glory of the one true God and our Savior! We must engage these Satanic invaders with full force! I call upon the leaders of all Christian nations to take up arms and destroy that ship! I call upon the president of the United States of America to authorize the use of our nuclear weapons if they are needed. *We must destroy that ship!*"

Standing at the foot of the stage listening to the speech was three-star Army General Terry Knepper. His presence at the Fellowship America convention had more to do with political networking than any personal fondness for Rev. Graves. But that speech was too much for him to complacently ignore. He immediately leapt to the stage and smothered the podium microphone with the palm of his hand. "Allen, have you flipped?" he asked incredulously. "I got a call from the Pentagon telling me to keep my forces ready, not to fire off nukes unless so ordered by the president himself!"

"Then get me through to the President. I can persuade him to give you permission."

"Allen, with all due respect, if it wasn't for that ship heading toward us, I'd swear that you've gone off your nut to hit us with such a story. I suggest that you just sit tight and let us military folks deal with this, okay?"

In a hurry to get back to his speech, Rev. Graves switched to Negotiation Mode. "You've read the Book of Revelation, haven't you, Terry?"

"Several times, but—"

"Terry," Graves cut off the General, "the president is as devout a Christian as you and me. When he learns that these aliens have brought a fake Jesus with them as reconnaissance, he will understand the direness of this situation. You've GOT to help me get through to him! Dammit, I helped him get elected!"

Gen. Knepper frowned. "Don't say another word into this microphone!" He took out his cell phone and said into it, "Colonel Dietz." After a brief pause, he commanded, "Russell? Have you heard about anything unusual happening at the CSA? ... There is? ... Well, shit, Russ, why the hell do you think the security guards can handle this themselves? Where's the Homeland Security people at the airport? ... *At the convention with me*— well, that's just fucking beautiful! Okay, Colonel, listen to this: there's a potentially explosive situation there with those four suspects, and I'm ordering you to have your units move into the CSA and clamp it down tight! Place those four people in your custody until further ordered."

"Five people," Rev. Graves added spitefully, "including Marilee Navidad!"

The General fumed. "You catch that Russ?" he asked the phone. "Okay. Move out now. That is all." He hung up and turned to Graves. "That's the best I'm going to do for you until WE BOTH get back to the airport. Unless I see Four Horsemen galloping across the sky or something, I am not going bother our president at this time. Understand?"

"I will be vindicated," Graves stoutly declared. To the audience, he announced, "My friends, obviously we need to conclude our little get-together now. I must return to the airport and personally confront the Antichrist. With your prayers and faith, we will crush the Antichrist and pave the way for the return of our Lord and Savior, Jesus Christ! Let us now pray." Everyone bowed their heads as Graves closed his eyes. "Dear Lord, now more than ever we need your guidance and strength in what is mankind's darkest hour. Your eternal enemy is in our midst, spreading his terrible lies and turning people away from your glory. Look upon us with favor, O Jesus, that we may triumph over this evil so that you will return your heavenly rule over our world. In Jesus' name, amen!"

When they made their way into Rev. Graves' limousine, Gen. Knepper asked the Reverend, "Once we get this 'Antichrist' into our custody, what the hell are we supposed to do with him and those others?"

"Since Marilee and Charlie Schwitters are human beings," Graves replied stiffly, "your people could try them for crimes against humanity and stick them in the worst shit-holes you can find. As for the others, my people need to eliminate all traces of their existence for the good of all humanity."

Terry looked at Graves with alarm. "You talk as if, you want them killed."

"It's purification," Graves replied. "Once you see them for yourself, you'll understand."

*****

Up in the Reconnaissance Ship, Xashan leapt to her feet. "Did you hear that? Reverend Graves wants to kill all of us!"

Sitting next to her in the communications room, Toochla looked up from her notes on her impending call to the Earth people. "I heard it," she calmly replied.

"He is completely mad! Mad and murderous!"

One of the communications crew offered, "Any of their weapons they could launch at us, we can easily thwart. They may hamper our rescue efforts, though."

"I will do my best to prevent any hostile exchange," Toochla said. "Most humans can be peacefully reasoned with if you approach them the right way."

"Attention, all personnel," Captain Mrovinta's voice announced over the intercom, "rescue number one from Portland, Oregon, United States of America, will commence in fifteen minutes. We will need to be within range of the region's nuclear missiles to achieve success. All personnel on High Alert." Then came a personal call to Toochla. "Toochla," Mrovinta asked, "are you prepared to initiate official contact?"

"I am, Captain" Toochla replied bravely. "Please remember that this is without precedent. I cannot predict how Earth's leadership will respond."

"So noted, Researcher," Mrovinta replied benignly. "The High Council wishes us all Good Fate."

As customary, all in the room chorused, "Good Fate to us all."

*****

So far, as Iannis had predicted, the crowd outside paid no attention to the Islamic Resource Center as they gazed westward waiting for something to happen. Inside the Center, Ahmed had the TV turned on—all channels, even the cartoon channels, were covering the historic event. Jazari kept a wary eye on the playground area; the chain-link gate was still locked tight, but some people could scurry across the parking lot that lay between the playground and the Center's nearest door. It was a mere ten yards. But much could happen in even less space in mere seconds.

Didier explained to their hosts, "Everyone in this area will be able to see the ship with their naked eyes. It will look just smaller than the moon in the sky, and is roughly arrow-shaped. Once it is within a seven degree arc over our heads, they will open the Gate. We will have one minute to enter it." Iannis added something in Greek, which Didier translated as, "As for yourselves, you must be discrete when you allow us into the playground. We have no idea how this crowd may react when they see the Gate open."

Iannis' head jolted up. "They will open the Gate in five minutes," he announced. "Let us be prepared."

Hushed and scrambling, the guests in the Center gathered their bags of souvenirs and clothing. Ahmed had his key to the playground lock ready. Taza looked at him and said sincerely, "If only the original Muslims were as nice as you!"

Ahmed smiled. "I came along at a more mature time," he modestly replied.

Jazari looked longingly at Didier. "Will I ever meet you again?"

Didier smiled grimly. "It is too hard to say. But I will always be happy to see you again."

Clodagh had just finished packing her things when she heard excited shouting out front, followed by collective gasps. Peeking out the front curtain, she saw many fingers in the crowd pointing up to the western sky. "Here comes the ship!" she announced as she hurried to join the others at the rear exit.

Ahmed said, "I'll go out first alone. As soon as I open the gate, walk quickly, but don't run. I will lock it behind you. May Allah bless all of you."

The exit door opened. Ahmed stepped out and looked in the opposite direction that the crowd was looking. Fortunately, most people, despite the commotion, were still respectful of not trespassing on the Center's parking lot. Then Ahmed looked in the same direction as the crowd—sure enough, there was a dull gray, triangular object coming right toward the Parkrose neighborhood. Careful not to attract attention, he walked to the playground gate and slipped the key into heavy-duty padlock. He opened the gate, and looked toward the others expectantly. The guests quickly walked single-file from the Center exit to the playground entrance, each shaking Ahmed's and Jazari's hands, except for Taza who gave them each a hug.

But no one, not even Ahmed, took into account the distinctive squeak the playground gate made when it was opened. The squeak rose above the crowd noise, and caught the attention of some young men near the parking lot entrance. Dressed in dirty jeans and t-shirts, and holding beer cans, it was obvious that they knew more about fixing cars than they did about diversity training. To them, it was a suspicious sight—two Muslims (an ethnic group they neither understood nor trusted) leading four strangers with several shopping bags into an enclosed playground, instead of paying attention to the approaching ship. "Hey!" one of the rednecks called to the group. "What the hell are you doing?"

All six were startled by the gruff, booming shout. For all his talent and expertise in peaceful negotiation, Ahmed knew that he had no way of explaining this to anybody, let alone several hostile rednecks, without giving the game away. As the four guests were already within the playground fence, Ahmed shoved his daughter in, and followed her. He was barely able to get the lock latched before the rednecks rushed to the gate. Soon there was shouting and forceful chain-link rattling surrounding the six as more curious people came up to the fence. Iannis shouted, apparently to no one, "We are ready. Open the Gate! NOW!"

The Ship's communications room received the signal from Iannis' earpiece. Mrovinta gave the order to open the Gate. Toochla and Xashan were in the Re-entry Chamber, ready to receive their guests. Seeing the commotion surrounding the rescu-ees on the Chamber monitor, Xashan lamented, "And this is the *easy* rescue!"

"Just be prepared," Toochla replied patiently.

To the astonishment of the crowd, and the relief of the guests, the time/space vortex opened up on the patch of concrete that was the four-square court. The shouting ceased as the Gate widened to a diameter of ten feet. As the four guests started to enter it, the shouting and rattling renewed with a vengeance from the frenzied crowd. Two of the rednecks clambered up the fence, and the one nearest the top pulled out his multi-tool and snipped at the protective razor wire at the top. With a gap in the razor wire safely made, the redneck deftly began to climb through it. After Didier escorted Taza and Clodagh through the Gate, Iannis grabbed Ahmed and Jazari by the shoulders and forced them through the Gate as well. The first redneck had jumped to the ground and sprinted through the Gate, to the cheers of his buddies. He had just made it through when the Gate closed. The crowd fell silent.

Seconds later, the Gate re-opened. Out of it ran two four-legged, four-armed Baasians in protective suits, restraining the terrified redneck intruder. They unceremoniously tossed him away from the Gate and scurried back in. Didier appeared at the Gate, saying to the astonished crowd apologetically, "Really, they are very nice people!" before Iannis grabbed him and pulled him back inside, crying "Get back in, you fool!" Then the Gate closed, leaving behind a very gobsmacked crowd.

Safely inside the Re-entry Chamber, Ahmed and Jazari, hugging each other in fear, got their first look at the Baasians. From behind a protective glass window they saw two Baasians looking back at them curiously. "Oh!" one of them, Toochla, exclaimed. "It looks like we have two more guests. This is rather awkward."

Iannis bowed slightly toward Toochla. "They are the people who protected us," he explained. "This is Ahmed and his daughter Jazari. It would have been extremely ungrateful to leave them at the mercy of that mob." Didier said to Ahmed and Jazari, "These two Baasians are Toochla and Xashan. They are our main contacts with the Baasian people, and very good friends."

Toochla bowed her head politely, then touched the control panel on her side of the window. Before this, Ahmed heard only a strange gibberish. Now when Toochla spoke, her voice came through in English. "We welcome you," she said. "We also thank you for sheltering our human friends. We apologize for the inconvenience to you."

Ahmed and Jazari gazed in awe at their hosts and the chamber they were in. Ahmed looked pleadingly at Toochla. "You are not taking us back with you to your planet, are you?" .

"Certainly not," Toochla calmly replied. "We will try to get you home as soon as possible. We need to wait for the rest of your species to calm themselves. It is too dangerous right now."

"But where are we going?"

"The city of Colorado Springs, where the rest of our people are being held. We will be there in half an hour," Toochla said. To Didier, she said, "When the decontamination process is complete, I will need you to come with me to the communications room. When I establish official contact with Earth's leadership, it would be reassuring to have a human at my side."

Didier was bemused. "But why not Iannis? He is our human representative."

"We need someone who can speak English without intermediary translation. The rest of you humans will need to stay in the recreation area until this is over. Xashan will attend to your needs."

The Frenchman sighed with resignation. He turned to Iannis. "You are a brilliant man," he complained good-naturedly, holding up a pinching thumb and index finger. "Couldn't you have learned just a *little* English?" Iannis could only laugh and clap him on the shoulder.

Clodagh stood closer to the window and asked Xashan nervously, "Are Yeshua and the others well?"

"They are all well for now. The people holding them are much more benign than their previous captors. We are hoping we can negotiate their release."

"Have they figured out who Yeshua really is? I keep worrying about what they may do to him."

Xashan grinned. "It is so unexpected," she responded. "After they overpowered their captor, Charlie Schwitters actually brought Yeshua, Drasher, and Clover into a crowded area and explained their presence publicly. The people wanted to hear Yeshua make a speech about himself. So far, that crowd seems to be placated."

Clodagh smiled. "Yeshua can still hold a crowd," she boasted for him.

Ahmed had calmed down enough to have his curiosity piqued. "Who Yeshua 'really' is?" he asked Taza. "Why would the crowd want to harm him?"

Taza sensed suspicion in Ahmed's voice. She hesitated before she tactfully answered, "The Baasians have a great wealth of information about our history. I think you'd better prepare yourselves for some big surprises!"

CHAPTER TWENTY-THREE: CONFRONTATION

At the same time that Rescue Mission Part One was completed in Portland, General Knepper's army troops arrived at the CSA and blocked all the entrances and exits. One platoon stormed into Baggage Claim Area A, alarming the crowd. Charlie Schwitters, who was fielding questions about Clover looked at the commotion and wailed, "Here we go again—shit!"

Platoon leader Sgt. Eric Funt shouted out, "All right, everybody. Don't move." Marching straight up to the Wanted Five with his pistol drawn, he commanded, "Charlie Schwitters and Marilee Navidad: you, the alien, the cave girl and the Antichrist are under arrest. Come with us. Don't make this any harder than it already is."

At the term "Antichrist," an alarm rang in Charlie's mind. Marilee was shocked. She knew that her now-ex-boss Rev. Graves wouldn't take her defection lightly. But sending in the US Army? "But he is not the Antichrist!" she protested, embracing Yeshua in comfort.

"National Security," Sgt. Funt stiffly said. He strode up to Drasher and held out his hand. "Give me that thing in your hand," he ordered.

Brad, the guard, tried to intervene. "It's not a weapon. We checked it out."

Funt shot Brad a nasty look. "This is now out of your hands, mister," he snarled. Returning to Drasher, he said, "Give it to me while I'm still a nice guy!"

Drasher calmly turned off the device and handed it to Sgt. Funt. That was the cue for half of the platoon to swarm around the Wanted Five with their rifles drawn. Clover again clung to Charlie, knowing how loud weapons with tubes on their ends could be. Sgt. Funt called to the audience, "As of right now, I want all cell phones and cameras turned off. Anyone caught with a recording device on will be arrested." A cacophony of beeps, chimes, and jingles ensued.

"Okay. Now everybody line up, starting at the baggage belt. For security reasons, we need to delete all images and audio recordings you have made here. If you've already posted their images or movies on the internet, you'd better let us know, because we're going to make you log onto those accounts and delete them."

"Since when does the Army take orders from Reverend Graves?" Charlie protested.

Funt stuck his pistol up to Charlie's nose. "You ready to see God, atheist?" To his troops, he said, "Harrison, Trimble, you take the alien back to the base. You four, take Schwitters and Navidad down to the Homeland Security office. You four, take the Antichrist and Lilith to the truck. All of you will wait for further orders. Move out!"

The troops grabbed their prisoners. Clover screamed and cried as they tried to detach her from Charshwit. It took the butt of a rifle to her ribs to loosen her. The audience saw this brutality, gasped, then shouted protests. The rest of the soldiers cocked their weapons, and the audience to cowered into silence. Then Charlie's voice broke the silence. "Put me on the truck as well!" he demanded.

Funt glared at Charlie. "Dude," he chuckled, "I don't think you want to go on the truck."

Charlie, restrained by two soldiers, was defiant. "Because Graves is going to destroy the evidence, isn't he? Well, I'm fucking tired of dealing with that psychopath! He wants me out of his way? Fine! I'd rather be dead than see him provoke a war with the Baasians!"

"It's not me provoking the war, Mister Schwitters," Rev. Graves' voice boomed unaided from behind the crowd. The crowd parted in awe as he, General Knepper, and their entourage walked toward the captives. "I must say, I'm impressed with how you have charmed all these people. Very seductive. You are quite the impresario, Charlie. You really have them believing that these Baasians are coming in peace. If it wasn't for the fact that they brought along a false Jesus and you have a record as a sex offender, I'd have believed it myself."

To Marilee, he said with icy regret, "I'm sorry, Miss Navidad, but your gullibility has cost you dearly. I pray that you come to your senses before it's too late."

"Too late for what?" Marilee asked meekly.

"Final Judgement," Graves replied simply. To the crowd, he announced, "Which is coming soon now. It is the same for all of you. I was here earlier today to interview this man who calls himself the real Jesus, and what he told me was far different from what he has told you. He told me that he wants to destroy all of Christianity!"

Yeshua exploded into a furious rebuttal. Unfortunately, in his anger he had forgotten that he didn't have Drasher's device to talk into, so the people only heard Aramaic in rapid-fire. The audience reared back in shock. Charlie saw this and announced to Graves, "He says you're a lying sack of shit."

"Always the comedian, eh Charlie?" Graves retorted mildly.

"Actually," volunteered a male Israeli accent, "that is very much what he said."

Graves stiffened. "I take it you're another comedian, sir?" he asked in that direction.

"No," replied the man, who stepped forward. He was well-dressed with a large beard and black horn-rimmed glasses. "I'm a Biblical scholar at B'nai Brith. That was definitely Aramaic he's been speaking, only it's a dialect that I've never heard before. I don't know if he is the historical Jesus, but I don't think—"

"He said anti-Christian things, did he not?" Graves abruptly asked the man.

The B'nai Brith scholar stammered, "Well ... what he said wasn't evil ..."

"But it was anti-Christian, right?" Graves demanded.

"It was anti-YOU!" Charlie answered.

Graves turned toward Gen. Knepper, whose attention was captivated by the sight of Drasher, who looked back at him meekly with a fresh oxygen mask over her mouth. "General," Graves requested testily, "can you have your men get Charlie and Marilee out of here?"

Knepper broke his gaze away from Drasher and looked at the rest of the captives, especially Yeshua and Clover. Not a single one of them looked threatening. "Allen," he replied in a calm-before-the-storm tone, "all I see here are four scared people and an alien who has trouble breathing. Why are you diverting my troops away from their duties? My *grandchildren* could take these people on!"

Rev. Graves started to look persecuted. "Do the math, Terry!" he insisted. "A false Jesus, an ape-woman, and an alien meeting an unrepentant child molester for his help. Nothing good could possibly come from that!"

The general turned back to Drasher. "Do you speak any English?"

"Little, yes," she politely replied.

Choosing his words carefully, Gen. Knepper asked her, "Why are you here?"

"We study your planet while we terraform another planet for us."

"There is no intention of war?"

Drasher shook her head. "No."

Knepper pointed at Yeshua. "Is he the real Jesus Christ?"

"Not as in the Bible," she answered. "Jesus ... comes from him."

The implication of this was potentially devastating, but the General persevered. "Do you have proof?"

"Much proof on our Mothership. We may show you."

Countless more questions swarmed into Knepper's mind, but he knew he had to stay focused. He sighed heavily and said to Graves, "Well, Allen, I can see where the bombshell is in all this."

Graves spread his arms emphatically. "Well, there you go!" he said wide-eyed. "As a man of great faith, you know where your duty lies, General."

Knepper nodded slowly. The captives exchanged nervous glances. Graves stared penetratingly at Knepper. Finally, the general answered thoughtfully, "Yes. And I would be betraying that faith and my duty if I were to act as irrationally as you want me to act, Reverend!"

The captives' expressions lifted as Graves' face fell. Even Clover sensed that this bad man was no longer in charge. "Terry," Graves said incredulously, "you can't side with them!"

"No, but I'm not going to muck this situation up any further than it is now," Knepper declared. To Drasher, he asked, "The ship that's coming is here to pick up you and your friends?"

"Yes," Drasher said.

"Alright, you all can wait in the Executive Lounge of this airport until it gets here. Sergeant," he said to Funt, "these people are now guests, not prisoners. I expect them to be treated as such."

"Yes, sir!" Funt replied with a salute. Far more amicably, the sergeant said to Charlie, "Well ... awkward! This way please."

Seeing that the soldiers were called off, Clover ran to Charlie, gripped his arm, and snarled at Funt. Charlie kept himself between the two as they walked and told Funt, "First impressions, Sarge. That's how she determines friend and foe."

When the guests were out of earshot, Knepper led Graves into the men's room and whispered gruffly, "If you want to salvage your reputation, you'll let them get on that ship as quickly and quietly as possible. What the *hell* were you thinking when you had them brought here?"

"If I didn't have to host this convention," Graves replied defensively, "I would have flown to Portland by myself to investigate them. If anyone is to blame for this fiasco, it's Marilee Navidad! She's the one who betrayed me!"

"Let me rephrase the question," Knepper said smolderingly. "Why are you so interested in these people that you would order them brought to you during your convention? I seriously doubt that it has anything to do with Armageddon."

Almost robotically, Graves replied, "It's for the sake of all Christianity, Terry. Just the presence of those people could destroy our religion! Just think of the chaos that would result if—"

"Bullshit!" Knepper spat." There's slime all over this, Allen. Just like your involvement in that Niger thing several years ago, there's something more to this than you're telling! Well, if you get called on the carpet by the Feds about this, don't count on me to help cover your butt. And if you accuse me of treason or blasphemy, I'll haul your ass into civil court and make you back your accusations!" Exiting the men's room, General Knepper stalked away through the confused crowd in the direction of the CSA Executive Lounge.

Reverend Graves stood motionless in the restroom for several moments before he reached for his cell phone and called his personal pilot. "Justin, is the jet fueled up yet?"

"Yes, Reverend. But there are orders for all nonmilitary flights —"

"I know about that! You let me worry about getting clearance. You just have your hand on that joy stick, ready to get me to Zurich!"

"I'm sorry, Reverend, but that could end my career."

"I could make a few phone calls and end it myself with even *greater force*, Justin! Now do as I tell you!" He hit the "End Call" button and strode out of the restroom.

Noticing that the crowd had dissipated, he heard an announcement over the PA system:"Your attention, please. The following message is from the President of the United States."

"My fellow Americans, I have just received a communication from the occupants of the approaching spaceship. They assure us that they have been surreptitiously observing our world for many millennia for scientific research and are very peaceful. They have visited every three hundred years or so, and have adopted several humans throughout our history for humanitarian purposes, some of whom have returned to Earth with them. The humans in their care personally assure us that they have been treated kindly and with dignity. These aliens have no intention of invading Earth or harming our people. One of their own has been stranded on our planet and they wish to retrieve her before returning to their own planet. The stranded alien is now in protective custody at the Colorado Springs Airport, along with three fellow human travelers. As leader of the Free World, on behalf of the people of Earth, I welcome these visitors in hope that they may share with us the knowledge of our own past they have recorded. I implore all people to keep a respectful distance from the ship when it lands."

Without a word, Reverend Graves and his remaining entourage made their way toward his private jet. As he walked, Graves sent a text message to his close ally, Air Force General Livingstone:

"I need flight clearance now from Colorado Springs Airport. Very important, explain later."

*****

"You're kidding!" General Knepper muttered as he joined the Five Guests about to enter the Executive Lounge. "They're going to *land* that thing? How in hell are they going to take off again without destroying everything around it?"

Drasher overheard him. "Will not harm." She explained briefly in Baasian, which Charlie translated as, "I cannot divulge our technology, but I can say that the ship can float using the sun's gravity."

"But why do they have to land it? Can't it just stay orbiting?"

Again Charlie translated Drasher's answer: "'We access the Reconnaissance Ship through temporary ... er, Gates-' I think she means wormholes. 'For the more frequent personal contact we are anticipating, it is easier to open those Gates to the Earth's surface from down here than up there.'"

"Wow!" was all Knepper could say as they entered the lounge and took seats. Charlie chose a two-seater couch, which Clover joined him on. Knepper sat across from them, separated by a teak coffee table. "I take it," he observed to Charlie, "that you have some translating device that allows communication among you?" Charlie, Yeshua, and Drasher pointed at their earpieces. "Okay," Knepper said. Turning to Marilee, he asked, "Maybe I can get a coherent answer from you. Why did Rev. Graves bring these folks here?"

Marilee summoned her courage. She had nothing to lose. "One of the Baasians shot two muggers who attacked Charlie Schwitters. The police could not identify the weapon that shot the muggers, so they called Homeland Security. Well, someone at Homeland Security called Teller Munitions about the weapon, so they sent Ed Harper to arrest them using Ed's Homeland Security credentials. When Ed and his people saw Yeshua, Ed called Rev. Graves."

Knepper did a slow burn. "Ugh, of all people to handle this, they had to send Ed Harper!"

"You've heard of him?" Charlie asked.

"I met him in Iraq early on in the Occupation. Let's just say he's not exactly welcome back there! He once worked for Homeland Security. But by then he had taken a job with Teller Munitions, an international arms dealer, of which Reverend Graves is a stockholder."

Charlie's eyes flared. "And Teller Munitions wanted a cool new toy?"

"That's a good bet. He still gets contract work from Homeland Security for some especially dirty work, and he's not above claiming that he is officially one of their agents. So how badly did he treat you guys?"

"Pretty rough. He was especially mean to Clover and me."

Marilee added, "Rev. Graves instructed me to tell Ed Harper that he never wanted to see them or Yeshua again. He repeated it when I asked him explain what he meant. The way Ed reacted when I told him, I assumed that meant he wanted them dead."

"How did Ed react?"

Marilee shuddered. "He seemed cheerful. In my old neighborhood in Luzon, I saw that same expression in the faces of the gang members who assaulted my older sister and me. That is why I decided to go against Rev. Graves and help these people."

The general nodded knowingly. "That certainly explains a lot." He looked at Yeshua, seated next to Marilee, and finally had the nerve to ask, "Look, I'm a lifelong believer in Jesus Christ. Are you certain that you are the one that the Gospels are based on? Frankly, if you are, that scares me to death."

Yeshua shrugged and said something in Aramaic. Charlie translated: "Just because I cannot do miracles like the Gospels claim does not invalidate righteousness. Just face life bravely."

Knepper said sourly to Charlie, "I guess being an atheist, this doesn't concern you that much."

"General, if believing in Jesus was the doorway to a happy afterlife, I'd be waiting in line with the other saints. But seeing the likes of Reverend Graves bullying his way to the front of that line shattered that belief for me."

General Knepper leaned toward Charlie, causing Clover to huddle closer to Charlie with an uneasy growl. "Personally, I would have liked to keep his presence here a secret. But I guess that's impossible now, thanks to you."

"If we kept trying to hide like we did before, General," Charlie curtly responded, "Ed Harper and his people would have caught us, and we would never be seen alive again." Drasher said something in Baasian, and Charlie translated, "And if they did any harm to Drasher, that ship would be arriving under less peaceful terms!" Drasher nodded in confirmation.

Knepper backed off somewhat. "I don't mean to belittle your efforts to help these visitors, Mister Schwitters. But what should we do when the whole world finds out that the Jesus they have been worshipping is still alive and just another human?"

Charlie leaned back exhaustedly. "Well then, General, I guess we'd better get ready for the most massive *plotz* in human history!"

"That's a pretty cavalier attitude, Mister Schwitters," Knepper said, offended.

"Sorry, General," Charlie said, rubbing his eyes. "You're talking to a man who's running on about three hours of sleep and twenty-four hours of incredible stress. As a science teacher, I've picked up an attitude about having to deal with religious zealots, several of whom destroyed my life and career. I don't mean to take it out on all religious people."

Thinking better about it, Knepper said, "Well, I'm so used to dealing with power politicians like Rev. Graves, I ought appreciate honesty a little more." He rose to leave. "Go ahead and rest, all of you. My men will keep you safe. Drasher, if your ship is going to be around awhile, I'd love to learn more about your people."

After the General left the room, all was quiet. Lulled by the serene view of the Rocky Mountains through the huge lounge windows, coupled with the wonderfully soft couch cushions she now sat upon, Clover fell fast asleep next to her Charshwit, who found himself dozing off.

CHAPTER TWENTY-FOUR: REUNION

Charlie was jolted awake by Clover's excited squeals. Reorienting himself, he looked out the huge windows to see half the sky blocked by a gargantuan, crudely metallic ship. The color of the ship was matte black, which explained why it was able to avoid detection when it landed on the moon. On the ship's keel were numerous hexagonal ports each the size of a soccer field, emitting a white glow. Charlie and Marilee gaped stupefied as ship gracefully passed over the airport toward the designated landing space thirty miles away. Charlie looked at the ground underneath the ship and was astounded to see that there was only slight wind disturbing the trees, flags, and debris. The back of the ship measured about a mile across and three-quarters of a mile high, with 10 massive, square exhaust ports. He turned to Drasher. "Okay, I give up. How is that giant ship staying afloat?"

Drasher smiled. "Your sun's gravity. That is all I am allowed to reveal."

Charlie shook his head. "I doubt that'd I'd understand the technology anyway!"

The ship coasted away with a soft, deep rumble. Marilee nervously asked, "So what happens now?"

Drasher answered, Charlie translated. "'We will need to be transported out to the landing sight when Captain ...' Mrovinta? Is that right?" he asked Drasher, who nodded affirmatively, "'when Captain Mrovinta gives her permission.'" Drasher added one more sentence in English: "You are welcome to join us, Marilee Navidad."

"I don't know," Marilee replied with an apprehensive smile. "I've been through so much ..."

"Do you have kids?" Charlie asked her.

"Two boys, yes."

Charlie grinned and said, "You'd be the coolest mom in the world if you've been on a spaceship!"

Marilee sighed. "I'm just not sure how my husband is going to accept all this. He is a devoted follower of Rev. Graves. I know he's going to have a fit when he hears about what I've done."

"Well, all bets are off about how anybody is going to react with that ship arriving," Charlie philosophized. "Keeping a cool head and paying attention to the moment is about the best advice I can give right now."

Clover had her face pressed up against the window, looking longingly at the ship as it lazily faded into the distance. She knew from past visits that it meant she would be going back to the Mothership, her home. She had mixed feelings, though. She had grown quite fond of Forest Park and wouldn't have minded living there for the rest of her life.

Yeshua, meanwhile, was fascinated by the winged flying machines on the runway that were of his own species' design. Standing next to Clover, he noticed some similarities between the activities of the ground crew and the crews in the Mothership preparing the Reconnaissance Ship for another mission. Then he noticed a disturbingly familiar jet taxiing away from the airport. He pointed at the spectacle and announced to the others, "Graves!"

Marilee nodded in astonishment. "That is his plane, yes!"

Charlie asked, "Didn't he get the memo about nonmilitary aircraft being grounded?"

Marilee shook her head sadly. "No laws apply that man. He can make a few phone calls and do anything he wants."

"In other words, he's not done with us yet."

Again, Marilee nodded.

Drasher's eyes could see much farther, however. She saw the jet start to accelerate for takeoff, then suddenly lose power in all four engines. The others looked in astonishment as the plane coasted helplessly down the runway, into the distance. She smiled and said, "My people are not done with Reverend Graves yet!"

*****

"What's happening?" Rev. Graves bellowed from his seat in his jet. "Why are we stopping?"

"The fuel injection system just went kaput," Justin called back in bewilderment. Graves angrily released his seatbelt and bolted into the cabin to investigate. "The plane was just inspected," Justin explained. "There was nothing wrong with it!"

They both looked out the right side window at the receding spaceship. Then, a very strange voice came over the ship's intercom, saying in English, "We wish to talk to you, Reverend Allen Graves."

"Who is this?" Justin nervously asked into his headset.

"My name is Mrovinta, captain of the Baasian Reconnaissance Ship. We do not wish war with you humans. We do, however, have serious conflict with you, Reverend Graves, about how people under your command treated our people. We demand that you explain your decisions and actions to us."

All Graves could think of saying was, "I don't what lies your people have been reporting to you, but I had nothing to do with their treatment!"

In response, Rev. Graves' voice played through the speakers. It was his last conversation with Marilee, culminating with his soon-to-be-infamous order, "I never want to see them again ... *I never want to see them again!* Ed will understand." Dead silence within the jet. Then Mrovinta's voice resumed. "That is what prompted this visit, Reverend Graves. We have been monitoring your hearing device; everything you have heard in the past day, we have recorded. For now, I must supervise this ship's landing and rescue proceedings. In the immediate future, how you and your associates conduct yourselves will have an impact on relations between our two species. We WILL talk later! Mrovinta out." Dead silence again.

Graves returned dumbfounded to his seat. His entourage looked at him warily; no one dared to say anything. In a fit of impotent rage, Graves yanked out his hearing aid and flung it across the seats. For the rest of the day, Graves kept a vow of silence.

*****

As soon as the designated landing site became obvious, the race was on for all the media stationed in Colorado Springs. Since air travel was restricted and the main roads (plus their detours) were furiously clogged, it was a slow race for reporters and their crews. Even when they arrived, none were allowed within a six-mile radius of the site. The local National Guard was positioned around the site with their vehicles and weapons ready. Several miles beyond them, the Marines were ready with their antiaircraft weapons. All had been told to hold their fire until ordered.

If the landing site was starting to resemble an impending war zone, the rush of civilians toward the site resembled an approaching circus. Every UFO enthusiast, every paranormal true-believer, every sci-fi convention regular in the Western Hemisphere converged on Colorado Springs, many forgoing their jobs and other commitments to do so. There was an especially huge crowd—about 40,000—in a caravan from the Burning Man Festival in central Nevada crawling toward the site.

Gen. Knepper returned to the airport Executive Lounge. "Well," he announced reservedly to the Five Guests, "it's landed."

Yeshua heaved a sigh of relief. Charlie and Marilee caught their breath in nervous anticipation. Clover hid behind Drasher and growled nervously at the General. Charlie asked Knepper, "So how do we get there from here? Rev. Graves' limousine?"

"Helicopter," Knepper answered, unamused. "There is one large, excited, potentially dangerous crowd swarming into Colorado Springs from all corners. We'll be lucky if nobody gets killed. The Guard is sending over one of its troop choppers now." Noticing Clover's suspicious stare, he pointed at her and asked Charlie, "Is she going to give us much trouble? I've got enough to deal with without her flying off the handle on the way there."

"She loves flowers, or anything that smells nice. If you got her something from one of the gift shops here and gave it to her, she'll be a lot more trusting of you." Drasher nodded in concurrence.

The General got out his cell phone. "Dietz? Go to one of the gift shops in the terminal and get some flowers, or something that smells pretty ... It's for the cave girl ... It's to gain her trust, and nothing more on my part! Got it? Thank you." He hung up and said to the others, "The governor of Colorado will be meeting us there to officially greet the people in the ship."

Drasher looked uneasy. "She is one of Graves' people?"

Gen. Knepper now looked uneasy. "Graves is one of her biggest supporters—privately, of course. Is that going to be an issue?"

"I do not wish to offend, General. Even before we met Charlie Schwitters, my leaders did not trust Reverend Graves. He talks like the leaders who killed our planet."

Knepper's blood ran cold. "There's a lot I don't know about your people," he said diplomatically. "As a general in my country's army, I will do my best keep peace between our peoples—within reason, of course."

Drasher smiled reassuringly. "You are good, General Knepper. I will do my best to keep peace as well."

There was a knock on the door. Knepper opened it and accepted a medium-sized teddy bear that smelled like lavender. He tried to relay it to Clover, who backed away warily. Charlie intervened. "Hand it to me," he said. The general did so. "Now, shake my hand," he said. The general shook Charlie's hand as Charlie handed Clover the bear. Clover reluctantly accepted the toy, then smelled it —lavender! She gave the general a half-smile. "I think she'll be cool now," Charlie said.

The general softened. "You really have her down to a science, don't you?"

Charlie shrugged modestly. "Well, I *am* a paleoanthropologist."

The lavender teddy bear was some comfort to Clover, but she was uneasy during their heavily-armed escort through the terminals, with crowds staring at her and pointing. The people with the strange equipment, pointing sticks with meshed balls at the end and shouting questions to her group made her even more uncomfortable. The National Guard helicopter, though, was the deal breaker: outside on the hard asphalt, that huge, whirring blade scared her to pieces. Seeing no other alternative, Charshwit picked her up and carried her onto the huge beast, where she sat terrified with her hands clamped over her ears. The only thing that kept her from breaking down entirely was the polite, but loud, conversation Charshwit had with Knepper. Though an old-earth Creationist himself, the general was interested to learn more about this 500,000 year-old living fossil he was escorting.

The Reconnaissance Ship stood out from the edge of the Great Plains grasslands like a three-mile-long sore thumb. Finding a spot to land the helicopter, however, proved tricky. The terrain was uneven, and the long grass could conceal deep holes. Then there were the crowds: thousands of people had already made their way to the site, and the Army had their hands full keeping them at bay. The soldiers braced themselves as the chopper landed safely in a bare spot—no telling how the excited crowd was going to react when the passengers stepped out.

The disembarking was well-thought: the first ones out the door were six soldiers brandishing automatic rifles. Next out was Gen. Knepper, who surveyed the surroundings to make sure all was safe. He waved his hand into the doorway, and out walked Marilee, assisting Yeshua, who still didn't have a walking stick. Next came Charlie and Clover, the latter all-too-relieved to get out of that infernal monster. Finally, Drasher emerged, still clutching the oxygen tank. She looked nervously at the cheering crowd and gave them a brief, coy wave before joining the others.

Through instructions given to her through her earpiece, Drasher led the way to where the Gate would open. They were still about half a mile from the ship when Drasher motioned the group to stop. She drew a straight line in the dirt with one of her toes. Charlie explained to the General what was going to happen.

Given the order, the six soldiers assumed a defensive stance in a semicircle on their side of the line. When all was ready, a brilliant light blue vortex gaped open, to the gasps and cheers of the distant crowd. Drasher led the way in, followed by Charlie and Clover, then Yeshua and Marilee. As if trading off, seconds later out of the Gate appeared two Baasians and two humans: Captain Mrovinta and Toochla, plus Iannis and Ahmed. They introduced themselves to Gen. Knepper, who graciously received an earpiece of his own. After hearing all their voices instantaneously translated to English, the General invited them to a nearby RV office for a casual get-acquainted meeting.

Now safely inside the Re-entry Chamber, Charlie and Marilee marveled at their surroundings while Xashan politely told them to wait for about 15 minutes while their outer bodies were purified of all Earth bacteria. When that was completed, Drasher was led back to her quarters for some much-needed recuperation. The humans were escorted to the Recreation Room, where the rest of the humans were ensconced. Clover excitedly hugged Xashan, and Yeshua and Clodagh embraced for the longest time. There followed more introductions. Jazari looked eagerly at Clover and asked, Taza, "Is this the 500,000-year-old girl?"

"That she is," Taza replied proudly.

Jazari again looked at Clover, who was feeling a little uneasy about this newcomer. Jazari gasped, "She's *cute!*" She asked, "Is she friendly?"

"She will be to you," Taza answered, beaming.

Over a foot taller than the hominid, Jazari bowed slightly and extended her hand in hopeful friendship. "Hi," she said.

Clover's face lit up at the word that Charshwit had greeted her with. Seeing another new friend, Clover clasped the hand and wheezed "Hi!" in return. This newcomer looked like another Taza to Clover, and that was okay by her.

Marilee, after getting used to the exotic decor of the Rec Room, couldn't help but notice how close Yeshua and Clodagh, the Dark

Ages English woman were—as if they were spouses. Noticing how engaged the others were in conversation, she was starting to feel like a fifth wheel, although she had been provided with an ear translator. Timidly, she took Xashan aside and asked, "Would it be okay if I left now? I don't think I belong here."

Xashan blinked in surprise. "I am sorry you feel that. You played a crucial part in saving our friends. You are an honored guest."

"I'm very honored!" Marilee responded. "Your people are extremely kind, and it's really exciting to see your ship." She took a deep breath, then explained, "All the other people you have gathered are independent, innovative thinkers—I'm not! Before today, I was happy to be an assistant to Rev. Graves, until I saw what a monster he really is. I'm just a born follower with nothing to say on my own!"

Xashan smiled and knelt closely to Marilee. "I am a born follower too!" she said, to Marilee's amazement. "So many of our people think that I am the co-leader of the Human Study Project because I am the life-mate of Toochla, its leader. It is Drasher who is second to Toochla, and I can only envy her innovative mind. In our culture, leadership is just another skill or talent. We respect it, but we don't worship it. Marilee, just because you are a follower doesn't make your courage worth less. We honor you because you had enough courage to reject the rule of a criminal leader and do good. My people would love to hear your story!"

Tears welled up in Marilee's eyes. Wiping them away, she asked, "You really mean that?"

"Absolutely."

"So would we," said Clodagh, who was standing in back of Marilee with Yeshua. "Yeshua explained what you did, and we are so grateful!" Later that evening, Marilee found herself spending the night in the ship on a spare bed in Yeshua and Clodagh's room.

*****

About the same time, Charlie found himself nodding off while the conversations flowed. The time was roughly nine P.M., Mountain Daylight Time. "Heavens, *Monsieur* Schwitters," Didier told him, "you have had a long day. You need to sleep!"

"Oh, well. If you insist." He yawned. "So where do I sleep?"

Xashan picked up on it. "We have a room for you, Charlie Schwitters, if you do not mind sharing it with Clover."

Charlie looked at Clover and smiled. "I can handle that."

Clover instinctively knew that Charshwit was ready for bed. Enthusiastically, she led him by the hand out of the Rec Room. Jazari saw this and did a double take. Turning to Taza, she asked, "Those two are really going to share a room?"

Taza smiled and replied, "Clover hates to sleep alone. She sleeps with me a lot, because she loves how I brush her hair. She is a very good roommate." Jazari could only shrug in response.

Clover led Charlie to their room and slid open the panel door. At first glance, the room seemed rather spartan. Then Clover touched a metal plate on the wall and rubbed her finger upward, turning on a long, tubular light in the ceiling. Looking up, Charlie was astonished to see the ceiling completely covered with small, stout plants growing upside down—they smelled vaguely like anise seed. There were several more plants growing up the walls from ruts in the floor. There was a rectangular mattress on the floor that looked like a huge yellow marshmallow. Between the plants on the left wall was a smaller panel door, which Clover slid open. Charlie looked in the small room, watching her demonstrate the functions of the items inside. She lifted the lid to what he surmised to be a toilet and made a low grunting sound. Charlie nodded.

Now he noticed how familiar this ancient hominid woman was with advanced technology. She was The Expert as she continued to show Charshwit the various appliances. Next she opened up what looked to Charlie like a porcelain pizza oven. She pulled a wide tray out halfway, then nonchalantly removed her bodysuit and placed it on the tray. Unashamedly naked, she tugged at Charlie's flannel shirt and pointed at the tray. "Oh, this must be the laundry thing—okay," he said, stripping off the shirt. "Man, I'm surprised nobody has tossed me through a car wash yet!" He placed the shirt in the tray, then Clover gave him an expectant look accompanied by an all encompassing gesture. "All of it?" He took off the rest of his clothes and placed them in the tray. When he peeled off his briefs, Clover made a disgusted expression leavened by her sweet smile. "Whew!" Charlie said as he placed the fermented underwear into the tray. "Those are rancid enough to wilt all the plants in the room!" Satisfied, Clover pushed the tray back in, closed and sealed the door, then touched another metal plate. A soft low hum emanated from the laundry device. Since there was no window to it, Charlie listened curiously to what it was doing; he couldn't hear any water splashing. "Damn, I wonder if this is like that ultrasound clothes washer I've read about?"

Clover grunted softly to Charlie, pointed at the door and rubbed her arms in a cleaning gesture. Charlie nodded then pointed at himself and Clover, and made the same rubbing gesture. A big, mischievous smile came over Clover's face as she slid the room door closed. She maneuvered Charlie into the center of the second room over a small, grated drain hole, hit a round button on the wall, then quickly stood close to him, face-to-face. A large, slimy blob of mildly sticky, sweet-smelling goo descended on their bodies. "Aaugh!!" cried Charlie, to Clover's great amusement. She rubbed the goo over his body, and Charlie rubbed it on her in return. Clover reached up and worked the goo into Charlie's long hair, being careful to avoid his eyes. He felt the goo turning more liquid as they scrubbed. Then, to his astonishment, she scooped up a handful from around her feet, put it in her mouth, swished it inside vigorously, then spat it into the drain hole in the floor.

Charlie imitated Clover's dental hygienic maneuver, only to receive a sharp pain in his mouth—he knew he was long overdue for a dental appointment. He held his painful cheek. Concerned, Clover touched his shoulder and cooed at him. "I'm fine," he assured her as the pain subsided. He spat out the remaining goo and looked for a towel. But there were no towels in the room. There was also no need for towels: feeling his skin and his hair, Charlie found that he was already dry—and clean! "Whatever that stuff is," he proclaimed, "I want it!"

Clover giggled with delight at Charshwit's reaction to the body-cleansing solution. Then she opened the door back into the main room, turned to him and pointed at herself with a grunt. She pantomimed drinking from a cup and pointed inquiringly to Charlie. "Sure," he replied, "I could use a drink." She smiled and exited through the main door stark naked. Charlie's first instinct was to stop her, but then he figured that nudity, at least for humans, wasn't that big a concern to the Baasians. His fatigue now reasserting itself, Charlie gently laid down on the large mattress, which was soft, but firm.

Clover trotted happily down the main hallway of the residential part of the ship to where the vitamin-enriched drinking water, specially formulated for the human guests, was dispensed in small, sealed jugs. On the way back to her room, she encountered Jazari and Taza. Jazari immediately averted her eyes from Clover's naked body. Clover stopped and looked confusedly at her new friend, wondering if she did something wrong. Taza grimaced at Clover and swept her hand across her own private area. Getting the hint, Clover bowed her head and grunted in apology, then continued on. Taza said to the embarrassed Jazari, "I'm so sorry. Clothing is optional in the living area. Clover didn't grow up with clothing, so she sometimes forgets how more modern people react."

"That's okay," Jazari replied, relieved. "It was just such a surprise."

Following not far behind the Arabic ladies was Didier, who was on his way to his own room. His reaction was the same as Jazari's, only more pronounced. "Oh, my!" he cried, shielding his eyes. This amused Clover to no end. She made a roaring sound and pranced around him in a mock-attack, laughing hysterically at his eighteenth-century propriety. "Clover!" Taza yelled sharply, with a finger pointed farther down the hall. Clover giggled mischievously, amiably patted Didier on the back, then continued to her room.

Clover was anticipating consummating her love with Charshwit, now that they were finally in a safe place. When she returned to her room, she saw that he was sprawled on the mattress, fast asleep and snoring. Her shoulders slumped in disappointment, but she understood. Her man needed rest after being the Hero all day, and she began to feel tired as well. She set the water jugs in a corner of the room, curled up next to him and started to fall asleep. Charshwit woke up enough to put his arm around her shoulder and kiss her on the forehead. Less than a minute later, both hominids were blissfully asleep in the warm, plant-filled room.

Alone in her flat, Drasher had more trouble finding rest. Thanks to Charlie's desperate gamble back at the airport, she had become the first Baasian seen in public on Earth. She was worried about how well Mrovinta, Toochla and Iannis could initiate negotiations with Earth's authorities. She was worried about how the High Council may punish her for breaching protocol out of self preservation. She was troubled by the possibility that Rev. Graves could reassert his influence over his own leaders and endanger her whole species. Sheer logic dictated that she should be angry with Charlie Schwitters for talking her into that breach and shame for weakly following him into this current state of affairs. But it was that one moment in that hidden room when Charlie pleaded, "I don't want you to die, Drasher!", that negated all of those feelings. The concern that now dominated her thoughts was her growing love for Charlie Schwitters.

Made in the USA
Monee, IL
19 July 2025

21077323R00125